The Adventures of Benjamin Skyhammer

By Nicole Sheldrake

Published by Nicole Sheldrake at Createspace

This is a work of fiction.

For Ben

पिङ्गल

Table of Contents

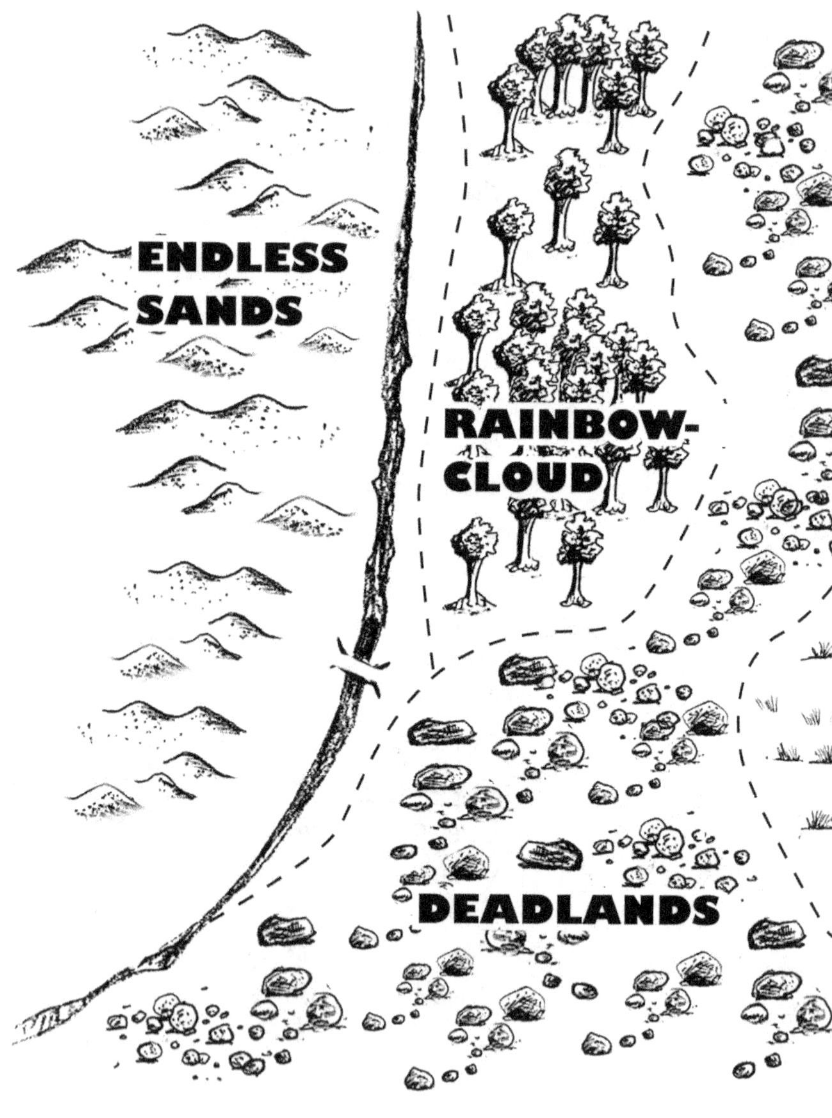

ENDLESS
SANDS
RAINBOW-
CLOUD
DEADLANDS

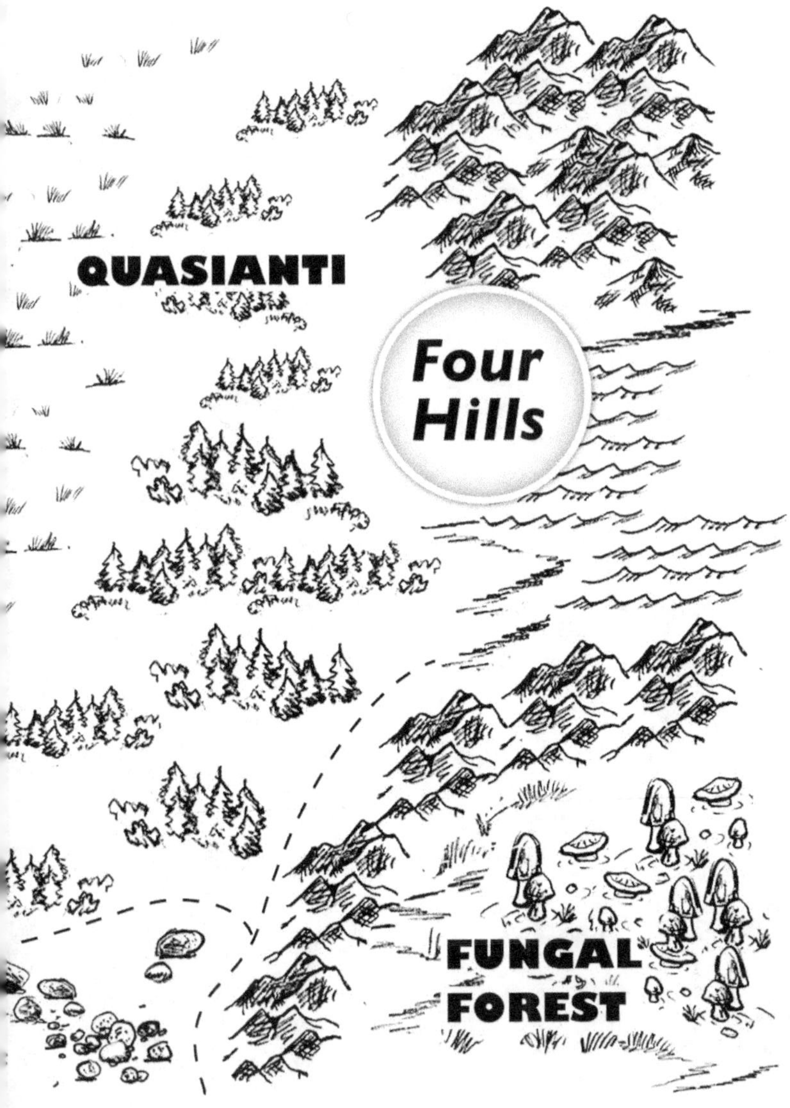

QUASIANTI
Four Hills
FUNGAL FOREST

Chapter 1

Benjamin Skyhammer backed away from the door, one hand on his sword, the other on the strap of his backpack. He couldn't go in.

Light stretched out from under the wooden door. The room was supposed be empty; light indicated human magic. No oil lamps or candles ever warmed the room; Higgins always spelled a light for him. But his Relic-hunting partner couldn't have arrived yet and besides, she would never shut the door like she had something to hide.

Skyhammer frowned, fiddling with the corner of the newspaper tucked under his arm. The visitor could only be Kelhenia, the Relic collector. She had arrived early. Kelhenia would take the Relic from him with ease; a sketch and a breath on her magic slate and it would be hers.

Skyhammer glanced down the corridor, toward the building's exit. Without magic powers, he could not defend himself from Kelhenia's spells. He needed Higgins and her powerful magic to protect him. Here, within the Royal Circle of magic, he was powerless against any other human. He gritted his teeth. A weakling, that's what he felt like. Outside the Circle, where no one could perform magic spells, Skyhammer's sword, ingenuity and six-foot-two height were assets. Every time he returned to the Royal Circle to sell a Relic, he felt as though he had turned into the runt of the litter.

"About time you got here, Skyhammer. Not thinking about leaving again, are you?" Kelhenia's peevish voice floated out of the office. "Where's my Relic?"

He started in surprise. Her hearing was the only thing sharp about her. When would Higgins arrive? He sighed and opened the door. When he caught sight of the Relic collector, he raised his eyebrows. Kelhenia had changed one of his plain wooden chairs into a bright pink armchair, wide and soft enough for her enormous bottom. She'd left the rest of his office the same, empty except for a second chair and a simple wooden table. Office was a bit grand a word for this place, he admitted to himself, glancing at the bare brick walls and shuttered windows. With Kelhenia here and Higgins not, it felt more like a prison.

As he shut the door, Kelhenia closed the golden circle of her Retrograph Whorl. With a look of disdain on her face, she crossed her arms over her wide-sleeved lilac jacket. "Well?"

"Good morning to you too, Kelhenia." He strode to the table in the middle of the room, nose wrinkling at a waft of her heavy floral perfume. Eyes trained on the jiggling jowls of the woman across from him, he dropped the newspaper on the table.

"I said. Where's my Relic, magic-less scum?" Kelhenia slipped a red, rectangular glass slate from her pocket.

Skyhammer's eyes widened. She planned to perform a spell on him! With a swift, automatic movement, his right hand gripped the hilt of his longsword. After a moment, he released it. Hauling out his sword and attempting to slice her in half was one option but, like most humans who lived in the Royal Circle, she would have a magic shield protecting her, a second, invisible skin. Once, he'd seen a cat jump on a human inside the Royal Circle. The pieces left after were too small to bother picking up. He swallowed, heart pounding. Would she transform him?

"How'd you like me to fix those big ears for you? Wouldn't take much. You could do it yourself - oh wait. No, you couldn't, you have no magic power!" She cackled.

Skyhammer rolled his eyes. He didn't consider himself good-looking but over the years he'd grown attached to his spiky brown hair and prominent ears. With a desperate glance at the other chair, he realized that even if he was fast enough to hurl it at her, he was only delaying the inevitable. It felt like giving up.

Kelhenia's sausage fingers drew white lines in the impressionable blood-glass, creating a sketch that looked as if fingernails had pressed hard into sunburned skin. She blew across the drawing. Skyhammer tensed. Maybe the sword had been worth a try after all. Too late now.

As her breath erased the drawing, the table disappeared. The newspaper plummeted to the wooden floor and landed with a soft smack.

He clutched the straps of the backpack and exhaled, relieved. "It's in here," he muttered.

Kelhenia sniggered. "Well? Aren't you going to put the table back?"

Two years. Two years he'd been selling the woman Relics

and every time they met, she had to taunt him about his lack of magic powers. His teeth clenched. It wasn't his fault he was born without magic. If Higgins had been here, Kelhenia would be oozing effusive gratitude. She did pay more than other Relic collectors but as of today, he decided, interaction with Kelhenia wasn't worth the money. He dropped his backpack on ground and followed that with a swift kick.

"How dare you abuse *my* Relic!" Kelhenia leapt up, face red, fingers starting to trace another pattern on her magic slate.

"It's not yours yet." Skyhammer knelt and opened the clasp of his bag. Maybe he could distract the collector. Higgins wasn't due to arrive for another ten minutes.

Kelhenia gasped as he withdrew the Relic.

Thick cyan liquid filled a simple red clay bowl to the brim. Five inches above the deep bowl, a stream of the liquid erupted out of the air and poured down like wine from an invisible bottle. The liquid fell in perpetual motion from the source to the bowl but never had Skyhammer seen it overflow.

Kelhenia's greasy red lips made an O as she stared at the Relic.

Grinning, Skyhammer rose, holding it in one palm. His other palm cut into the stream of liquid.

The collector squeaked, one hand rising up as though to stop him.

Viscous blue liquid continued to pour over Skyhammer's hand and straight down into the bowl as though the stream was a rope that Skyhammer had displaced. He lifted his palm. The source stayed a constant five inches above his hand and the liquid continued to flow. Despite Kelhenia's presence, he had to smile. Every Relic he captured amazed him with its impressive design and surprising function. The Moksha, the now-vanished species that created the Relics, possessed a more powerful magic than any human, or other magic-wielding species, alive. Neither magic nor brute strength could alter or destroy the Relics.

"I must have it," Kelhenia whispered.

Skyhammer tilted the bowl until it reached the same height as the source. The stream adjusted, pouring horizontally.

Kelhenia reached for the bowl. He hopped out of reach.

"Really?" She snorted in contempt. "Higgins isn't here to protect you and I'm tired of paying your rates. You should be paying me for the privilege of taking this Relic off your hands." A cruel smile twisted her face. "Which animal would you like to be this time?"

"What are you talking about?" Skyhammer stammered. How did she know? Last time he visited Market Hill, a pack of kids only a couple of years younger than him, maybe 16 or 17 years old, thought it would be funny to transform him into a snake. His serpentine body had allowed him to escape from the kids but he'd waited for hours outside his office door for Higgins to arrive and change him back.

"Everyone knows, stupid boy. Most people born without magic power don't survive as long as you have. Freak. Oh, you're the useless Keeper of the Retrograph Vault, too. And besides, the joke was funny." She waved her slate in his face. "Now give me the Relic or I will transform you into a . . . let's see . . . a slug. Then I'll take the Relic anyway."

Skyhammer held out the bowl and accompanied it with a frustrated glare. Where was Higgins?

"That's the least you deserve for making me come down to this filthy place. Lucky for you I don't want to waste my energy on a transformation. This is the last time we'll meet, Skyhammer."

He felt relieved yet confused. Had she found another source of Relics?

"The ceremony is in less than two months." She paused, noting his continued confusion. "You don't even know about the ceremony? You really are sub-human." She rolled her eyes. "Afterwards, humans will be able to perform magic anywhere on Pingala instead of only within the Royal Circle." She popped the Relic into a basket she created from Skyhammer's other office chair. "I'll be able to find my own Relics and you'll be totally unnecessary." Kelhenia tossed him a scornful smile and left.

What ceremony? Visions filled his head, of humans spreading out across his planet, Pingala, transforming the world with their magic powers and taunting him everywhere on the planet he travelled. Nowadays most humans depended so heavily on magic that they refused to leave the Royal Circle, for which Skyhammer counted his blessings. After this ceremony though, they could fly to wherever they wanted; Relics located in the uncharted territories that took Skyhammer weeks to reach would only take them a few days. He caught his breath. They might even find the mesh glove - the one Relic he knew could bestow magic powers - before him. Then he'd never be able to find Spark, never be able to use it to give her magic, never be able to make her love him again. He glowered at his backpack. That blue liquid Relic was worth at least 200 gold coins. He should have waited for Higgins. Waited for her protection. Again.

With a growl of frustration, Skyhammer threw himself into the remaining chair and began to open his Retrograph Whorl. Only with his Retrographs could he see the image of the bowl and blue liquid Relic now.

First raising his right arm to straight with his index finger pointed, he moved his arm in a widening spiral. A shower of gold sparks trailed his index finger until a glowing ring, four feet in diameter, hung in the air in front of him - his Retrograph viewing Whorl. Skyhammer dropped his arm. A static, three-dimensional image of the last Retrograph he had viewed popped into the center of the ring. An image of Spark looking down at him, her long black hair just reaching her pert nipples, laughing blue eyes in a thin white face. Her room, low ceiling, soft lighting. The Relic Academy. Four years ago. His first love, his first everything.

"Skyhammer!"

Higgins. His Relic hunting partner's footsteps pattered down the hallway. She thrust open the door and stepped into the room, magic slate in one hand. "Where's the table?" She glanced around. "And the other chair?"

Skyhammer flushed. He peeked around the edge of his Retrograph Whorl at Higgins, relieved that it was impossible for any human to see another's Retrographs. Although Retrographs were taken exactly one minute apart, they still recorded a lot of information about a human's daily activities. The Retrographs were taken automatically from the point of view of what humans joked was their third eye, a spot right between their eyebrows. A vault deep under a lake stored the Retrographs, some distance outside the Royal Circle of magic. The whole system was a Relic of the Moksha. Grateful though Skyhammer was to have access to his Retrographs, every time he opened his Whorl it puzzled him that he had no magic powers like other humans but did have Retrographs. Not that it seemed to trouble others. Most humans, and other species, agreed that the Relics were a different kind of magic.

Higgins' wide green eyes appraised his rosy face. She smirked, which made his face even redder.

"I met someone in the hall who has something of ours when I believe she should not." She spoke as though admonishing a small child.

Skyhammer stood up, closing his Whorl with a jerk of his hand.

Fingers a blur, Higgins sketched and blew on her slate.

Through the doorway floated Kelhenia, squirming with indignation as she hovered a few feet off the floor on her back. Her mouth moved but no sound came out.

An enormous grin split Skyhammer's face.

"She didn't come quietly, as you can imagine," Higgins said. "That made me happy." Her fingers moved again and the collector dropped to the dirty floor in a heap. Her basket sailed toward Skyhammer. The blue liquid Relic floated into his hands and the basket returned to its chair shape.

"Please forgive me, Higgins." Kelhenia cowered, drawing her knees up to her chin in a foetal position. "I shouldn't have taken it. I will pay; here I have the money." She fumbled in her jacket.

Higgins' face turned purple. "You try to steal a Relic for which my friend and I risked our lives, and now you expect to just buy it and be on your way?" She inhaled a slow and loud breath.

In a surprisingly quick movement for a woman her size, the collector leapt up and drew out her slate. "You dare to -" she spluttered, fingers dancing across her slate.

Skyhammer stepped back.

Higgins shook her head, muttering, "Incredible," fingers already moving, lips pursed.

Kelhenia blew on her slate at the same moment as Higgins.

As though he had stepped into sunlight then back to shade, Skyhammer's skin went warm, then cold, the effect of Kelhenia's attempt at a spell. Higgins had shielded him already; thank the gods.

Kelhenia disappeared for a brief moment. Skyhammer's table reappeared, supporting a leather bag and a wooden cage. Inside the cage, a fat snake writhed. Attached to the cage was a FOR SALE sign. Kelhenia's shield had not slowed Higgins' spell.

Higgins marched up and put her face close to the snake. "You won't forget the difference between a Wizard and an

Enchanter level human, will you? Somewhat similar to a magic-less one and an Enchanter, don't you think? Hope you like rodents." She straightened up then lifted the leather bag and presented it to Skyhammer. "With Kelhenia's compliments."

The snake hissed.

After shoving the bag into his backpack, he exhaled a huge sigh of relief. "Thank you." He sat down on the wooden chair.

"Oh the pleasure was all mine, believe me. She had it coming." At another breath on Higgins' slate, the cage, sign and snake disappeared. "Not sure if the market stall that receives her will be grateful or angry. Oh well." An escaping strand of curly strawberry-blonde hair stuck out above her ear. Clad in loose brown leggings and a blue knee-length tunic, she plopped into the pink chair. "Have you heard about the Ceremony?" Her left foot tapped the floor in a constant beat.

Skyhammer nodded. "I heard collectors won't need us because they will be able to use their magic powers to go and find their own Relics." He scowled. "The Royal Circle will no longer confine the poor things' use of magic." Leaning back in the chair, his chin sank down to his chest.

"So?"

"That means, in addition to magic users bugging me everywhere on the planet, we are out of a job -"

Higgins sprang to her feet. "That idiot wench didn't tell you?" Her eyes alight with excitement, she grabbed the newspaper and shook it in his face. "About how the other changes to magic powers affect you?"

Chapter 2

Countdown to ceremony: 55 days

"It's magic. How could it possibly affect me?" Skyhammer asked.

"The Ceremony will make magic accessible all over Pingala, yes, but it will also bestow magic powers." Higgins moved her face so close that the tips of their noses almost met. "Skyhammer, the Ceremony will give you magic powers." She sat down with a triumphant smile.

Skyhammer couldn't stop shaking his head. Half of him yearned to believe the ceremony would give him magic powers, the other half feared the usual disappointment. Forcing his head to stillness, he whispered, "Tell me."

Higgins spread the newspaper out on the table. The first few pages were taken up by drawings, one per page.

"The ceremony." A serious look came over her face. "These pictures are of a Relic that the Byndari found. A wall. It's part of the Pinnacle -"

"The one in the middle of Anusaka Ocean?" Skyhammer interrupted. "There's always a storm around that spire of rock, no one can get near there."

"None of the human, Katipo, Flyer or Aridizan species," Higgins agreed. "But in their amoeba form, the Byndari can swim near the base of the Pinnacle, since it's underwater. There was an earthquake a couple of weeks ago and a piece of rock fell off the Pinnacle." She slapped the paper in excitement. "It's a Relic!"

"Guess that proves your theory that the Pinnacle is a creation of the Moksha."

"Not really. There's something at the top that the Moksha are trying to hide with that wild storm but I don't think they actually created the Pinnacle itself." Higgins bent over the newspaper. "Anyway, the piece of wall has carvings on it! The Byndari engaged their best artist to make these drawings since the Wall is still at the bottom of the ocean."

Skyhammer pulled his chair beside her and peered at the drawings. Crowns, human figures, spiders? "I'm confused." The artist was talented though; he could tell that the carved figures were sculpted onto the wall in relief.

"Start here." She flipped back a page. "Each drawing is a detailed rendering of one of six panels from the wall."

Skyhammer stared at them and blinked his eyes. He couldn't focus. His mind raced with the possibility of magic powers.

Higgins' hand squeezed his shoulder. "Want to get out of here? I can explain these later."

He nodded.

"Record each panel with your Retrographs first," she ordered.

His brain felt fuzzy. If she actually had to remind him to record the drawings, he must really be out of it. He watched each panel for at least a minute, then opened his Whorl to double-check they had been recorded.

She was withdrawing her magic slate as he closed his Whorl. Her fingers danced over the blood-glass and her lips puckered, then she blew over the sketch to ignite the spells. Skyhammer's backpack rose into the air. He held out his arms so that its straps could slip over them with his eyes glued to Higgins' slate all the while. It fit snugly in her palm and was about the same shape and thickness. He imagined the soft, warm edges of a slate in his hand and pursed his lips-

"Let's go!" Before returning it to the leather pouch on her hip, Higgins blew one more time over the slate, returning the pink chair to its original wooden form.

They left his office and entered the dark corridor that connected all the offices on the ground floor. The brick building had no other tenants yet the owner charged Skyhammer an exorbitant rent. Another bonus for not having magic. Money wasn't an issue for him though; he was a very successful Relic hunter and, when his Relics were actually paid for and not stolen, he made a lot of money.

"We'll fly back to the harbour." A rolled-up blue and green carpet, about seven feet long, hovered outside Skyhammer's door. After they passed the carpet, it began to float down the hall behind Higgins. "Then we can sail up the coast a bit, relaxing until the ceremony happens in two months. That way we can be here when the King moves the Royal Circle to the Kingmaker Tower and simply fly there with it."

"No." Skyhammer stopped with his fingers around the handle of the door to the street. He turned to face her. "We have to get the mesh glove."

An astonished look crossed Higgins' face. "Haven't you been listening to me? The ceremony will give you magic. You don't need the glove anymore. If we go all the way out to the Uncharted Territories we may not get back in time for the ceremony. And the King has decreed that everyone should be in the Royal Circle for the ceremony."

He rolled his eyes. "We'll be back in time. We know exactly where to go."

"You do," she grumbled. "You won't even tell me how you got the glove's location from that Aridizan Relic protector."

Skyhammer said nothing. That Aridizan had seen the mesh glove. The Relic was located over a ravine that required two people to get across. The Aridizan had been stuck in town recovering from the loss of her partner to the ravine. Weaselling the glove's location out of her had taken a lot of alcohol and money. Killing her so she never revealed the location to anyone else - well, he avoided thinking about that. Although it had kind of been an accident. Not his best moment. Guilt pricked him for hiding from Higgins what he had done. He hardened his heart. No matter the cost, that glove and the magic powers it bestowed were destined to be his.

"Once I explain the ceremony to you, you'll realize we don't need to go. Open your Whorl now and I'll show you!" Higgins began circling her arm.

Skyhammer caught her wrist, then dropped it. "Higgins. I believe you." A note of desperation tinged his voice. "I do. You believe this ceremony will give me magic. But I can't just wait and see." He looked into her eyes, searching. Would she understand? "You know what my life has been like." He took a deep breath. "Meeting Spark, then having her disappear without a word. Getting chosen as Keeper of the Retrograph when it was the last thing in the world I would have expected or wanted." He felt a tide of words rushing up his throat. Words he'd never said to his best friend. He guessed she probably knew how he felt but they'd never talked about it. "That was it, the Keeper thing. I couldn't live there next to the Retrograph Vault, alone in the middle of the forest. For the rest of my life? I want magic powers. That's all I've ever wanted."

Higgins remained silent, her gaze fixed on his face.

"I feel like everything has been snatched from my grasp, you know? Like I've always been given something with one hand while the other takes something else away. I was born with the Retrograph ability but not magic powers. I fell in love with Spark and she left me. I was accepted to the Relic Hunting Academy, did the training, then got chosen as Keeper. Expected to squander my life as a figurehead guardian of a Relic, with no idea of how it works." His bitterness threatened to overwhelm him.

She began to nod.

"Now you say there's an opportunity for me to get magic powers at this ceremony when I've just learned from a reliable source that the mesh glove Relic is accessible." He sighed. "Can you see why I would be excited about the ceremony but still want to attempt to get the glove?"

"It's dangerous out there." Higgins massaged her eyes with her fingers. "What do you want to do?"

"If we leave now, we can be back here in 40 days." He couldn't go without her. No one else would hunt with him and he needed a second person to get across that ravine.

She sighed. "Fine."

Skyhammer hugged her.

"Get off me, you great lout." She pushed him away, smiling. "You said 40 days and I'm holding you to that."

"Of course, Jacqueline." He'd known her for six years and still had never managed to guess her first name. At the Academy, it had started as a way for her to tease him. All this time later, and he was beginning to think she actually didn't want him to know it. That made him all the more curious of course. He hauled open the door to the street. "Let's get back to the ship and get that glove."

"You guessed Jacqueline last year," she chided him. "You need to start writing them down. This is why we have Retrographs. Human memory is very unreliable." Higgins followed him out into the streets of the Four Hills business district called Market Hill.

It was mid-day and dark. Across the street, a floating lamp illuminated the bald head of man clad in tight red leather closing his Retrograph Whorl, then stepping onto a thick dark blue carpet suspended a few inches off the dirt road. He kneeled, looked up, and the carpet shot straight into air.

The pinch of envy was hardly noticeable anymore. Instead Skyhammer glared at Floatilla, the floating city above them that occupied the Royal Circle of magic. The bald man's carpet soon joined the flow of travellers going between the human capital of Four Hills and the floating city.

Floatilla was bound to Four Hills or, more accurately, to the King. The King was the physical center of the Royal Circle and the source of human magic. To perform magic spells, humans had to be within ten horizontal miles of the King. Long ago, humans had discovered that the Circle extended hundreds of miles into the air above the King and had built a floating city so more people could live in the Royal Circle and move with the King if he had to go anywhere. He rarely left the Palace, however. It was a lot of work to coordinate the movement of Floatilla and make sure that no one was left behind or hurt.

The floating city almost filled the column that was the extension of the King's Circle into the sky above. A half-mile gap remained around the outside for safety. A column in the middle allowed for transportation of goods and people. Layers of cities, each built on a thin disc of wood, housed powerful magicians closest to the outer edge and less powerful ones in the central slums. The outer walls of each layer were made of glass, the wooden frames faded by sun, wind and rain to a pallid gray.

Skyhammer tilted his head back, always impressed despite himself by the sheer scale of Floatilla, and the organization and amount of magic power it took to keep so many humans and buildings and everything else in the air. He wondered if any of the King's Mages who managed Floatilla ever used up their daily quota of magic power and let something, or someone, drop. Eight or so miles away, sunlight illuminated mountains to the north-west and the ocean to the south-east. He opened his Retrograph Whorl and took a wistful peek at the sunny plains of his last Relic hunt.

A movement out of the corner of his eye alerted him in time to jump backward, out of the way of a group of young women walking by while looking at their Retrographs. They hadn't noticed him. Since they weren't travelling by air, they must only be Conjurer level humans.

His gaze followed them up the street towards the peak of

Market Hill. A block up, just outside of the poorest area of Market Hill, humans conducted their business, along with a few adventurous visitors of the Katipo, Aridizan and Byndari species. Carpets flew back and forth a few feet above theirs heads. Almost all the humans had their Retrographs open while they walked, making the street look as though it was populated by roving golden apples on two legs. Skyhammer had to admit he liked being able to appreciate women's legs and hips without disapproving looks being sent his way.

"Ready?" Higgins voice interrupted his thoughts. While he'd been sending negative vibes to Floatilla, she'd spelled her blue and green striped carpet to carry them back to her yacht, which was docked in the harbour at the foot of Port Hill.

"Skyhammer! Wait!" A carpet with a bold daisy pattern, carrying a human female, plunged almost into the ground in front of Skyhammer.

Chapter 3

Countdown to ceremony: 55 days

The woman stumbled off her carpet, the ruffles of her loud pink dress billowing in the wind.

Skyhammer reached out a hand to steady the new arrival, one of his Relic informants named Bernice Young.

Bernice pulled back, avoiding his touch. "The Aridizans know where the glove is," she announced as she performed a spell to tidy her mussed red hair. She tucked her slate away. "They're sending a Relic protector team out to claim it."

Butterflies of fear fluttered in his stomach. Unclaimed Relics were silver-coloured and changed to a species-specific colour when claimed. If any other race subsequently touched the claimed Relic, their life ended in a wet and immediate explosion. If the Aridizans got there first he would lose the glove forever.

"Bernice." Higgins put her hands on her hips. "This is an unexpected surprise."

The informant glanced at Skyhammer, who gave an almost imperceptible shake of his head.

"I just wanted to warn you that Relic protectors are after the glove as well. They've taken the eastern route but there are only three of them."

The eastern route took longer, Skyhammer recalled but if only three protectors were travelling, they could move quite quickly.

Higgins laughed. "If I didn't know better I'd think you cared about our well-being."

"I do care." Bernice's smile didn't reach her eyes.

Higgins stepped onto her carpet. "You told us because you want the 1000 gold piece reward that Skyhammer promised for information leading to his retrieval of the mesh glove. If the Relic Protectors claim it, you'll never see that money."

Bernice looked into Skyhammer's eyes. "If you want that glove, leave now. And for *some* reason they've got it out for you especially, Skyhammer."

Skyhammer saw Higgins' puzzled face and spoke before she

could ask any controversial questions. "They know I want it and what I'll do to get it. Thanks, Bernice."

The informant nodded and zipped away on her carpet without another word.

"Why would they have it out for you?" Higgins asked him as he seated himself on the carpet, leaning against his backpack.

He shrugged. "Relic protectors always have it out for me. I'm the best Relic hunter on Pingala which means I deprive them of Relics *they* think they should be protecting." Relic protectors believed in a ridiculous theory, to his mind. Apparently the Moksha were planning to return to Pingala - if indeed they'd even left, no one knew - and the Relic protectors possessed an almost religious fervour to ensure the Relics stayed exactly where they were found. Why the Aridizans thought an intelligent species like the Moksha couldn't find their own Relics again was beyond him.

Higgins sat cross-legged facing him. "That's nothing new. But Bernice gave the impression that this was more than the usual protector versus hunter competition." She blew on her slate, lifting them into the sky.

Skyhammer stared down at his feet, determined not to look over the carpet's edge as they rose higher and higher above Market Hill. Damn her curiosity! His toes wiggled in anxiety within his boots. He couldn't reveal the murder to Higgins. "They know the glove is the Relic that will give me magic and the only one I will do anything to possess."

Higgins' lips pressed together in a resolute line. "Then let's claim that Relic and get you some Moksha-damned magic!"

* * *

Twenty days later, Skyhammer flicked a giant scorpion, dead, off the tip of his longsword and back into the jungle before joining Higgins on the ledge overlooking a long-sought valley. They exchanged excited grins.

She passed the telescope to Skyhammer.

"That knoll on the other side of the ravine. Dead center of the valley. . ." She waited.

Skyhammer jammed the scope to his right eye. He moved the lens to the left. The glove came into focus. He gasped. The

mesh glove was right there in front of him, glittering silver in a
sunbeam. He squinted, puzzled. The glove appeared to be stuck
on a stick, swaying in the wind. Not a stick, he realized as he
examined the whole area around the glove. A bone. An arm
bone. On a little stone table that looked like the same stone as
the platform. Whoever had worn the glove last had died here.
He thanked the gods that claims wore off after a hundred years.
His hands shook. Magic power was finally his. He felt ready to
burst with excitement.

"We still have to claim it, my friend." Smiling, Higgins pulled
the scope from his hands and returned it to her backpack.

With its sheer sides and flat middle, the valley looked as if it
had been created when an enormous coin had been hewn out of
a mountaintop. A ravine ringed the stone platform that held the
glove but the rest of the ground was covered in bright red grass.
Skyhammer imagined it seen from the sky as a red eye peering
straight up amidst the green of the surrounding mountains. "So
how do we get down?" His fingers itched to grab the scope again
and stare at the glove.

"I'm all for rappelling." Higgins strode to the edge and
peered over.

Skyhammer's jaw clenched as he pictured the distance from
the ledge to the valley floor. "Are you sure we couldn't find a
path?" His eyes scanned either side of the ledge then he pointed
to the right. "Stairs! I'm sure there are stairs right there."

Higgins chuckled.

"You knew they were there all along, didn't you?"
Skyhammer glared at her. "Imp." He took a deep breath and
surveyed the terrain.

"I see..."

"They're coming..."

Skyhammer nodded for Higgins to continue.

"...trouble," she finished. To their left across the valley,
three figures in grey clambered down the cliff face.

"The Aridizan Relic protectors." His hand gripped the hilt of
his sword.

Higgins grimaced. "We've got some running to do then." She
started towards the staircase.

He followed, a broad smile spreading across his face.
"Nothing like a race to make a hunter's day. We've never been

beaten by protectors before and we certainly aren't going to start now. Come on!"

* * *

As Skyhammer ran across the valley floor, he alternated his gaze between the space just ahead of his feet and the three Aridizans who were a third of the way across the valley, streaking towards the ravine. Two-thirds the height of a human, with deeply wrinkled black skin and grey robes, the Aridizans looked like old men but could run like the wind.

Higgins ran a couple of feet to his right. "Not slowing down back there, are you?" She grinned, pulling ahead.

Skyhammer ploughed after her. The woman could run. Even at five feet eight inches tall, with larger hips and thighs than was currently fashionable, his colleague moved with ease and grace. The wind pushed at his back, carrying a cinnamon scent from the red grass crushed by their feet.

The lip of the circular ravine was fast approaching. He glanced one last time at the Aridizans. They were almost at the ravine as well. The protectors would be prepared for the crossing and fuelled by anger about how he had killed one of their own. He forced his legs to move faster. After a lifetime of wanting magic powers and three years of searching for the glove, it now sat less than fifty feet away. He not only deserved to claim the glove but *needed* it. To them it was just another Relic to protect. For Skyhammer, the glove would change his life.

At the ravine's edge, he halted next to Higgins and stared down, frowning. The top of the ravine was about 30 feet wide all around, like a moat surrounding a castle. Smooth and steep sides drew closer together at the bottom where frothy white water tumbled in a ten foot gap. The water must have originated in an underground river on the far side of the ravine. He could see it disappearing into a dark hole in the outer wall, farther to his left, closer to the Aridizans.

Skyhammer shrugged off his backpack. He pulled out a long length of rope and a grappling hook. Higgins removed her own rope from her bag.

"I'll throw the hook as close as I can get it to the left of the table," he said. "Then we'll pull to the right until it hooks around one of those stone legs."

Higgins nodded. "Get on with it." She glanced over at the Aridizans.

He swung the hook in a circle over his head a few times to build up momentum. The first throw landed too far from the table. He hauled the hook back, yanking it across the ravine so it wouldn't get caught in the current.

Cheers erupted from the Aridizans. He didn't bother to look at them, just raised his arm and swung the hook again. This time it landed right next to the table. He risked a glance at the Aridizans. Two of them stood on opposite sides of the ravine's outer wall, securing a rope across the ravine and the central area. The third Aridizan had divested himself of his grey cloak and was hopping from foot to foot as his partners adjusted the rope.

A burst of rage exploded in Skyhammer's chest. Why hadn't he gone and killed the Relic protectors before they could cross the ravine? He had focused on the glove so much that his desire for it commandeered his strategic planning. Too late now.

Skyhammer ran to the right, Higgins close behind him. After about 10 feet, he felt a tug on the rope. It had hooked onto the table.

"Can you hold it?" He looked at Higgins.

She shook her head. "Not without something to brace me. I'll hold the end while you climb down and back up the other side. You're fast." She gave him a smile of encouragement and tied her rope to the end of his.

One last time, he looked over at the Aridizans. The naked Aridizan hung by both his hands from the rope, nearing the middle of the ravine. He moved in a steady progression, hand over hand towards the glove. No time for Higgins' plan. He had to get across faster than that.

Skyhammer secured his longsword across his back. He took a deep breath, tugged the rope one more time, then dropped it. Higgins pulled it tight, holding it at waist height.

He took off, running towards the ravine, beside the rope. This was his only chance to catch up to the Aridizans. At the edge, he jumped.

In mid-air Skyhammer grabbed the rope with both hands. Higgins released the rope. As he dropped like a rock down to the water far below, momentum carried him towards the inner wall of the ravine. During the few seconds he soared through the air, he bent his legs and pulled himself another couple of feet up the rope, towards the glove.

It was enough.

First his feet, then his forearms slammed into the rock wall, just above the water on the inner side of the ravine. His forehead smashed into his wrist. Elation filled him, covering up the pain. Relief that the rock hadn't split his skull open followed. His hands began to slip and his body dropped towards the frothy water. He looked down. Now that he was closer, he could see fish with more teeth than body swimming just below him. One jumped out of the water and snapped at his backside. He hauled himself up, stretching out his legs. A voice called out from behind him, far away. He couldn't hear the words over the rushing water. Hand over bleeding hand, Skyhammer pulled himself up the rope. Ignoring the ache in his knees, the scrapes on his arms and the burning in his hands, he fixed his mind on a vision of the glove, sitting on its platform, waiting for him.

At the top, he lifted his right leg over the lip of the ravine, swung his left leg over and rolled onto his stomach. He had made it. The glove was his. Next time he wanted to fly, he'd just be able to cast a spell and rise into the air. He grinned.

A flash of black over to his left.

Inhaling a deep breath, he sat up and looked over at the platform.

The cloak-less Aridizan grasped the mesh glove with both hands, happiness suffusing his wrinkled black face. A wave of dark gray spread like ripples on a pond over the glove, changing its sheen from silver to gray.

Skyhammer rose, staring at the Aridizan holding *his* mesh glove. It wasn't supposed to be this way. *He* needed the glove, had searched for it ever since he and Spark had read about it in that ancient book. He hated the little Aridizan with a sudden, dark fervour. With the glove, and thereby magic, out of his reach, Skyhammer would remain sub-human. He had never realized how certain of success he had been, how the rest of his life had depended on this one moment. He staggered, disappointment hitting him like a physical blow to his chest.

The Relic protector cackled. "Too late, Skyhammer. No magic for you. Did you really think we wouldn't find out that

you murdered her?" From a fold of skin, he produced a knife, its
blade polished to a blinding brightness. "She was innocent,
Skyhammer. Not only that, she was my wife," he hissed. "You
will not leave this valley alive." He dropped the glove and bore
down on Skyhammer.

Skyhammer fumbled to unsheathe his sword from its
inconvenient location on his back. He retreated left. The
Aridizan lunged and Skyhammer twisted right as his sword
finally came free. Then Skyhammer was upon the protector,
slashing and skewering like a madman.

"He's dead. Skyhammer!" Higgins' shouts cut through the
haze of anger and defeat that enveloped him.

He looked up. Higgins and the two Aridizans were staring at
him in shock. He fell to his knees, eyes locked on the glove. His
forehead bowed to the ground.

* * *

Minutes or hours passed. Skyhammer heard a voice calling
his name but he couldn't bring himself out of the darkness that
blanketed his soul. Bitterness squeezed his heart. His one
chance-

He raised his head. The ceremony. Higgins. Climbing to his
feet, he looked around. The Aridizans were gone. No, not quite.
They lay motionless at Higgins feet. She was watching him,
shouting at him.

"They attacked me! Are you coming back?" Concern
coloured her voice. "Climb across their rope. It can hold your
weight."

He began to walk, like a wooden doll, with jerky movements.
Each time his foot hit the ground, the word 'ceremony'
resounded in his head. His eyes did not leave his partner's face.
He reached the rope and swung out over the ravine. Straight
towards Higgins he climbed, hand over hand, until he reached
the outer wall and swung himself over the edge.

"Sit down," she told him in a sharp tone.

His legs obeyed, collapsing, before his mind had a chance to
process the order. "The ceremony." Now it was his only hope
for magic power.

Higgins smiled, sympathy filling her eyes. "We'll be back in timc for the ceremony." Her smile disappeared as she sank onto her knees beside him. "What did the Aridizan mean when he said you had 'murdered her'?"

Chapter 4

Countdown to ceremony: 35 days

He couldn't tell her the truth. She would never speak to him again, never forgive him for killing an innocent for a chance at magic powers. He couldn't forgive himself. "I'm not sure what he meant. When I left the Aridizan female, she was alive. Why would they think I murdered her?" She knew him so well. He could only hope that since they'd just been through a fight, she was not as sensitive to his emotions as usual.

Higgins rubbed her eyes. "Perhaps they just wanted to blame someone for her death and you were the last person to see her. I guess they couldn't know that you'd never do something like that." She gave him a tired smile.

Skyhammer looked down, ashamed yet relieved. "Yeah, they don't know me as well as you do," he muttered. "I don't deserve a friend like you."

"Don't say that!" Her smile dropped away. "You deserve the same as every other human on this planet. I hate those people who say that you are sub-human. Makes me crazy."

He nodded again but inside he disagreed. To be born without magic powers made him not fully human. It was a fact.

"Let's start heading back," she said. "Ten days to the coast, then another ten sailing back to Four Hills, if we have good winds."

"Before we go."

Higgins swung her backpack over her shoulder. "Yes?"

"The ceremony? How does it work?"

She opened her Whorl and started walking. "If you look at the first picture. . ."

Skyhammer returned his sword to its usual spot on his left hip, then put on his backpack and hurried after her, opening his Whorl as he caught up. He flicked to the Retrographs of the drawings in the newspaper.

"I'll keep watch as we walk." Higgins closed her Whorl.

He peered at the first drawing, his excitement growing, then flicked through the others as she talked.

The words tumbled out of her mouth; her voice filled with

excitement. "This ceremony isn't just about human magic powers. Every magical species on the planet - humans, Aridizans, Flyers, Byndari, Nasuchu, and Katipo - is part of the change. Each has its own Royal Circle of magic and as a result of the ceremony, every species will be free of that magical confinement, able to do magic anywhere on Pingala."

Higgins' eyes shone as she explained how each of the six drawings outlined the ceremony's goal. "Although the Kings and Queens don't know exactly what will happen when they get inside the Kingmaker Tower, the drawings clearly show that everyone will have magic afterwards. Did you see the fifth panel that showed a large sphere inside the Tower with symbols of a crown and a bolt of lightning at the bottom? The King's Wizard thinks those symbols represent the spread magic from the Royal Circles."

Skyhammer inhaled, closing his Whorl for a moment to enjoy the wind on his face and the sun warming his skin. "How do you know this?" He glanced at his partner.

"I was with Polygon before you and I met up in Four Hills." A faint stain of pink bloomed in her cheeks.

Skyhammer smiled. "And how is the King's Wizard these days?"

Higgins' eyes glazed over a little. "She's wonderful."

"What about that boy you met at the inn that morning? Conquered and moved on already?"

"He was a cutie, right?" She grinned then opened her Whorl and glanced at her Retrographs for a few seconds. "Yes, indeedy he was."

Skyhammer shrugged. "Can't say I noticed."

"Wasn't in the mood for male company that day." She closed her Whorl.

Higgins' dalliances, male or female, never lasted long. "The panels? How big are they?"

"Oh huge!" She threw her hands in an immense arc. "Twelve feet tall and ten feet wide, I think Polygon said."

Although the Moksha did seem to have a penchant for making large objects, Skyhammer decided he wouldn't be surprised if Polygon had overestimated the size in her excitement. Tracing imaginary lines across the sixth drawing, Skyhammer pondered for a minute before speaking. "Magic powers, anywhere in the world for any race." He stopped walking.

Higgins stopped too, a concerned look on her face.

His voice filled with wonder. "All humans have magic and can do it anywhere on the planet," he repeated, looking straight at Higgins. "No one without magic. Even those who now don't have magic will get some?" He was whispering, questioning, scared of daring to hope.

Higgins' smile spread across her face like sunrise. "Yes! There are no symbols of humans without magic powers in the last panel." She threw her arm around his shoulders and pulled him close for a brief hug. "You will have magic powers!"

She smelled like vanilla, delicious. When she released him, he felt disappointed. He still couldn't believe it. In thirty-five days, he would have magic powers. Disappointment about his failure to claim the glove was crowded out by a growing excitement. "But how can we be sure?"

"Polygon saw it in person."

"The King moved Floatilla?" The coordination it would take to move the whole floating city boggled his mind. But of course the Floatilla citizens would be happy to go, if it meant confirming their ability to do magic anywhere in the world.

"Well, he had to be sure. They nudged the edge of the Royal Circle just close enough that the half-mile buffer zone included the piece of wall. Polygon went down to confirm its authenticity."

"Why wouldn't the Byndari just move it somewhere more accessible than the bottom of the ocean?"

"They want to keep it in their country, I guess. They've never had their own Relic before." She shrugged.

"So if the wall landed on the ocean floor, how did Polygon get down to see it?" He imagined the King's Wizard transforming herself into a giant triangular fish with pointy teeth and bulbous eyes.

"Created a spherical shield and displaced the water. Easy spells for a Wizard. So?"

"So what?"

"Do you believe it?"

He opened his mouth to say yes, then closed it. He chose his words with care. "I believe, because this ceremony involves all the species instead of just one Relic and me, that there is a good chance I will get magic powers from the ceremony."

She snorted with laughter. "Good answer."

"This is it though."

"What?"

"My real last chance. If this ceremony doesn't work, then I will never get magic power. There hasn't been a whisper of any Relic that bestows magic besides the glove. The Byndari only found the wall because of the earthquake."

"We'll just have to make sure the ceremony is a success then," Higgins said, linking her arm through his. "Hey, what do you say to spending a night in Edgeton? We have to pass by it on our way to the coast and I could sure use a hot bath."

"A hot bath, eh? Or a hot night with the young buck that brings the bath water?" He smirked.

She shrugged. "See how I feel when I get there I suppose. Race you to the staircase?" She took off.

Buoyed by his new opportunity to gain magic powers, Skyhammer tightened his backpack's straps and ran after his partner, grinning like a kid who had magically replaced his dinner vegetables with cookies.

* * *

"The Apricot's Pit or the Boar Snout and Cheese?" Skyhammer inquired as they made their way between buildings to the main road of Edgeton, a supply outpost on the route to the uncharted territories.

The trek back from the valley had taken just over a week. Their first sighting of Edgeton brought the inevitable anticipation of a bed, hot water and a change in diet from roots and roasted jungle monkey.

Higgins opened her Retrograph Whorl and flicked through some images. "The Pit's got better beds and we deserve some comfort."

Skyhammer grinned. Trust Higgins to be familiar with the creature comforts of each inn in Edgeton. His expression darkened. Although magic didn't work out here beyond the Royal Circle, everyone in Edgeton knew what he was. At least in this remote village on the edge of the uncharted territories, residents knew of his Relic hunting prowess and respected that a little. He smiled. They respected him because he was handy with his sword and that was enough for him.

The Apricot's Pit was at the other end of town. They walked along the dirt road, off to the side to avoid the oxen and horse dung that was ground under the wheels of carts. The stench revolted him. Skyhammer couldn't imagine why anyone would choose to live in a dirty, stinking town. The residents clearly didn't see a link between visual and olfactory pride. In contrast to the smell, striking designs carved into the door and window frames of the buildings made each one appear to have a different animal face looking out over the main street. All created without paint, just using wood grain and carving techniques.

Each building had a veranda that faced the street, where men and women sat chatting, some heads blocked by their Whorls. Their voices fell silent, Retrographs closing, as he and Higgins approached. Eyes narrowed and lips curled with disgust. More than usual, he noted. Whorls and voices started again after they passed.

At the Pit, they went straight to the back of the bar, discarded apricot pits scrunching under their boots. The inn catered to humans and the bar was filled with chattering Relic hunters and locals. Patrons snacked from bowls full of freshly-picked apricots. By the time they reached the long wooden counter at the back, the bar had fallen silent. Although they disliked him, usually the locals just ignored him. Their silence was strange. Skyhammer couldn't wait to get to his room.

Higgins did the talking. "Two rooms, please, Speckle." She put on a charming smile.

"None available." Speckle, the proprietor, looked Higgins up and down appreciatively. Even after a few weeks in the jungle, her strawberry-blonde hair was free of bugs and leaves, her rosy face shone with health, and her green trousers, blue tunic and black boots were clean and unrumpled.

Skyhammer watched Speckle admiring Higgins, then looked at himself in the mirror behind the bar. Perhaps it wasn't his lack of magic powers that scared off the ladies. Higgins, with a change of clothes, could be accepted in the presence of royalty. He on the other hand . . . Skyhammer picked a leaf out of his mop of brown hair and scratched his bristly jaw. Looking down, he noticed sweat stains and dirt caked into his long-sleeved black shirt and black, pocket-covered trousers. He looked up. Higgins was watching him in the glass. He gave her a rueful grin.

Higgins threw her most appealing smile at the proprietor. "Speckle, we got cash."

Speckle shook his head. "Try somewhere else." He shot a dark look at Skyhammer and moved down the bar.

Skyhammer turned and marched toward the door. Speckle too? He and Higgins had stayed at the Pit plenty of times. Speckle had always bought him drinks in return for tales about his Relic-hunting adventures. He'd even dared to think that Speckle might be a friend. But now . . . he glared at the orange door. I didn't choose to be born without magic powers, he raged.

Angry mutters trailed him through the bar.

"If Skyhammer'd done his job we wouldn't be in this fix!" a voice shouted out behind him. The room got so silent Skyhammer could hear the mice rustling amongst the apricot pits.

Skyhammer stopped. Turned around. A thin man stood behind him, a beer in one hand, the other propping him up on a table surrounded by his drinking cronies.

"I've just been out Relic hunting. That *is* my Moksha-damned job."

The drunkard snorted. "Guess it depends on whether you're a Relic hunter or the Keeper of the Retrograph Vault, Skyhammer. You're a good Relic hunter but a shite Keeper. And now look what's happened."

Murmurs of agreement floated up around Skyhammer.

"What are you talking about?" He looked around, puzzled.

The man rolled his eyes. "Guess you been out of town for a bit." He swayed closer to Skyhammer.

The crowd watched in silence.

"Someone's altered the King's Retrographs. Someone got into our Vault and changed a Retrograph. The King's! Makes you even more useless, I'd say. Didn't think it was possible. Nasuchu take you." He shook a knobbly finger in Skyhammer's face then fell back into his chair.

Skyhammer's mind whirled. Impossible! No human could tamper with Moksha Relics and the Retrographs were definitely Relics. Recalling where he was, he glanced around the room at faces filled with hate and disgust. Except one, of course.

Higgins strode past Skyhammer, whispering, "He's drunk. Retrographs changed? Give me a break. You don't need to listen to them." She held open the door, stepped outside, then let it slam shut behind her when she saw Skyhammer wasn't following.

"You realize, Keeper," the man spat the title onto the filthy floor, "that this puts us in a pretty pickle."

Skyhammer stared at him, frozen.

The man spoke as though to a very young and stupid child. "You see, there's a powerful magician somewhere out there. The most powerful magician in the world, since he or she can perform magic on a Relic of the Moksha. Now . . ." The man looked around at the silent bar, relishing the attention. "Listen up, Keeper. On one hand, we got this powerful magician changing a Retrograph. Altering a Relic of the Moksha. Possibly changing others. Possibly destroying Retrographs."

There was a collective gasp.

"Who knows what this Sorcerer can do? Plans to do? Lucky for us, we have a protector." The man's face twisted with disgust. "Skyhammer! Keeper of the Retrograph Vault! Who ran away to hunt Relics, leaving the Vault unprotected." His voice rose. "Who does not have any magic powers to fight back against this Retrograph Sorcerer! *This* is the person we retain to protect our Retrographs from the world's most powerful magician!" The man slapped his hand on the table. Spittle had collected at one corner of his mouth.

The door opened.

Skyhammer and all the faces in the bar swivelled to look.

Higgins stuck her head inside. "Are you coming or what?" She glanced around the silent room, then at Skyhammer's bewildered face, and frowned, eyes narrowing.

Skyhammer forced his legs to move. Someone had changed the one of the King's Retrographs? No species' magic was powerful enough to affect a Relic; that was one of the few certainties of life. If so, what other Relics could this Sorcerer affect? He opened the door and escaped the hateful and repressive air inside the bar.

On a bench outside, he collapsed beside Higgins, dazed.

"What was that all about?" she asked. "You can't actually

believe-" She saw his face and stopped talking.

As they both opened their Whorls, he told her what the man had said.

Were any of *his* Retrographs changed? He flicked through them. Yes. His eyes widened.

Chapter 5

Countdown to ceremony: 28 days

A knot twisted his gut. Their fear and hatred he understood; he felt the same. The thought of someone looking at one of his own Retrographs - he felt sick. A person, probably human since only humans had Retrographs, could see every minute of his life, every time he was bullied, every moment with Spark, every time he failed, the day even his mother rejected him forever. All the embarrassing or intimate moments captured by Retrographs were on view. He shivered. It was as if someone had run their hands over his naked body as he slept, a stranger touching what wasn't theirs.

"We'll never find a place to stay. You can bet the whole town feels the same way." Higgins was still madly cycling through her Retrographs.

"Hig-" He choked on the words.

Higgins closed her Whorl, turning towards him. "Did you find something?" Her voice trailed off at the end. "Oh no." She seized his arm. "What did you see?"

"Ceremony. The drawings."

"What about them?"

"The drawings were face-down."

"What?"

"The Retrographs I recorded before we left Four Hills. I recorded at least one Retrograph of each drawing. And they've all been turned over." What did it mean? He opened his Whorl again and flicked through all the Retrographs of the drawings. Each drawing had been picked up and laid face down. The sense of violation overcame him once more. This Sorcerer was meddling with memories of his life, Retrographs that he could never get back. Sure he could look at the drawings again but what was to stop the Sorcerer from changing anything else? He went back and examined older Retrographs, looking for changes but also seeing them anew, as a stranger would see them. He shook his head as something occurred to him.

"Why me and the King?" he asked.

"We don't know for sure that you're the only two."

"True, although we'd hear about it soon enough of anyone else's got changed, I think."

Higgins nodded. "And why only the drawings?"

"Huh. I wonder which Retrographs of the King's were changed." He closed his Whorl. A vegetable cart trundled past, stirring up clouds of flies.

"He'll be wanting to speak to you anyway. Being Keeper of the Retrograph Vault and all."

Skyhammer sighed. "Did you see their faces in the Pit?" He twitched. "That Sorcerer has got a whole pile of hate coming his way. At least they'll never accuse me of changing the Retrographs."

"Well, of course. You don't have magic and you weren't even near the Vault when the changes were made. And why would you change your own?" She paused. "Although, no one else knows yours have been changed too."

"Higgins?"

She looked at him, her face open and concerned.

"Why the drawings? Why alter the one thing that's left to give me magic?" He could hear a whine colouring his voice and hated himself for it.

She struggled to keep a cheerful expression, he saw.

"Coincidence? I don't know," she said. "Until we talk to the King and find out if any other Retrographs have been changed, we should probably just not think about it."

"Oh sure that'll be no problem." Skyhammer stood up. They both knew he'd never be able to put it out of his mind. "It's getting dark. Let's stay here tonight, if we can find an inn that will admit the dastardly Keeper of the Retrograph Vault."

* * *

"Finally. An innkeeper with some sense." Skyhammer leaned his back and elbows on the front counter.

They had been to all of Edgeton's inns that day and this one, Whistlepunk and Daughters Inn of Grace, was the only one who agreed to take them. For a ridiculous price. He wrinkled his nose at the damp odour permeating the rickety inn. Located a few minutes' walk from the main road, it sat on the side of a hill, hidden by scraggy trees and bushes.

"Yes, thank you, Mrs. Whistlepunk." Higgins counted out coins into the innkeeper's hand.

Skyhammer watched as she re-counted the coins. "Do you know anything about the King's changed Retrographs, Mrs. Whistlepunk?"

The innkeeper of Whistlepunk and Daughters Inn of Grace shook her head, eyes fixed on the money.

Higgins argued they had no other choice but Skyhammer suspected there was more to Whistlepunk's agreement to take them in than the coin she was getting. The woman would not meet his gaze.

"Maddie!" Mrs. Whistlepunk bawled over her shoulder. "Take our guests to their room!"

A young girl scurried out from the back room and up the stairs. Skyhammer and Higgins followed her to their room on the third floor. They reached the top of the steps in time to see into which room the girl disappeared.

Tossing a grin at Higgins, Skyhammer raced down the hall and through the door, yelling, "Bottom bunk's mine!" He threw his backpack onto the lower bunk then stood still. What if the Retrograph Sorcerer was looking at his Retrographs right now and thinking how immature Skyhammer was? He straightened up.

Higgins sauntered in. "Get off. You had the bottom last time." Higgins threw her bag next to Skyhammer's then heaved his up top.

"Water hose is down there." The girl ran from the room.

What did the daughter fear, Skyhammer wondered. Besides her mother. He turned to Higgins. "Did you know they had a shower?"

She smiled.

He closed the door and looked around. A wooden table against one wall with a chair pushed beneath it. Bunk beds against the opposite wall and a window at the end. Everything shabby but clean. "Whistlepunk wouldn't look me in the eye."

"I noticed." Higgins wandered over to the window and peered out.

"Anything?" He opened his Whorl and examined the changed Retrographs again.

She frowned. "Some people are coming and they don't look pleased."

Skyhammer grinned. "That's one good thing at least!"

"On the contrary..." She scrutinized the road outside. "I think I know why she rented us the room."

Skyhammer moved to the window and watched the band of humans marching up the road to the inn, led by the thin man from the Pit's bar. Every man and woman in the group held a sword or a cudgel; some also carried bows and arrows. He opened the window a little, keeping the pane of glass between him and the crowd.

"Looking for me?" he shouted.

The group halted and they all looked up at him, scowling.

The thin man stepped forward, sober this time. "We know you're jealous of our magic powers, Skyhammer," he yelled. "But to sabotage the ceremony for the rest of us?"

Skyhammer's jaw dropped.

"We know what it means when all the Retrographs of ceremony drawings are being turned over. Not only those belonging to the King but also to Enchanters, Mages and even Wizards! We don't know how you did it but we can't allow you to ruin our chance to do magic outside the Royal Circle!" The leader waved his hand over his head and the crowd around him took off, running towards the Inn.

"Moksha's balls!" Skyhammer swore.

They strapped on their packs.

"Move fast." Skyhammer dashed into the shower room across the hall. "In here!"

Higgins squeezed into the tiny room with him and glanced around at the drainage hole in the floor, the single tap and the hose sticking out of one wall a foot above Skyhammer's head. "Not such a great hiding place, my friend." She wriggled past him to the window. "Ah!"

"You go. I'll be right behind you." The branches appeared strong enough.

Footsteps pounded on the stairs.

She unlatched the window and slipped out.

He hurled himself out the window after Higgins and onto a tree branch. She had already shimmied down the tree and was clambering up the steep hill behind the inn. An arrow shot past him and embedded itself in the tree trunk. The townsfolk had moved faster than he anticipated. Shouts erupted from outside the inn below. More arrows whizzed by. He jumped down the last few feet of the tree and took off after Higgins who was just disappearing over the top of the hill. Shouts and arrows fell off behind him.

Skyhammer caught up to Higgins on the riverbank. The trees ended and a great beach of white boulders stretched to his left and right. Water crashed around enormous stones in the river's bend to their right, then straightened out for a few feet and disappeared around another bend.

"Are you thinking what I think you're thinking?" Higgins bounded from rock to rock like a mountain goat.

"Floaters. Haven't used them since the repairs from our encounter with Aridizans at that lake a few months ago." Skyhammer hoped they'd found all the holes. Glancing over his shoulder, he exhaled in relief. No sign of them yet.

At the river's edge, both opened their backpacks and brought out six small sacks each. "Start blowing. They'll be here any minute." They stood back to back so they could keep watch, and blew up each of the sacks to watermelon size.

Higgins attached two of the sacks to the ends of her backpack on the outside and stuffed the other two inside the backpack at the ends, creating an X shape with her gear in the middle. While Skyhammer did the same, she scanned the trees.

"They're here!" An arrow flew by her head. "Get in!" she yelled, sliding backwards off the rock into the water and pulling her pack in after her.

Skyhammer followed suit, a hail of arrows clattering on the rocks behind him as he sank into the icy river. The cool water was a relief after the scorching sun. He kicked strongly to the middle of the river, catching up to, and then passing Higgins as arrows continued to rain down. With one hand grasping the bag as a shield to protect their bodies from the arrows, the current soon pulled them out of range.

Higgins raised herself on her bag. "They're still coming fast!"

"How are we going to get out?" Skyhammer had started shivering. His skin felt like it was growing a layer of ice. A low roar had started. "There's a waterfall around the next bend!"

"Let's just stay in the river, close to the bank, and float down a bit farther until we can get out and run from their arrows!" Higgins' teeth chattered.

They paddled downriver in the glacier-cold water, and when Higgins started turning blue, Skyhammer called a halt. He glanced upriver. No one in sight. The mob must have given up.

"I think we have enough time! Let's go!" He heaved his backpack onto the bank, then himself. He turned to reach a hand out to Higgins.

"Skyhammer!"

Higgins was past him, down the river, nearly at the bend, kicking frantically. The current had pulled her out into the middle again. He inhaled sharply. The waterfall! He bolted across the rocks towards her, but she had drifted beyond his reach.

"Kick, Higgins!" She was a good swimmer! Surely, she could. . .

She disappeared around the bend, too weak with cold to paddle. He raced back to his bag, tossed it in the water and paddled as hard as he could after her. Rounding the river's curve, he saw her head bobbing some ways ahead of him. The roar of the waterfall grew deafening. He kicked and paddled furiously until he was in line with her. But now the river dropped away and verdant land spread out below the waterfall's edge.

"Higgins, hold on to your bag!" he shouted.

She looked over and nodded, winding her hand into the pack's strap.

There was no fear on her face, he saw with pride, just a quiet determination to live through this next challenge. His heart lifted and together they sailed over the edge of the waterfall. His body dropped straight down. The roaring filled his head; eyes squeezed shut, he imagined he was hurtling straight into the screaming maw of a monster. He plunged into the maelstrom of liquid. Moving darkness surrounded him when he opened his eyes. Holding his breath, lungs aching, he let his buoyant pack take him to the surface.

* * *

Skyhammer scrambled out of the river and lay on the bank, panting.

There had been no sign of Higgins when he surfaced. He sat up, straining to hear over the rushing water. His eyes roved over the rocks.

"Higgins!"

She floated face up in a little eddy downriver, her upper body splayed limply across the pack. One hand was still tangled in a strap. She lay too still.

Skyhammer splashed through the water towards her, heart clenched with fear. Upon pressing his ear to her lips, her breath tickled him. Overwhelming relief made him grin. He stroked her cheek once, then lifted her out of the icy water.

As he rubbed her hands and feet, he thought about the mob that had just tried to kill him. And Higgins! Those damn short-sighted people, of course they would think it was him. Even though he had no magic powers. As Keeper, he was the only person with access to the Retrograph Vault. Proof enough for them. It galled him that they were right on one level - he was jealous of their powers. But thinking that he would sabotage the ceremony?

He had to find this Sorcerer and stop the changes. Moreover, he had to find out why the Sorcerer was only changing the Retrographs related to the ceremony. This person could be planning to sabotage the ceremony and he could not let that happen.

Chapter 6

Countdown to Ceremony: 15 days

The residents of Four Hills got fed up with explaining the capital's name long ago.

"Where's the fourth hill?" Tourists shaded their eyes in an attempt to spot it.

Locals always had an answer ready. "Now, there's a story! You remember the great Goblin War of 3040, don't you? The Goblin bodies were piled so high that they created a little hill. From that point on, the town was called Four Hills. Of course, the bodies eventually were buried but the name stuck."

Or, "The name has been pronounced wrong for thousands of years. Originally, it was 'heels', four 'heels', and this was because a beautiful princess came from a far-away land to marry the prince of Quasianti. The marriage was arranged, as all such are, and the prince's father had died while on his way back home. Luckily he had sent word ahead that the princess was coming so the people gathered to greet her. The carriage drew up in front of the palace and the princess's hand poked out of the dark interior. The prince grasped it eagerly and led her down the stairs. A gasp rose from the onlookers at her beauty as her head and shoulders emerged and then they gasped again as an exact copy of her body emerged backwards from the carriage. You see, the princess was a conjoined twin. The women were in perfect health and conjoined at the buttocks so they could only see the other's face using mirrors. Many doctors had offered to separate them but they loved each other so much that they did not want to be apart. They both adored beautiful shoes and so the prince had a pair of exquisite jade stilettos made for each of them when their first child was born. And thus, the people called the palace 'four heels', and those two women ruled benevolently with the King until the end of their days."

Four Hills' locals held an annual contest to see who could come up with the most creative answer and they enjoyed hearing any stories the tourists had learned.

* * *

Two hours out from Four Hills, Skyhammer could see, from the prow of Higgins' sloop, a dark column hovering in the distance. Floatilla.

Skyhammer thought it looked like a giant shiny earthworm hurtling towards Four Hills.

"Isn't it beautiful?" Higgins rested her forearms on the railing next to him, a delighted smile etching her face.

"I suppose." Skyhammer craned his neck to see the top. He'd never been up. What would the world look like from so high? Everything below you would seem very insignificant. He chuckled. Below Floatilla resided the King, the most significant person in the citizens' lives. If he died, the Kingdom had ten days to find a replacement, or the Royal Circle disappeared and no one could do magic until a new King was made at the Kingmaker Tower.

"What is it?" Higgins couldn't take her eyes off the city. One hand crept to her hip, fondling the glass slate resting in a low-slung pouch.

"Just feeling sorry for the King." Unable to leave the Palace, the King had it worse than Skyhammer. At least he could escape the Royal Circle whenever he wanted and exist outside, where magic was not the most important part of daily life.

Higgins nodded. "Can you imagine if he just ran out of Four Hills and didn't tell anyone?"

"A lot of people would come crashing down." He grinned. "Might be good for them." He pictured the King making a dash for freedom one lazy afternoon, buildings and people plummeting to the ground as he fled, like a storm front chasing a dolphin across the sea.

Higgins frowned. "There are good people up there too. You're as bad as them sometimes."

"Ouch!" Skyhammer nudged her with his hip. "Too cruel."

"I'm one of them." Higgins' voice was low.

"You're the only good one."

When the ship entered the shadow of Floatilla, they both stared up to where it started, a couple hundred feet above their heads. Skyhammer looked behind him, back out where sunlight still danced on the waves, where freedom beckoned. When he turned back, Higgins' magic slate was in her hand and the ship was rising above the water and gaining speed. Her sails disappeared and the wooden deck beneath Skyhammer's feet became slate.

They had decided to disguise the ship and themselves as soon as they arrived back in the Royal Circle. If humans outside the Royal Circle were ready to murder Skyhammer over the changed Retrographs, then inside the Circle would be a million times worse, Skyhammer figured.

"Skyhammer!" Higgins pointed over the bow, a puzzled look on her face.

He followed her finger. "I see them!" A black line of flying objects resolved itself into five airships, each twice the size of Higgins' yacht.

Higgins brought her boat to a halt. The contingent of airships surrounded them. Skyhammer felt the strange warming of his skin that meant Higgins had put a body shield in place. It calmed him. To be accosted so soon after entering the Circle did not bode well.

"King's Guard," Skyhammer noted as the airships came close enough for him to discern the orange and black chevrons on the side. He stood with Higgins at the wheel and watched as three flying carpets left the airship that hung just off their bow. The three orange carpets landed on the deck. Off each carpet stepped a King's Guard, male, wearing the black and orange livery of the King. Skyhammer could see a slight shimmering around each man; they were all shielded, slates strapped to their palms.

"Higgins and Skyhammer. Welcome back to Four Hills." One of the men stepped forward. "I am Captain Acidophilous, head of the King's Guard. The King has sent us to escort you to the Palace. If you will proceed at our pace, it would be appreciated. I am leaving these two guards on your ship to protect you."

Skyhammer and Higgins exchanged a glance.

"Captain Acidophilous, I'm Captain Higgins." She emphasized the 'captain'. "I'm sure there's some mistake. We don't need an escort to the Palace. Both of us have been there before and the King knows us. And *I* don't need your men protecting me."

Skyhammer smiled to himself. Acidophilous could not be

aware that Higgins was one of the most powerful magicians in Quasianti, probably second or third only to the King's personal magician.

Acidophilous looked from Higgins to Skyhammer then back at Higgins. "Captain Higgins, this force has been sent to protect you and your ship. Since you've been away you may not know-" He hesitated. "There is a sizeable contingent of the population who believe that Skyhammer is responsible for the King's changed Retrograph. They wish to-" He paused again. "Take revenge. Of a sort. The King would like you to reach the Palace alive. I do not doubt that you can defend yourself but there are several hundred people back in Port Hill who are raring to try your defences."

Higgins' eyebrows rose.

Skyhammer gulped. And he would've only had Higgins to protect him, had the King not sent his guards. He was suddenly thankful to see the airships and Acidophilous.

"We appreciate your support." He smiled at Acidophilous.

The head of the King's Guard looked at him unsmiling, then bowed to Higgins. "At your service. We are flying at two knots. Do not leave our formation no matter what happens once we get to the port. We will leave guards with your ship then take you to the Palace in our airship. Nice to meet you, Captain Higgins." He stepped on his carpet and was gone.

Skyhammer scowled at the Captain's back. Even from the captain of the King's troops sworn to protect him. Let's see them fight a jungle cat and survive in the desert for three weeks, he grumbled to himself. If this Retrograph Sorcerer sabotages the ceremony, they may have to learn.

The two other guards nodded to Higgins, ignoring Skyhammer, then moved to opposite sides of the ship.

Higgins led the way back up to the wheel deck.

Skyhammer perched on the bench off to the starboard side. Chin resting on his palm, he opened his Retrographs and flicked through them, then closed the Whorl. Restless, he jumped up and moved to his hammock, lolling and watching Higgins spell everything in sight.

Her slate was in constant use now. She laughed as she made a drink fly into Skyhammer's hand. He didn't begrudge her playfulness, of course. He set the drink down next to the hammock with a curt thanks.

"We're entering the Bay of Biscuits."

Skyhammer tore his eyes away from her slate and looked ahead. The port was just ahead, embraced by two headlands lined with dark, mussel-covered rocks. Floatilla loomed overhead.

Higgins brought the ship down into the water next to a dock. The airships matched their movements, staying in exact formation around them.

A bolt of fire sizzled overhead and struck a shield above them, creating a huge shower of sparks. Skyhammer started.

What he had thought was traffic in the air above them now converged into an all-out attack. Forty or fifty carpets hovered above them. Each spell that struck the shield burst into sparks. Encapsulated in a sphere of light and noise, Skyhammer couldn't see beyond the tight circle of airships that held the King's Guard.

"Are they strong enough?" Skyhammer shouted to Higgins.

She laughed. "They're Mage level magicians! They do this for a living! And they've trained together. They can hold off pretty much anything, especially a rag-tag bunch of humans."

"Captain Higgins!" one of the guards shouted.

Higgins and Skyhammer hurried over to him.

"We're getting you off this ship and onto one of ours for the rest of the journey. You have one minute to gather your things. We'll take care of your ship while you're gone."

They raced down to their quarters and grabbed their backpacks. Noise from the exploding spells made conversation almost impossible. It seemed to be getting worse.

When they arrived back on deck, the guard had unrolled a carpet.

"This will take you to our Captain's ship over there." He pointed to an airship hovering about one hundred feet off the bow of Higgins' ship. "I've spelled it with shields and directions. Get on."

A second after they stepped on, the carpet leapt into the air.

Clutching his backpack, Skyhammer fell to his knees and closed his eyes. "I hate the Royal Circle," he groaned. All this Nasuchu-damned flying.

Skyhammer opened his eyes only when he felt the carpet

touch down on the airship's deck. A pair of boots barred the front of the carpet.

"Glad you could join us, Captain Higgins. Please come this way." Acidophilous. The boots marched towards the command deck.

Overhead, spells continued to bombard the shields. Most of the ship's main deck was covered by seated troops, slates in hand. Maintaining the shields, Skyhammer supposed. There were two rows of ten guards. He strolled behind Higgins and Acidophilous.

"We have orders not to harm any citizens, so we are attempting to bring them down to the ground," Acidophilous explained. "They are not amenable." The group paused to watch two of Acidophilous's troops cast a spell at an attacker and force her carpet down to the docks. "They have had a chance to blow off some steam though, so that should help."

When they reached the command deck, Acidophilous pointed to two chairs with a good view of the ship. "Please have a seat. We are leaving for the Palace." He called movement orders out to his commanders and the guard magicians.

All but two airships began to rise.

The attackers' spells stopped coming for a brief moment, and Skyhammer caught a glimpse of the people who had so much hatred for him. Most of them, now looking confused, sat cross-legged in the middle of single- or double-person carpets. They looked like ordinary men and women and an interesting mixture of rich and poor.

Who was the Retrograph Sorcerer who had turned humans into panic-stricken and angry citizens? One person with more power than all the King's Guards put together, that's who. It was not who the Sorcerer was, but what he or she had done. Performed magic on a Relic. It took great confidence or arrogance to change a Retrograph, to change so many people's Retrographs. And to give the impression that they were going to sabotage the ceremony! Skyhammer knew the Sorcerer had to be higher than Wizard level to affect a Relic; he had sold Relics to collectors whose first action after buying was to take each Relic to a Wizard level magician and see if they could take the Relic apart or change it in any way.

Skyhammer clenched and released his fists, watching the

veins on his forearms pop out. Being dependent on someone other than Higgins made him nervous.

The airship sped forward, rising at the same angle as Port Hill. While Higgins watched up ahead, Skyhammer looked over the ship's side onto Port Hill's collection of bars, warehouses and run-down buildings. Only those that didn't have at least an Enchanter level of magic power lived on the ground. But they were looked down upon less than those who lived outside the Circle altogether. Even if, like Skyhammer's family, they were farmers who supplied the capital and Floatilla, and couldn't afford to move inside.

Port Hill's buildings were made of cheap materials - all other resources went to supplying the floating city. No plant life grew under Floatilla; the city gripped the land in shadow except around sunrise and sunset.

Skyhammer's stomach rumbled. Would the King feed him or just kill him straight away? If the King went to so much trouble to protect them from the attackers, Skyhammer reasoned, he probably did not believe that Skyhammer was the Sorcerer. Perhaps his Royal Highness thought Skyhammer knew the identity of the Sorcerer and would try to torture the answer out of him. Skyhammer, nervous now, began to crack his knuckles, over and over. Higgins glared at him and he stopped. He'd never heard of the King torturing anyone. But that didn't mean it hadn't happened. His breath was shallow and quick. He forced his mind to stop imagining tortures and focused on the airship.

The attackers had stayed in the port presuming Skyhammer and Higgins still to be with their ship, Acidophilous told them. The magicians on board the airships were resting now, although some still maintained the shield. Skyhammer, staring hungrily at all the slates, encountered a number of baleful looks coming from the main deck. He glared back.

Once they had left Port Hill behind, Market Hill rose to their left and Palace Hill lay ahead. The area between all three hills was hard bare ground in the barren shade of the floating city. Mostly carpets zipped through the air between Floatilla and the Hills. Low-level magic humans and a few members of other species travelled the roads on wagons or horseback. Each species' magic powers only worked within that species' Royal Circle.

Higgins sat down beside him and began to spell clean their packs and clothes. After a couple of minutes, she stopped and surveyed them with a critical eye.

She sighed. "It'll have to do - oh!" She made an adjustment on her slate.

Skyhammer watched Higgins' face. She was grinning; her head held high and her fingers spread, suffused with power.

"Does the amount of magic you can do increase?" he asked. "As you get closer to the King?"

"No." She shook her head. "But the feeling is like a high. I feel I could do so much more, sometimes I feel like I'm about to explode with magic. I envy the people who are near him all the time."

His mood blackened. He opened his Whorl and watched again as the glove was snatched from him forever.

"I wish you could feel it too," Higgins blurted out. "I'm scared that the ceremony will be sabotaged."

Skyhammer's lips twisted. "Me too," he whispered under his breath. "Me too." Skyhammer closed his Whorl.

The airship started to climb the long, steep hill topped by the Palace. Halfway down, a high stone wall encircled the hill, intersected only by a gate and guardhouse. Below the wall, the ground was brown and bare. Inside the wall, the grounds were lush. Gardens bursting with bright flowers, paths lined with low bushes, ponds hidden under hanging tree branches. The palace covered the top of the hill like a carefully crafted pile of round, hard candies. The buildings were fat, squat cylinders of orange and pink stone, piled next to and on top of each other. Farthest away was a tower made of four purple cylinders, the tallest structure on the Palace grounds.

The airship sailed over the wall, the guard at ground level saluting as they went by.

Skyhammer stretched, then shouldered his backpack as the airship touched down outside the Palace doors. Was the King really protecting them or did he too believe that Skyhammer wanted to sabotage the ceremony?

Chapter 7

Countdown to ceremony: 15 days

"Lady Higgins and the Keeper of the Retrograph Vault, your Majesty." The servant bowed low as they strode by him into the Crystal Room and handed off their backpacks to another servant.

"Come in." The King stood at the opposite end of the room, hands resting on his protruding belly. His crown sat askew on his short, blonde hair. Baggy, orange pants and a matching silk top in the royal shade gave him the air of a pumpkin. If his pointy nose had been green, the picture would be complete. Skyhammer couldn't discern if the King's expression was disapproving or concerned.

Between Skyhammer and the King, six straight-backed chairs encircled a large round table in front of open balcony doors. Next to the King, plates of cheese, bread and olives flanked by bottles of wine covered a corner table. Along one wall, a third table held a scattering of papers.

Guards stood on either side of the doorways. Gaudy orange wall hangings enlivened two of the purple, stone walls. The third wall had two rows of hooks. Seven sword-shaped spaces lightened the walls above the hooks.

Skyhammer bowed and Higgins curtsied before the King.

"Get something to eat and we'll get started as soon as Poly arrives." The King sat down at the central table. "Now that they know you're here, the mob will be converging on the Palace. We don't have much time."

Skyhammer piled his plate with food, then gazed at the sword wall for a moment, disappointed. He'd been looking forward to examining the King's sword collection. He must have moved the display. Skyhammer wandered onto the balcony. Outside, he ate in great gulps, looking out over the Crystal Lines. The gleaming white fissures zigzagged for miles behind the Palace. The fissures were largely unexplored but most people were okay with that; the strange screams and freakish howls that frequently rose from their depths put most adventurers off.

In the distance, he saw a sliver of light - a glimpse of the sky between Floatilla and the far-off mountains. Would he survive another magic attack long enough to be out in the wilderness again? To his relief, the King acted welcoming, so he must not think Skyhammer was the Sorcerer. What did the King think? They would find out shortly. Skyhammer glared at Floatilla, bustling like a beehive above him, and couldn't imagine how the King survived living in its constant shadow. Opening his Retrograph Whorl, he took a longing peek at Higgins's boat.

"Skyhammer!" The King beckoned him over to the paper-strewn table. "Record these with your Retrographs. You'll need to examine them later when we discuss the Byndari."

Skyhammer finished chewing an olive. The King didn't know about Skyhammer's changed Retrographs. He stared at each of the five drawings in turn, making sure his Retrographs recorded them. Again. He shivered, nervous again. A powerful Sorcerer was out there somewhere. Someone with no regard for Skyhammer's life or desire for magic. If they were willing to sabotage the ceremony, then perhaps the Sorcerer could already do magic outside the Royal Circle.

When the door swung open, Higgins was updating the King on the events surrounding the glove and the attack in Edgeton. Skyhammer straightened up and turned around.

"Lady Polygon, your Majesty," the servant announced, ushering the King's Wizard through the doorway. She curtsied to the King, long skirts spreading out over the floor and lengthy brown hair falling across her face. Polygon, though only in her late twenties, was one of the most powerful humans in the realm: a Wizard level magician.

Until now, Skyhammer realized. He wondered how that made her feel. The King's Wizard supposedly protected the King, but now an unknown, more powerful human was out there - a Sorcerer level magician. One who had the gall to change the King's Retrograph right under Polygon's nose. That had to make her pretty nervous.

Higgins rose from the table and walked over to Polygon. The two women embraced, holding each other a few seconds longer than necessary, Skyhammer noted. He shook his head. Higgins still carried that torch?

"We've got a lot to discuss," the King called. "Let's get going."

Polygon and Higgins joined Skyhammer and the King at the table.

A guard entered and whispered in the King's ear.

The King sighed. "A small crowd is gathering outside the Palace. They want us to give them Skyhammer." He paused, eyes flicking briefly to Skyhammer. "They think if Skyhammer dies they can find another Keeper who can do magic and protect them from the Retrograph Sorcerer."

Skyhammer, chewing on a hunk of cheese, halted mid-bite and stared at the King, wide-eyed. He swallowed. "Do they know how much time it'll take to find a replacement?" Exasperated, he shook his head.

"I don't think they care," Poly said, looking at him coolly.

Eyes narrowing, Higgins laid a hand on Skyhammer's arm. "They can't have him. And they can't get to him through the King's defences. The sooner we get through this meeting, the sooner we can get out of the Circle."

The King nodded to the guard. "Keep us updated."

The guard saluted and left. But not before throwing a furious glance at Skyhammer, who slumped back in his chair, stunned. He looked around. The King and Higgins focused on Polygon. What if the guards felt the same way as the mob outside? He pushed the thought away. He needed to concentrate on this conversation.

"Polygon, give them the details."

"Yes, your Majesty." Polygon faced Higgins and Skyhammer. "You know about the ceremony already. The drawings the Byndari made of the wall Relic have been circulated to all six countries. Here in Quasianti, we've seen them in the newspapers at least once a week since we received them."

Skyhammer rubbed his heel against the leg of his chair. Thinking about the changes to the drawings in his Snapshots made him anxious. The Sorcerer possessed a scary amount of power.

"The Byndari told us about the Relic and the ceremony seven weeks ago," Polygon continued. "Three weeks ago, the King opened his Retrograph Whorl and discovered--"

"An outrage!" The King leaned forward. Flecks of spittle flew from his lips as he spoke. "The morning of the alterations, the Byndari ambassador had dropped by for a chat. We sat at this exact table and looked over the drawings." He shook his head. "That evening when I went back to review my Retrographs, the Byndari ambassador had a sword from my display thrust through his chest and so did I!"

That was certainly more frightening than having a couple of drawings turned over in a Retrograph. Skyhammer couldn't think of anything to say.

"I'm sorry to hear that, your Majesty," Higgins said. "Was anything else changed?"

"Oh yes. Every page of every drawing of the wall that I have in my Retrographs has been turned over. And the one that isn't turned is always the last one showing all the species with their magic powers all over the world. That drawing has a sword through it as well!" The King's face grew redder and redder as he spoke.

Polygon signalled a servant to get the King a drink.

"I've been King for forty years and these last seven weeks will be the death of me." He downed his wine in one gulp and held out his glass for more.

"Your Majesty, is the Sorcerer threatening you or the ceremony or the Byndari?" Higgins asked.

Polygon answered. "We have no idea. Of course, we thought the Sorcerer was Skyhammer at first. No one else has access to the Vault. But since he has no magic and was away Relic hunting when the Retrographs were changed, we didn't think it was probable."

The King and Polygon glared at Skyhammer, who shook his head.

"It didn't stop there unfortunately." Polygon cast a spell to warm her wine. "The Sorcerer has begun changing other humans' Retrographs."

"He changed mine," Skyhammer said. "Turned over my drawings as well."

"That's what's been done to everyone's Retrographs," Polygon continued. "The Sorcerer is only focusing on the drawings."

Higgins spoke up. "Turning them over is like trying to get rid of them."

"That's what we think. And we guess the Sorcerer is a

human, which makes trouble for us with the other species." The King slid a half-eaten piece of cheese around his plate. "We're at peace with most of the other species. And the ceremony requires all our cooperation. The Byndari have talked to the other Royals and obtained their agreement, even the Nasuchu."

"The Nasuchu?" Higgins sniffed. "I guess Byndari aren't exactly palatable to those cannibals."

"Also," the King's Wizard continued, "Floatilla is bursting at the seams. Overcrowding is increasing the spread of disease-"

"It will give us a chance to seize resources from nearby countries," the King added, eyes gleaming.

Uh oh, Skyhammer thought. He didn't need to look at Higgins' face.

"You're planning to invade our neighbours? After cooperating for the ceremony?" A flash of anger then disgust crossed Higgins' face before she could control herself. "I apologize, your Majesty," she said, sitting back into her chair. "Your decisions are not up for discussion." She stared down at the table.

"Quite so, Lady Higgins." The King's face was stern. "Apology accepted. Conditions are deteriorating inside Floatilla and as King, our first duty is to our people. But as you can understand, this relates to the Retrograph Sorcerer's next move. If the Sorcerer is a member of one of the races from whom we are planning to appropriate land, our plans could be foiled if our Retrographs reveal them. But we cannot invade if the ceremony does not happen. What if the Sorcerer can modify the Kingmaker Towers in the same way he or she can alter our Retrographs?"

"I had a thought earlier," Skyhammer said. "If the Sorcerer is planning on sabotaging the ceremony, then maybe he or she doesn't need planet-wide magic. Perhaps they can already do magic outside the Royal Circle." He stiffened in alarm as three guards burst through the door. Two of them took up a position by the wall, the other approached the King.

"Your Majesty, the group outside is growing. No spells have been cast, yet but we fear it may happen soon. If it continues to grow at the current rate, we may have a mob attack on our hands."

The King glared at Skyhammer. "You'd better not be more

trouble than you're worth." He turned back to the guard. "Keep us informed. If they attack, you have our permission to defend with whatever force necessary."

The guard left.

"So you see, Skyhammer and Lady Higgins." The King clasped his hands over his belly. "We have an unknown element in this Sorcerer. Extraordinarily powerful, arrogant enough to threaten us through our Retrographs-"

"What did you bring us here for, your Majesty?" Skyhammer couldn't wait any longer.

"Isn't it obvious?" Polygon snorted in derision. "If the Sorcerer is changing our Retrographs, then they could be inside the Retrograph Vault. And since you are the only one who can get in the Vault . . ."

Skyhammer nodded. It made sense.

A shadow blanketed the room. Every head swivelled toward the balcony doors.

A cloud of humans on flying carpets blocked the light from outside. They hovered about fifty feet away from the balcony but close enough that Skyhammer could see the fury and hatred in their faces. They disappeared behind a wall of light, spells exploding against the Palace's shield.

Skyhammer leapt to his feet. He had no way to fight these people, no magic powers. They had the Palace surrounded and there was no escape. He looked over at Higgins, desperate. Inside him, anger surged at how useless he was, at his dependency on other people.

Standing up and putting her hands on his shoulders, Higgins pushed him back into his chair. "Please tell us more, your Majesty," she said. "I'm sure your guards can handle the people outside."

Slumping in his chair, Skyhammer eyed his Majesty.

The King signalled for the balcony doors to be closed, then leaned forward, his eyes locked on Skyhammer's. "Go to the Vault. Find the Sorcerer. Bring him back. Alive, preferably, but dead if necessary. You have 15 days."

Their solution was to send a magic-less human to fight the most powerful Sorcerer alive? The King had guards. They could go and wait outside the Vault; the Sorcerer had to come out sometime. "But your Majes-" He paused, cocking an ear towards the door.

Voices, loud, yelling, the boom of exploding spells. Everyone stood up.

"Grab-" The door to the hallway opened and slammed shut, cutting off the King's words.

Two guards faced the doorway, casting spells frantically with their slates. The third guard strode up to the King - Acidophilous.

"Your Majesty, treachery has broken our defences." Acidophilous scowled at Skyhammer.

"Tell me," the King ordered.

"A few guards agreed that it was better the Vault Keeper died. They argued with other guards. While distracted, the mob seized the opportunity to get through. The traitors were slain and we are in pursuit of the attackers. They are headed here. They know you are here. They are also trying to break the shield so the attackers outside," he gestured to the balcony without taking his eyes off Skyhammer, "can get through as well."

Skyhammer and Higgins exchanged glances, then fetched their backpacks.

Polygon clasped her hands around Higgins' for a brief moment. Their eyes met, faces softening. Higgins smiled and whispered a few words to Polygon.

Skyhammer frowned. "How do we get out of here, your Majesty?"

"There's a secret passage behind that wall hanging." He pointed to his left. "It leads-"

The balcony and hallway doors exploded open at the same time. The hallway teemed with attackers fighting guards amongst sparks of light. Attackers on carpets outside the balcony door zipped through the air, chasing and being chased by guards. One of the attackers spotted the open door and zoomed towards it.

The King sprang into action. "This way!" He grabbed Skyhammer and Higgins by the arms and dragged them to the wall hangings.

"Guards! Form a defensive semi-circle around the King now!" Acidophilous commanded.

The six guards did as ordered, slates at the ready.

Attackers poured through both doors, filling the room. The

guards' shield seemed to be holding.

Skyhammer froze, back against the wall, screams of pain and anger filling his ears. The guards were orderly, professional and well-trained but there were just too many attackers. He began to shake, overwhelmed by all the magic flashing around him.

Poly had raced ahead of them and ripped off the wall hanging. She pushed it into Higgins' hands. "Carpet. You'll need it at the end of the passage." Polygon did an about-turn, whipped out her slate and proceeded to cast spells so fast that her hand was a blur.

The King tapped a pattern with his fingers on a section of the wall that was darker than the rest. A door swung back to reveal a passageway. He seized Skyhammer and pushed him into it.

"What about you, sir?" Skyhammer said.

The King looked at him. "They're not going to kill their source of magic, Skyhammer. Now find that Sorcerer!" The King touched Higgins on the shoulder. She stood hip-to-hip with Polygon, furiously casting spells.

Then the semi-circled guards turned to face Skyhammer.

A soft, "Oh," of fright escaped Skyhammer's lips. He stepped backwards into the passageway.

Acidophilous caught hold of the King and wrestled him into a corner, out of the protective circle. "I'm sorry, your Majesty. He can't be allowed to live."

Desperate but determined expressions on their faces, the guards raised their slates, eyes on Skyhammer.

Chapter 8

Countdown to ceremony: 15 days

"Stop!" Polygon shrieked.

Before any of the guards could move, she pushed Higgins into the passageway. Then the King's Wizard let loose a barrage of spells. The guards stumbled back.

Skyhammer caught Higgins as she staggered into him. The door to the passageway was closing.

Through the thinning crack, they watched Polygon send another volley of spells at the guards who all returned fire simultaneously. Polygon's body flew back against the closing door with a wet smack. The door shut. The attack faded to a low murmur.

Skyhammer and Higgins paused in the dark. He listened to her breath. Ragged. Like his. She sniffed. The guards would get into the passage soon. They had to leave. He couldn't move. He inhaled deeply. Musty air. He heard Higgins move. A light blossomed in front of him. A river of tears flowed down Higgins' cheeks. She had loved Polygon, he knew.

Skyhammer patted Higgins on the shoulder. "We have to get out of here." The floating light moved a couple of feet ahead of him, illuminating the purple walls and floor farther into the passageway. He didn't know what to say to Higgins. They had to keep moving.

"-t's go," she whispered, her voice clouded by tears.

Skyhammer followed the light. It stayed a few feet ahead of him. He turned once to make sure Higgins was following, and to take the orange wall hanging from her. Her tears had started again. She wiped them away with her sleeve.

The light led them down a few flights of stairs and past a couple of other passage entrances.

"How does the light know where to go?"

In a stronger voice, Higgins said, "I spelled it so it heads north and towards the nearest source of fresh air. We do need to hurry though. The guards will knows where the passage exits and they'll be forcing the King to open the door again soon. We'll be trapped."

They picked up the pace. After about fifteen minutes, the floating light turned right and disappeared. The corner remained illuminated.

"We're close to the outside!" Skyhammer rounded the corner. The passage opened up to a ledge with a view over the Crystal Lines.

"Nasuchu-teeth," Higgins swore. "We've got company. Already!" She withdrew her slate.

Skyhammer looked up. A horde of flying carpets was descending towards them. He dropped the orange wall hanging on the ledge and stepped on. "Then let's go! This is our carpet."

Higgins took a deep breath and stepped next to him. "Sit down. This is going be a crazy ride."

Before his bum had even touched the material, they were in the air and she had put up a green shield around them.

Skyhammer shut his eyes as they shot out across the Crystal Lines. If she had created a green shield, she must be expecting the colour to change at some point. Perhaps even to red. This meant she didn't think she could last long against her attackers. "We can make it to the edge of the Circle, right? Right?"

No response.

"Higgins? Higgins!" He opened his eyes and screamed in terror. They plummeted like a hawk to its prey while hundreds of dark shapes streamed down towards them through the sky.

"No, we can't," Higgins said through gritted teeth. "I can't steer this thing and fight them off at the same time."

"What can I do to help?"

Higgins laughed, a little manically, Skyhammer thought. "Pray." Their carpet dodged and weaved through a flurry of spells.

The fissures of the Crystal Lines lay only thirty feet below them now. Skyhammer looked up. A spell exploded against the shield, which dimmed to yellow.

"Oh buzzards," Higgins muttered.

"What?"

"Once that shield turns red, we're toast. I guess it's plan B." The wall hanging continued to plummet, Higgins' fingers flying across her slate.

"Uh, there's no exit down there, Higgins!" Skyhammer yelled. Three spells flared against the shield. It turned orange.

"There's only-"

"Plan B, like I said," she yelled back. She dropped them straight into a fissure of the Crystal Lines.

* * *

The fissure walls of jagged white crystal shot up around him. An eerie howling raised the hair on Skyhammer's forearms. Five feet of air protected their carpet from the walls on either side. It was a tight squeeze.

Through the orange shield, Skyhammer glimpsed three carpets following them, dark against the white background of the crystal walls. "At least three following, Higgins." Floatilla blocked the sunlight, so if a carpet flew directly above them, he couldn't see it.

She nodded, manoeuvring the carpet through the fissure's sharp twists and turns.

The carpet shook as another spell burst against the shield. One more and that deep orange shade would be red, Skyhammer thought. And they would be dead. He peered at the walls - there was something odd about them. They were moving.

"Did we lose them?" Higgins shouted.

Skyhammer turned around. "Looks like it." The space above him seemed to have become white but he found it hard to tell through the orange shield. He supposed the carpet might have gone under an overhang. "Stop the carpet, Higgins."

The carpet froze.

"Drop the shields."

"What? No way." Higgins looked back over her shoulder at him, a puzzled expression on her face.

"We need to see something."

Higgins cast a spell. The orange shield disappeared, to be replaced with a transparent one. "No way am I leaving us shield-less. Who knows what is dow--" Her mouth gaped open.

White spikes the length of Skyhammer's hand projected from the crystal walls. They swayed, like grass on the seabed. A tiny bulb at the end of each spike was lit from inside by a blue light. Skyhammer looked up and sighed. The spikes ten feet above the carpet had grown across the fissure, blocking it completely. They were spaced a little more than a fingers-width apart.

"Great. Above us, the spikes are bars. And maybe this is why people never come back." He found himself reaching out to touch one and yanked his hand back.

"What?" Higgins looked up and frowned. "We're trapped," she said glumly then attempted to smile at Skyhammer. "Our pursuers will think we're dead."

"Because we probably are!"

"We didn't have any other choice. And the bars haven't killed us. Just stopped us from going back up. We can still fly straight ahead."

He sighed. "At least the howling has stopped."

"What howling?"

He stared at her. "You didn't hear that horrible noise when we first entered?"

She shook her head.

"Okay," he said. She was probably so involved in flying and casting spells that she blocked out other sounds. He shrugged. "Well, that way is the Palace so the other direction must be the edge of the Circle. We can either go down more or continue at this height."

"We need to reach the edge of the Circle," she said. The carpet headed right. "I hear something now."

They both listened. Flutes, faint, played around them.

"There were holes," Skyhammer whispered.

"What?" Higgins swung around to look at him. "What did you say?"

"I saw holes in the spikes. I think the wind moving through them is making that music."

Higgins smiled. "It's beautiful."

Skyhammer snapped his fingers. "It also means that fresh air is blowing through here. And if there is air-"

"There must be an exit!" Higgins sang out.

"Well, Tabitha?"

Higgins rolled her eyes.

"Let's go then!"

"In a minute." Higgins' face creased in a small smile.

He felt confused. "I thought we just agreed--"

"We haven't even tried to perform magic on the bars. Maybe

the people who were trapped here before just didn't have enough magic power to get past the bars."

"Oh. It's worth a try, I suppose." Skyhammer sat back and opened his arms wide. "Be my guest."

Higgins sketched a few lines on her slate. A fireball burst against the bars a few feet above and ahead of them. Skyhammer shielded his eyes.

"No effect at all?" Higgins muttered. "I guess I'll try a stronger one."

Skyhammer didn't shield his eyes the second time. Again, there was no effect. "Try freezing them."

Higgins shrugged and sent a cloud of cold air up to surround the bars. Icicles formed on the bars, then dissipated. "That's-"

"Impossible?" Skyhammer asked. "These things are as impervious to magic as Relics. Maybe it is one big Relic." He slapped his backpack and gave her a smug smile. "Which gives me an idea."

Higgins looked at him.

"Fly this carpet to the edge of the Circle."

"You think it goes that far?"

"I think it does."

Higgins cast a spell. A silver light coalesced five feet in front of the carpet, hovering at eye level. "When that light disappears, we've reached the edge of the Circle."

Higgins set a dizzying pace. Skyhammer had to close his eyes.

After about ten minutes, the carpet stopped. "Are we there?" He opened his eyes and looked over the edge of the carpet. "Oh my."

At first, all he could see were exposed tree roots. The fissure's walls had opened up into a large cavern, not very deep, but quite wide. Roots covered the floor of the cavern but inverted, like the base of a tree felled by a storm. And instead of growing in dirt, the roots were growing in transparent crystal.

Higgins flew the carpet down until they were only two feet above the floor.

In some spots, there were serpentine gaps of a pond and feeder stream. Through these gaps, sky, clouds and animals were visible.

"Do you see what I see?" he asked. There was no forest for

hundreds of miles near the Crystal Lines as far as he knew. Maybe the crystal went right through the center of the world and they were looking at the other side of the planet.

"An upside-down forest?" She was shaking her head.

"Yep." Birds and butterflies zoomed over the water; a frog paddled below him. He stared at the frog's belly. "Is it real?"

"I've seen a lot of weird things in my time with you but this is, well," she frowned, "extremely disconcerting."

"How can we get out of here?" Skyhammer dragged his gaze away from the cavern floor and looked up again.

"We keep following the bars." Higgins pointed to the opposite end of the cavern, in the direction they were headed. The fissure resumed.

With a last glance at the inverted forest, Higgins flew the carpet back up to the bars and continued flying just below, the silver beacon bouncing along in front of them.

* * *

Skyhammer's body was shaking. An earthquake, he thought blearily, opening his eyes. No, just Higgins rousing him. "Wha-?" He must have fallen asleep.

"We're here." She gave him a final shake. "My light died."
He sat up at once.

Three feet in front of them was a wall of darkness. To their left and right, the blue-tipped spikes stuck out of the crystal walls, still swaying, eerily lighting the space around them. Above, spikes barred their path up and out. In the light cast from their side, Skyhammer could see spikes of a similar size protruding from the crystal walls and a track of bars heading off into the darkness. As though an enormous shadow covered the fissure ahead of them, the shadow being the absence of the Royal Circle of magic. "So the spikes react to magic," he murmured. "Fascinating."

"Now what, genius?" Higgins crossed her arms and looked at him. "We're trapped over there too."

"We've tried your way. The magic way. And failed. Now we try it my way." He stood up and drew his sword from its scabbard. Gripping the hilt double-fisted, he swung at the bars above him with all his strength.

Higgins yelped and fell to her knees as the sword rebounded off the bars with a clang.

Skyhammer halted the rebounding blade a foot to the left of her. "Oops. Should've faced the other way, I guess." He smothered a smile.

She glared at him. "So much for your way. Don't you think the explorers that got trapped here before would've tried that?" She stood up.

"No, I don't," he said calmly. "They weren't explorers. They were magic-wielding humans. Those types of people depend on magic all the time. They wouldn't have brought a sword or probably even known how to use one. They would've been confident that magic could get them out of any trouble they got into as long as they were within the Royal Circle."

Higgins considered this a moment, then nodded. "But that doesn't change the fact that your sword still didn't get through the bars."

Skyhammer grinned. "Not these bars, no. But those, yes." He pointed with his sword tip to the bars and spikes in the darkness ahead.

Realization dawned on Higgins' face. "Of course! The Royal Circle ends right here. Over there, the bars across the crevasse will be normal strength not magically powerful." She smiled and held her hands up. "Tell me what to do."

"Okay, Bethany." He raised his eyebrows in question.

She shook her head. "Not even close."

"Move the carpet forward until it is as close to the edge of the Royal Circle as you can get. Then stand at the back." He liked solving physical problems like this. Made him feel like he was back outside the Royal Circle, Relic hunting. Where ingenuity and muscle strength counted for something. And he especially liked solving a problem that Higgins couldn't. He chortled to himself.

Higgins did as he instructed, nudging the orange carpet right next to where the magic ended started.

After stepping to the front of the carpet, he positioned himself with one foot forward and one back. He stretched his sword out into the darkness ahead of him, close to the right-hand wall. In a quick, focused movement, he thrust the sword up then pulled it back, as if he was going to plunge it in to someone behind him. The sword sliced through ten of the bars on the shadowed side. When the sword crashed into the last bar still inside the Royal Circle, the blade rebounded against the bar, unable to break it. The movement pulled Skyhammer forward. For a few nerve-wracking seconds, he teetered at the edge of the carpet, gazing down into the well of blackness.

Higgins grabbed his hips and pulled him back onto the carpet.

He breathed a sigh of relief. He preferred the darkness to seeing the bottom. It meant he could delude himself into thinking the ground was just a few feet down. "Thanks. Ready for a second time?"

"Yup."

This time he sliced the blade of his sword along the left side of the bars. Cut-out pieces tumbled into the blackness below, leaving a dark hole. There was no sound of them hitting the bottom. Skyhammer shivered. Much deeper than a few feet then. He wondered what was happening above the Crystal Lines now that the Keeper was trapped in the fissures. Since no one had ever escaped from the Lines, his attackers would believe him dead, their mission accomplished. He resolved to prove them wrong. What a surprise they'd get when the Sorcerer changed more Retrographs.

Skyhammer fetched a length of rope from his backpack, then tossed one end of it up into the hole he had created on the non-magic side. Judging by how quickly it fell back down, he determined there were more bars above.

"That's a lot of cutting." Higgins had realized what he was testing. "And climbing."

He thrust his sword through the gaps in the bars above his head. "Oh, we won't be climbing." The blade went through to his hilt. "Need to find out one more thing first. Raise the carpet two feet higher please."

This put the carpet four feet below the bars. Reaching up, he threaded the rope end through a gap between the bars, then around the bar closest to the edge of the Royal Circle and back down. He tied a knot then yanked on the rope. The bar held.

"Lower the carpet to about ten feet please."

As the carpet sank, Skyhammer tightened his grip on the rope. When the carpet stopped, he swung in the air two feet above it.

The carpet rose so he could stand.

He tied the rope around himself. "Raise the carpet a few feet again." He thrust his sword into the dark hole he had made in the bars on the shadowed side and sliced down the left then down the right. Pieces of bar fell past his nose, clinking against the crystal walls as they continued down to the bottom of the fissure.

"And now, the grand finale!" He put away his sword and stood at the edge of the carpet, facing Higgins. He grasped the last bar that was inside the Royal Circle.

Chapter 9

Countdown to ceremony: 14 days

"Raise the carpet very slowly please."

Higgins nodded, her face serious. As the carpet rose, Skyhammer maintained his grip on the bar.

"Stop!" He sat down, still holding the bar. Leaning back, shoulders out over the fissure, he threaded his legs between his arms. A thrust of his hips lifted his body up and on top of the bars on the Royal Circle side. He poked his fingers through a gap and wiggled them. "Hi, Higgins!"

She rolled her eyes. "Nice work."

Once Higgins, their backpacks and the carpet were on top of the bars, they rose straight up the fissure.

"We can zip around to the mountain path and go straight across the mountains to the Vault." Skyhammer peered back across the Crystal Lines. The sun had set in the hours they'd been in the fissure. A few lights flickered from the Palace. Floatilla hung like a chandelier high above them. A lumpy dark line delineated mountains and starry sky.

The half-mile mile buffer zone was quiet this time of night.

"How many days would the mountain route add?" Higgins mused. "Six or seven, right? We can't afford that. We've already lost one day inside the fissure and we still have no idea who or where this Sorcerer is."

"We can't afford to die if they see us either," Skyhammer argued. His throat closed up at the thought of being in another magic battle, powerless to defend himself.

Higgins faced him. "It's night. No one will be able to distinguish us from other carpets. We stay in the buffer zone. Land in the village closest to the Retrograph Vault, walk through the village and we're in the forest and home free. No one'll track us in there." The carpet rose out of the fissure and headed for the mountains.

Skyhammer's thoughts leapt ahead to the Vault. Maybe the Retrograph Sorcerer would be there, waiting for him. The most magically powerful human in the world versus the human with no magic powers at all. But out of the Circle, maybe his magic wouldn't work. But maybe it would work and that was why the Sorcerer wants to stop the ceremony. So that other humans can't use magic outside the Circle as well! Or-- stop! Just wait and see.

****

"Think the Retrograph Sorcerer knows we're after him?" Skyhammer was grateful the sky had cleared. Stealing two horses on a cloudy night was hard enough but navigating their way to the Vault would've been almost impossible without the stars. Leaving a bag of money in place of the horses still made Skyhammer feel guilty, even though he had left quite a bit more than the horses were worth. They needed the speed though.

Higgins shrugged. "The King meeting with the Keeper is a pretty good sign, I'd say." She patted her horse's neck.

"He has to know the King would try to find him."

"Why do we think it's a him?" Higgins grinned. "I mean, would a man really have the balls to change the King's Retrographs?"

"Now, now, you don't have to bring your previous relationships into this-"

"At least I've *had* relationships," she shot back.

"Hey now! I had . . . one." Skyhammer chuckled as he held a branch out of the way for Higgins. "But what's the point?"

"Of relationships?"

He rolled his eyes. "Of overturning the drawings of the ceremony. Does the Sorcerer mean to communicate that he is sabotaging the ceremony? Or is there another meaning? Maybe he wants to destroy magic entirely. If he plans to kill the King with the sword, like in his Retrograph, that is certainly a way to destroy magic." He couldn't bear the thought. The ceremony was two weeks away. Magic power was two weeks away. He couldn't let this Sorcerer ruin his chance.

"Save that question for when we catch her."

As they continued through the dark forest, Skyhammer puzzled over relationships. Romantic relationships. Three years ago, he would've bitterly retorted that there was no point to relationships, only a maelstrom of pain and despair. Maybe a pointed stick in your heart. Funny that a woman with the name

Spark could so totally douse a flicker of love. But they had just been kids anyway. He was over it now. Not bitter at all. He unclenched his jaw. He didn't want these memories carrying him back to the Retrograph Vault and the Academy but they were like a tidal wave and he was the beach.

He'd never figured out why Spark left without saying goodbye. His Keeper of the Retrograph Vault ceremony was supposed to be the day they showed everyone they were officially a couple. She never showed up to the ceremony and never again at the Academy. In three years, he'd heard nothing.

In the beginning, he'd thought she had been kidnapped. The Academy's principal took him aside when she heard that rumour and told him that Spark had withdrawn from the school and wasn't coming back. The principal didn't reveal why.

He'd spent a week in the weapons room, going through sword forms and fighting anyone who came in. Slept there too. Even Higgins left him alone. Spark was the only other person he'd met that was born without magic powers. They'd planned to be Relic hunters together, him and Spark, looking for magic together. He wasn't going to hang around, visit the Retrograph Vault once a week, and eat himself to an early grave like the last Keeper.

Then Spark was gone. The only person who could understand, really, truly understand what it was like not to have magic powers. She'd dealt with her lack of magic with more violence but still, they'd finally found each other. How could she just leave like that? A jolt of hurt rocked him, surprising in its force. He thought he'd moved on. He imagined putting the feelings into a box and tossing them onto a bonfire. Better.

The light had brightened perceptibly and with it, Skyhammer's mood. They were nearing the Retrograph Vault. A loud growl erupted from behind him. Skyhammer twisted around, sword held high, eyes darting left and right. "I thought I heard a bear."

"You did. I'm un-BEAR-ably hungry!" Higgins rubbed her stomach.

Skyhammer groaned. "We'd better get you fed. Your brain's turning to mush." He led the way to an open glade off the trail.

As they chewed on spicy dried meat and sipped from their

water flasks, the twittering of birds rose around them, curious squirrels stopped by and the sun warmed their skin. The horses munched grass on the other side of the glade. Higgins and Skyhammer opened their Whorls.

Glancing over at his partner, Skyhammer was not surprised to see tears sliding down her cheeks as she flicked through her Retrographs. Polygon. He slid over beside her and put his hand on top of hers.

She smiled at him through her tears. "She was my best friend."

Skyhammer nodded. "She gave up her life for you. For what we're doing."

Higgins leaned her head on his shoulder. He inhaled her vanilla scent, wishing he could take her pain away or dull it at least. At last, she stood up, eyes dry, and closed her Whorl. "We have to find this Sorcerer before she kills the King and stops the ceremony." She pulled him up. "Let's go." Higgins led the way this time.

Tired from their sleepless night, Skyhammer stared at her horse's swaying rump, eyelids sagging, mind wandering. The drawings of the Wall were done by a talented Byndari artist. Skyhammer felt relieved that he had had a chance to view the drawings again at the Palace. The Sorcerer had turned over his first set of drawings. Would he . . .? He opened his Whorl and flicked to the drawings in the Palace. The first Retrograph appeared.

He straightened up so fast his lower back spasmed.

The Retrographs had been changed again. *His* Retrographs.

"Higgins?" he squeaked.

She turned in her saddle, concern crossing her face when she saw him. "What happened?"

Shaking his head, he stared at the Retrograph in front of him. The table in the Palace was still covered with the five drawings. But the papers had all been flipped over so only their blank backs showed.

"What is it?" Higgins pulled her horse up next to him and grasped his arm.

Eyes wide, unable to tear his gaze away from the Retrograph, Skyhammer whispered to her what had changed.

Her jaw dropped.

Skyhammer flicked to the previous Retrograph and gasped.

The pages had all been turned over in that one as well! And in the previous five Retrographs where he recorded the drawings. Would he ever see the drawings in his Retrograph again? His stomach clenched; so much of his past could disappear from his Retrographs. He never made an effort to remember anything he saw; why would he when he could just look at his Retrographs? What else had the Sorcerer changed?

Cautiously, he flicked back again. Nothing, nothing, nothing, then...

With a savage jerk of his hand, he closed the Whorl.

Higgins shook him, almost screaming in his ear. "What?!"

Skyhammer contemplated running away, back out to the jungle, the desert, any place where he could forget what he had seen. The Retrograph Sorcerer had touched him. Was watching him. Not just the King. He wanted a bath. Why did the gods insist on getting him more involved with the stupid Vault? He didn't want to be Keeper. Why didn't they just pick someone who was interested?

He stretched his arms up over his head, then dropped his hands to rest, clasped, over his skull. After a moment, he felt in control of his emotions, enough that he could explain to Higgins that in one other Retrograph there had been a change. One that involved her.

She clasped his hand for comfort as he described the round table with four slates on it. Two slates from the guards, one from Higgins and one from Polygon. Each slate had a knife plunged into its center. There were no marks of damage on the slates but it was obvious what the Sorcerer was trying to say. She was planning to destroy magic.

In a panic, Higgins opened her Whorl again. The drawings in her Retrographs were turned over as well, no other changes. "Why did the Sorcerer only change your Retrographs to show you the magic slates?"

"Who knows why that crazy person does anything," Skyhammer muttered. "But it's obvious they mean to sabotage the ceremony and destroy magic. Somehow the Sorcerer knows that the ceremony can destroy magic power as well as give it to people."

"But how?" Higgins asked. "And why change the drawings and the slates?"

Skyhammer shook his head, unable to answer. As he approached Murk Lake where the Retrograph Vault was located, a sense of guilt began to creep over him. He'd been gone for three years. It was his job to keep an eye on the Vault. But it wasn't my choice to be Keeper, he argued with himself. If I had stayed, maybe the same thing would've happened. I would've been unhappy anyway and maybe not paid attention as well as I could have. It's not my fault.

But was it a tiny bit his fault? He pushed the thought away. "Hey, we're only a couple hours away. Do you think there'll be anyone waiting for us at the Vault?"

Higgins didn't answer for a few moments. "Possibly," she finally replied. "When people's Retrographs started changing, they must have come out here to the Vault. It's the first place I'd look if my Retrographs were broken."

"Then they could possibly still be here." He looked back over his shoulder at Higgins.

"Oh yes. Maybe a lot of them, depending on how worked up they are." She frowned.

"If they're anything like those people in Edgeton, we need to be prepared."

"You still have to get into the lake to get into the Vault. When we get close, you go and have a look."

He felt nervous but not as much as in the Royal Circle. The humans waiting at the Retrograph Vault would not be as warrior-like as the ones who had chased them out of Edgeton. Around here, the villages were mostly full of farmers. Not the types to wield swords with any level of skill.

When he could see more light between the trees up ahead, he and Higgins dismounted. They tied the horses to tree branches. Skyhammer crept up to the edge of the forest. Hiding behind an oak, he looked out at Murk Lake. A carpet of vibrant orange moss banked the lake on all sides.

Except one. Towering above the trees yet sloped as if fearful, away from the lake, a cliff of dark yellow stone protected the west end. The lake was a truncated circle filled with gelatinous black liquid. The surface appeared to suck light into it. Murk Lake was a good place to hide the Retrograph Vault but it wasn't exactly welcoming. Skyhammer was surprised. And suspicious. Why was no one here waiting for him?

"Heard you were dead, I guess!"

He jumped at Higgins voice right behind him. "Don't sneak up on me like that!" He pushed her shoulder, relieved she wasn't a random vengeful human.

"Should such a great and successful Relic hunter be surprised that easily?" Higgins gave him a cheeky smile.

With a haughty lift of his chin, Skyhammer marched down to the orange beach. He stripped to his shorts. Higgins flopped onto the springy moss and opened her Whorl.

Skyhammer crept up beside her and put his mouth close to her ear. "Barracuda?"

"No! Who would name their child barracuda?" Her eyes remained fixed on her Retrographs. "Get going!" Then she grabbed his arm. "If the humans think we're dead, they'll be coming to try out for the Keeper position. Hurry."

He nodded. "And if their Retrographs change and they realize I'm not dead, they'll be coming here to get me." They couldn't use magic to attack him this time though. They'd have to catch him first.

Whatever material filled the lake, Skyhammer loved swimming in it. He and Spark had slipped away from the Academy and come here many times to swim. He skimmed along the surface, the black liquid far denser than water. No breeze made waves. The sun never affected the temperature; the liquid felt warm on his skin.

Upon reaching the center of the lake, he dived down. Eyes squeezed shut, he felt for the tip of a pointed rock far below the surface. The tunnel started a few feet below the rock's tip. Found it! Lungs starting to burn, he swam down the tunnel as fast as possible. His fingers hit a wall and poked into what felt like a moist cake. A strong kick sent his whole body through. His arms burst out into the cave on the other side and he remembered enough, even after three years, to let them break his fall so his whole body didn't crash painfully on the ground like the first time. First few times, he admitted to himself.

He was inside the Retrograph Vault. Would the Retrograph Sorcerer be waiting for him?

Chapter 10

Countdown to ceremony: 14 days

His shorts had disappeared. Naked as usual. They'd
somehow be back on his body when he left the Vault. He
wondered where his shorts were now. Nothing but a human
body could pass through the dense wall. Were they stuck inside
the wall? And nothing could come out, he had been told. Only
now did he wonder who had tried to bring something out.

Absolute blackness and silence engulfed him. Would the
Sorcerer be here? How else would the Sorcerer alter the
Retrographs? This was the only place in the world to view the
Retrographs. It was as impossible for the Sorcerer to be here as
it was for the Sorcerer to change Retrographs. In all of human
history, there had only been one Keeper at a time. As soon as
the Keeper retired from old age, or death, a new Keeper was
chosen. Once the Vault chose the new Keeper, the old one could
no longer access the Vault. So the Sorcerer couldn't be here.
And Retrographs couldn't be changed. Ha! Sighing, he rose and
shuffled down the tunnel, one hand on the wall.

When his fingers and toes grazed a spiky ridge encircling
the tunnel, he halted. From far below, a green light began to
climb the walls to light the cavern before him.

A step in front of him, the tunnel ended. The vast cavern
stretched up beyond Skyhammer's view, taller than it was wide,
and despite the light, he couldn't see the bottom or the top.
Glowing green tubes in vertical lines ran up the rock wall.

Floating isolated in the middle of the cavern, at the same
height as the tunnel, was a circular platform. From the bottom,
a spiral of rock pointed down. On top, an insect-like chair.
Silence filled the space. The Sorcerer wasn't here. Of course not,
he told himself. Only a Keeper can get in here. And you used to
think no one could alter Retrographs either. Get on with it.

Skyhammer gazed into the yawning gulf separating him
from the platform. His hands shook.

He took a deep breath and, grasping onto the ridge in the
tunnel wall, peered over the edge and down. Bottomless.
Shuddering, he moved back. Why did he even look when it

scared him so much? Destructive and frightening but he still did it. He stood up straight and exhaled all the air from his lungs. Then he stepped out into the empty space between the platform and the tunnel.

The lights blazed when his foot came down on the transparent bridge. He kept his eyes focused on the platform, pretending to ignore the great gaping void of nothingness below.

When he reached the platform, the walls began to rotate around it, spinning into a curtain of glowing green. Silence continued. The tunnel entrance was gone. How did the Vault know when he needed the tunnel back? He said a short prayer to the gods that this time, once again, the walls would stop moving and the tunnel would be available again when he was done.

Skyhammer examined the Retrograph viewing contraption, fashioned from a mysterious black metal. A tall black ring, a foot taller than Skyhammer, perched on its edge, about five steps in front of the chair. The chair had a square seat at thigh height and a rectangular back that reached to about three quarters the height of the ring. Two thin arms curved inwards, set with purple and blue buttons. The top of the chair's back bristled with rods and cubes of varying sizes. So far, no sign that anyone else had been here. He began to relax.

All the apparatus was made of an unknown material, unknown to Skyhammer at least and to every Keeper that had been entrusted with the safety of the Vault. Skyhammer ran his fingers over the buttons. No dust, but there never was, no matter how long between visits. He stood on the seat and peered up at the cubes and rods.

A cube was missing. He stumbled back, almost falling off the chair.

"It must have fallen off," he said aloud, as though that would make it true. There were usually five small black cubes attached to a rod that came out of the back of the chair. Only four were left. He searched the whole platform. Nothing. Maybe it had fallen into the abyss. No. The invisible field that kept humans on the platform would also keep objects on it.

His heart began to pound. He grabbed the arm of the chair to steady himself. An intruder in the Vault! An intruder who had taken a piece of the Retrograph machine. He collapsed onto the chair, mind racing. "A second Keeper?" he whispered. The silence was getting to him. He'd never spent this much time inside the Vault.

Skyhammer sat up and pressed a purple button on the chair's left arm. A list of names appeared within the black ring in front of him. The missing black cube didn't seem to affect the performance of the Vault. He scrolled through the names and picked one at random. A woman who lived in Floatilla, he discovered, scrolling through her Retrographs. He turned off the image, shuddering in disgust. He hated looking at people's Retrographs. No Keeper ever revealed that they could see Retrographs. Not even Higgins knew. Only another Keeper would know. The Keeper before Skyhammer was dead. The Sorcerer must be the new one.

A thought struck him. What if even he could do more than look? Perhaps the Sorcerer was just the first one to try changing Retrographs, not the only one with the ability. The image filled the circle again. Skyhammer rose from the chair and stood close to the picture. Pointing his index finger, he moved it right next to the image and then through.

His finger felt nothing. The image didn't change. He let out his breath.

Back in the chair, image gone, he stared unseeing into the soft green light of the walls. Someone had been here within the last three years. Someone had taken a piece of the Vault out. How was that possible? Who would break the Vault on purpose, then try to smuggle a piece out? Maybe he could take one as well and get magic powers. He stood on the seat once again and tugged and pushed at each of the four cubes, then tried to break a rod. The machine was unaffected. He slumped back into the chair.

For the first time ever he wished he had listened when the previous Vault Keeper had been droning on about the Vault. It didn't help that he was drunk eighty percent of the day and sleeping the other twenty percent. The result of a coveted, yet totally useless, position. The Keepers just kept an eye on the Vault. They knew absolutely nothing about how it worked-- like every other Relic.

He groaned. Maybe if he had been around, doing his job then

the Retrograph Sorcerer would've been caught soon after stealing the piece.

Maybe the Moksha had come back. He massaged his skull. They wouldn't break their own bloody Vault, would they? Who knew what the Moksha would do, though. They'd been gone millions of years.

The rod that was missing a cube didn't look damaged at all, he observed upon a second examination. In fact, it looked as though it was meant to come apart. There was a slot where some kind of hook could go into the rod. He compared it to the other black cubes: smooth all over, no sign of being able to come apart. How had the Sorcerer figured out that one was different? He would've had to spend a lot of time in here. The Sorcerer was a curious and intelligent person. And powerful.

Skyhammer walked to the edge of the spiral platform where he had come off the bridge. By the time he arrived, the walls had stopped moving and he could see the tunnel entrance across the chasm. He focused on the tunnel and stepped into empty air. When his foot hit the bridge, he whispered a quick thanks and hurried across. As he made his way back to the receiving cavern, he kept his eye on the ground. It was as clean and empty as ever.

Back out in the lake, shorts having reappeared, he floated, star-shaped, on his back. He wasn't ready to talk to Higgins just yet. Over the past two days, his world had turned upside-down. Words, ideas, events flickered through his brain. But he grasped nothing, like a fickle butterfly in a field of wildflowers.

Immutable truths. Only one Keeper? Untrue.

His thoughts landed. Orderly now, as though he was assessing a battle or planning a Relic hunt.

Relics unalterable? Untrue. Magic restrained by the Circles? True. Danger from angry humans? High. Likelihood of receiving magic powers? True. True. True!

He felt like he could soar above the lake, into the sky.

Likelihood of powerful sorcerer sabotaging the ceremony? Low, if Skyhammer had anything to do with it.

Strong strokes powered him back to the shore where Higgins was standing. As he got dressed, he told her what he had found.

"The Sorcerer and the Keeper who stole the cube is not

necessarily the same person," she pointed out.

They were walking along the moss beach toward the cliff. A Byndari named Hermit lived on top of the cliff, reclusive to the point of throwing stones down on people trying to get up the cliff. Byndari at the Academy just shrugged when humans complained about Hermit. They left him alone as well, in fact. He didn't seem to have any friends at all.

"You're saying that either there are three Keepers or the Sorcerer doesn't need to go in the Vault to change Retrographs." Skyhammer's imagination almost baulked at how powerful the Sorcerer would be.

"I'm saying we shouldn't rule anything out."

As he concentrated on keeping his balance walking across the springy moss, Skyhammer recalled the day that his class had gone to Murk Lake to do the test. Students at the Relic Hunters Academy were not given a choice to try out for the Keeper position. The test was part of their second year studies - if the Keeper position was open. Most kids wanted to be Keeper if they could. Who wouldn't want money, privilege and more importantly, access to one of Relics in the world that worked? And if you were studying at the Academy, you were already crazy about Relics.

Skyhammer didn't want to differ from other humans more than he already did with his lack of magic powers; he wanted to be a Relic hunter. The Retrograph Relic chose its own Keeper who always had magic abilities. As a human without magic, he was certain he wouldn't be chosen.

But of all the kids trying that day to swim through the wall at the end of the tunnel, he was the only one who could do it. When he tumbled into the receiving cavern, he had cried at the unfairness of it all. Now he would be expected to live in the King's Circle or near the Vault so he could do his duty to the blessed damn Relic that gave humans such a powerful gift. He would never be a Relic hunter. Instead, he would grow old and fat on privilege and power. So he sobbed alone in the cavern. Then he wiped away the tears and waited the required ten minutes before heading back out to tell his classmates and teachers what they already knew.

"Hermit must have seen something," Higgins said as they approached the cliff.

"Then why hasn't he told the Academy and the King?"

She shrugged. "He's a Byndari. Who knows why they do what they do?"

Carved into the yellow cliff face were a set of stairs. Although calling them stairs was a bit of a stretch, Skyhammer decided.

"Up you go!" Higgins looked at him.

Groaning, Skyhammer slipped his foot into a roughly hewn slot in the cliff and reached up to grab a metal spike hammered in some way above his head. He hated heights. "No wonder he never comes down." He heaved himself up the wall, chanting his internal mantra: "Don't look down, don't look down."

An hour later, Higgins swung herself over the cliff top and reclined beside a balled-up Skyhammer.

She whistled. "What a view, eh?"

The forest spread out in all directions. To the east, the enormous dark blot of Floatilla hung in the sky. To the west, the forest ended, a long ways off, and the grey range of the Nasuchu lands began. The Shard Mountains crept north. The wide blue above was studded with puffs of white cloud.

"Come on, let's go. I'm curious to see the inside of Hermit's place." She headed towards the house, wind ruffling her hair.

Hermit's house consisted of blocks carved out of the cliff. Since the cliff top was only about twenty feet long in all directions, the house was one room, half-underground. A tall urn stood at the back. Stairs led down to a door.

As they reached the entrance, a high-pitched squeak came from within. It rose and fell intermittently.

Skyhammer's face crumpled. "Oh crap."

"What's that?" Higgins' eyes widened. She stopped moving.

"His harmonica. Hadn't you heard him playing when you were here before? He's awful," Skyhammer whispered.

Higgins relaxed and continued down the stairs. She rapped on the door.

They waited a minute then tried again.

"Could he be ignoring us?" There was a dangerous catch in her voice.

"Possibly." He reached past her, turned the handle and pushed. "Let's just go in."

Higgins walked in, Skyhammer one step behind.

"Hello? Hermit?" To his left, the wall was hidden behind a number of large blocks of salt. Straight ahead, an enormous open fireplace lay dark, a poker on the ground next to it, a couch in front. The right wall reached to waist height then was open right up to the ceiling. A glass-less window. A harmonica lay on the window ledge, emitting a low squeak.

A glint on the floor drew Skyhammer towards the poker.

Crunch!

He froze.

Chapter 11

Countdown to ceremony: 14 days

Higgins hurried over. Skyhammer dared to look down. Beneath his feet was a pile of sand and other ocean detritus. The glinting object was a large oyster shell. Dried bits of seaweed, pieces of wood, small rocks, and any number of shells of all shapes and sizes covered the floor.

 Hermit was dead.

"Are you sure it's him?" Higgins knelt on the floor, leaning over what was left of Hermit.

Skyhammer had backed away, stepping off the remains of Hermit's boot-crunched body.

"That oyster shell sat on his left shoulder and he had," Skyhammer glanced over the pile of debris, "that gold-flecked rock on his right shoulder."

"Skyhammer."

"Mmm?"

Higgins rose from the floor. "The poker?"

"Ah." Skyhammer had been avoiding the heavy iron fire poker that lay next to the oyster shell and across the pile of debris. A Byndari's body consisted of an outer shell of sand and other ocean detritus that protected the millions of tiny and delicate water-borne amoebas from the murderous air. Repairing a hole in their shell was almost impossible; most Byndari died within a few minutes of being damaged.

"Someone killed him."

"Maybe he slipped and fell while poking the fire?" Hope filled Skyhammer's voice.

"Maybe."

They sat in silence on the couch.

"We haven't examined anything else." Skyhammer made no move to get up.

"There's no one here. Nobody comes here." Higgins stared at the harmonica.

"He didn't have any friends or anything." It puzzled Skyhammer that Hermit didn't even have any Byndari friends. Maybe the Moksha really had come back. They were the only beings powerful enough to get inside the Retrograph Vault and cruel enough to kill Hermit for seeing them do it. He rubbed his eyes. It was ridiculous to be blaming the Moksha for this.

"I don't want to stay here," Higgins announced. "We should push on to the Academy."

"Are you sure we should still go? The humans there will be just as angry."

"We need to tell the Byndari about the death of a member of their species," Higgins said in a stern voice.

Skyhammer nodded. "The Academy will send Byndari to investigate. Maybe they can tell us why he died or if and when he was killed."

"And they knew you at the Academy. We can speak to Rantama and Principal Floss about the situation. Maybe get some suggestions on who could have been near the Vault." Higgins shivered and headed outside.

Skyhammer cast a glance at the whispering harmonica on the window sill and then closed the door.

* * *

As they poled in a boat up the blue-green canal waters leading to the Academy's grounds, Skyhammer wondered if the student responsible for the canal boat loved the job as much as Skyhammer had. The boat was in the same excellent condition. The canal that connected the two lakes, Murk and Vatil, had been built by the Academy for handy access to the Retrograph Vault. Water that emptied from the canal into Murk Lake seemed to vanish under the black sludge. Maybe the Sorcerer was someone from the Academy. Principal Floss would be able to give them a list of the humans on campus. Although, they had no idea when the piece was taken or when Hermit was killed. If the two were connected, then if the Byndari could tell them when Hermit was killed, that would be useful information. Would Rantama still be at the Academy? He was looking forward to a chat with his Byndari friend.

Skyhammer's mind was awash with memories as he neared the Academy. Most were of his third year. Most included Spark. Stolen kisses, long discussions of childhood experiences, planning for a future of Relic hunting and always, always, dreams of what they would do when they had magic powers.

As the boat glided along the canal, Skyhammer smiled softly. High banks hid woodland and field but eagles and turkey vultures soared on the air currents high above. He recalled a sweet summer afternoon just like this one, soft blankets in the boat, and a warm girl in his arms . . .

The boat bumped into the lock leading up to the lake, jolting Skyhammer back to reality.

Higgins leapt up onto the lock and hauled the wheel to close the doors. As soon as the doors closed, she pulled the lever and the lock filled with water, raising the boat up to lake level. The Vatil, a fresh water lake and the heart of the Academy. Low buildings covered in greenery and flowers blossomed around the lake.

When he first arrived at the Academy, Skyhammer was astounded to find that everything was recycled and the school grew its own food. The dining hall served only vegetarian meals, making everything from scratch. Although students studied at their own pace, they were required to spend four hours each day maintaining the buildings and its environs and doing other daily chores such as cooking and washing. Remembering the taste of fresh-picked strawberries made Skyhammer's mouth water. Until the day he arrived at the Academy, he had only eaten scraps from his family's table or animals he hunted, or berries he picked in the forest.

Skyhammer had haunted the library most weekends, staying out of trouble. Extra time spreading nightsoil was the punishment of choice for professors but rarely did their keen pupils need discipline. Occasionally there would be structured group classes but if a student had a question, it was up to that student to go and find someone who could answer it. Rantama could answer most of Skyhammer's questions.

Skyhammer stared down into the crystal clear water, lost in thought. Next time he came back here, it would be with magic powers.

"Mr. Skyhammer. Miss Higgins. Rumours of your demise have been greatly exaggerated."

Skyhammer glanced towards the commanding voice then fumbled with his pole, almost spilling them into the water. He began to sweat. Ms. Floss, the school's principal, was as squat and muscular as she had been three years ago. Before he ran off without telling her. He'd forgotten about that until now. He poled furiously towards the dock where she stood.

"I'm sorry ma'am-"

She held up a hand. "I am prepared, in this hour of need, to welcome the Keeper of the Retrograph Vault. He has seen the error of his ways and comes back a humble man. I'm glad to hear it."

Skyhammer heard a soft snort from beside him and sighed. "Indeed he has, Ms. Floss. How good you are to accept this transgressor."

Higgins smiled up at the principal.

"I'm dying to hear all about how you escaped from the Crystal Lines." Ms. Floss's eyes shone with anticipation, then narrowed. "But you need to get inside before too many people see you."

Skyhammer tied up the boat.

"And we have some disturbing news for you, Ms. Floss," Higgins replied. She hopped up next to the principal and they headed off towards the main administration building, conversing in low voices. Skyhammer followed, glancing around. Perhaps the fever pitch of hatred for him had not yet been reached here but he wanted to be ready.

* * *

"Miss Higgins has informed me of recent discoveries, Mr. Skyhammer." Ms. Floss pulled the curtains across the windows. "You're in great danger here." She had taken them straight to her office.

Two female students tossed a disc across the large section of grass fronting the lake. Under a tree closer to the administrative buildings, a small ring of students bombarded a professor with questions, the whole group on their hands and knees examining something in the dirt. Each person's eyes had widened as Skyhammer passed, fear or anger painting their faces. He felt a new sense of respect for Ms. Floss. It was obvious she didn't think he was the Sorcerer if she was parading him across the Academy grounds. She was actually trying to set an example, he realized. Although grateful, Skyhammer kept his hand on the hilt of his sword. Here at least he could defend himself, not have to hide behind Higgins like a child. From the looks on their faces, the students and staff didn't agree their principal's opinion of Skyhammer.

Ms. Floss's office was minimal, a reflection of its occupant. Tables, chairs, papers, writing implements, shelves. No art, no personalization of space. With a shiver, Skyhammer recalled the few times he'd been there as a student. A stickler for the rules was Ms. Floss.

"And what-" Skyhammer began.

"I will order Gewiddy and Spelunk to Murk Lake to retrieve Hermit's body and maintain a watch over the Vault. When Spelunk returns, he should be able to tell us when Hermit . . . expired. Most unfortunate." Ms. Floss sat erect in her chair. "I also had word from Four Hills about your terrible deaths. You should know that a contingent of Floatilla citizens is on its way to the Retrograph Vault to try out for the open Retrograph Keeper position."

Skyhammer chuckled darkly. "Maybe we can make it to Keeper number four."

Ms. Floss frowned. "They asked for my help. As in, they want to stay here overnight. They'll be here tomorrow. They cannot find you here."

Skyhammer nodded. "We should -"

"The information on Hermit's death," Ms. Floss continued, "may be a clue to the Retrograph Sorcerer's whereabouts. You should not leave this office. I'll bring blankets in and set a couple of workers I trust to guard you. It's disgusting." She wrinkled her nose. "Some of the people here think that the Floatilla is right to kill you for possibly being the Retrograph Sorcerer. You will not come to any harm on my watch. Either of you."

Skyhammer swallowed, then nodded, grateful. Tough but fair. He hadn't appreciated that aspect of her when he was studying here. "Thank you-"

"You are both safe here." Ms. Floss steepled her fingers. "Until those Floatilla people arrive anyway. I will tell the Byndari to hurry back with the information."

"Thank you, Ms. Floss," Higgins said softly. "We appreciate your trust in us."

"Don't leave and don't let anyone in. I'll get you some food."
The principal left them alone.

Higgins and Skyhammer chatted while flicking through
their Retrographs.

"I'd really like to visit Rantama."

"Uh, letmethinkaboutthatno?" Higgins closed her Whorl.
"The Academy isn't the safest place either, according to Ms.
Floss."

"I'll be fine. I'll go after we eat and it's dark. I trust Rantama
and he may have some advice on how to find the Sorcerer."

"Okay but I'm coming."

Skyhammer opened his mouth, then shut it. There was no
use arguing with her. "Fine." He glanced back at his Whorl. He
kept going back to the Retrograph of the four slates with knives
stuck in them, mesmerized. Shocking, especially since the
previous and next Retrographs were perfectly normal.

A key turned in the door. Skyhammer closed his Whorl,
hand back on his sword hilt.

Ms. Floss slipped in, a large bag in her hand. As she closed
and locked the door behind her, she said, "A few people saw me.
And of course the kitchen staff was curious." She pulled food
out of the bag and onto the table - cheese, bread, fruit, some
kind of tart. "I'm not even sure if you should stay the night
here," she admitted, crossing her arms.

As Skyhammer and Higgins began to dig in to the food, Ms.
Floss sat down at the table with them. Stuffing a piece of cheese
in his mouth, Skyhammer sat back in his chair. Higgins
swallowed her bread.

"Maybe you could help us, Ms. Floss." Skyhammer described
the changes to his Retrographs once again. "Do you know of any
Relics that could make changes to Retrographs?"

Shaking her head, Ms. Floss began to pace the length of the
room. "Nothing springs to mind. I could check our records I
suppose. . ."

"And the changes are so specific," Higgins added. "And
consistent between your Retrographs and the King's."

"I guess." Skyhammer cut a slice of tart. "Both had people or
things stabbed and both had changes related to the Wall
drawings."

"What I don't get is why the Retrographs are changed at

all?" Higgins pushed back her chair.

Popping a grape in her mouth, Ms. Floss asked, "What do you mean?"

"If you're a powerful Sorcerer, intent on destroying magic or at least keeping it from being spread across Pingala, why would you bother to change the King's Retrographs? Why alert us? Why show us that you want to kill the King? Why not just do it?"

Skyhammer hadn't thought of that.

"Now the King will bring a ton of guards to the ceremony and make sure that nothing interferes with it," she continued, "He will take more measures to protect himself. It doesn't make any sense."

"You're right, Higgins." Ms. Floss leaned forward. "We also don't know if the Sorcerer can actually do those things - kill the King, sabotage the ceremony, destroy magic. We know he or she can change Retrographs but it doesn't necessarily mean anything else. They could be empty threats."

"We can't take that chance unfortunately -" Skyhammer began.

"I know that," Ms. Floss said, a dangerous glint in her eye. "I wasn't suggesting you stop looking for the Sorcerer. I just don't know where you should start looking for him."

Skyhammer shifted in his chair. Seeing the strong principal of the Academy at a loss for what to do was a little unsettling. "You were saying that maybe the Sorcerer was showing off. It's possible but I have to agree with Higgins that the changed Retrographs seem related somehow. Do you know any powerful magicians who graduated from the Academy and who may have been hiding the level of their magic powers? Maybe we should just head back to Four Hills and look inside the Royal Circle for the Sorcerer."

"And how about the Byndari?" Higgins asked.

His eyebrows raised in query.

"The Byndari ambassador was also stabbed in the King's Retrograph. Who doesn't like the Byndari? Who would be threatened by the change?"

"No one!" Ms. Floss burst out. "Being able to perform magic everywhere on the planet is good for all species."

"What if someone found out about the King's plans?" Higgins stared at Skyhammer.

Confused, Ms. Floss looked from Higgins to Skyhammer and

back. "What plans?"

"Plans to invade other countries as soon as the change is complete." Higgins crossed her arms.

Ms. Floss didn't say anything for a moment. "Well then. If a member of another species found out about that then they would definitely have reason to stop the ceremony."

"Only if they thought their species' magic couldn't defend them against a human invasion though," Skyhammer said. "Also, other species don't have Retrographs. How would they access the King's Retrographs? Or mine? We were in the middle of the forest when my Retrograph was changed!" Frustrated, he drummed his fingers on the table. They were getting nowhere. They had no information. If the Sorcerer was planning to stop the ceremony, maybe the best thing to do was to wait for him or her at the Kingmaker Tower and be near the King to protect him. Otherwise, they were just running around Pingala like headless chickens.

Skyhammer stood up, stretched and went to the window. Twitching the curtain aside, he peeped into the Academy grounds. Shaped like fat, house-sized cakes, each building's roof was moss- and wildflower-covered, their edges coming down to Skyhammer's waist. Each had a garden out front that was a mixture of vegetables and brightly coloured flowers. The impression was of low, verdant hills, now lit by the warm pinks and purples of a setting sun. Paths of crushed white stone wound between buildings. The view soothed him.

Shouting and the sound of people running came through the door.

Ms. Floss sprang to her feet. "Get your stuff. Out the window. I'm sorry," she hissed. She stood in front of the door, waiting for them to leave.

Skyhammer stuffed the rest of the bread and cheese into his bag and a tart into his mouth, then opened the window.

Loud knocking shook the door. "Open up, Ms. Floss. We need to talk with Skyhammer and Higgins!" a voice shouted.

Chapter 12

Countdown to ceremony: 14 days

"Alright, alright, I'm coming," Ms. Floss called, making shooing gestures at Higgins and Skyhammer towards the window.

Skyhammer mouthed a thank you as he swung his leg over the window sill and dropped to the ground. Now where?

Higgins came down like feather behind him and shut the window in silence.

The grounds were empty; most people in the hall eating their evening meal. They dashed around the corner of the building.

Pausing for a breath, Skyhammer heard the window fly open. Shouts of "They're gone," echoed across the quiet grounds. Ms. Floss's raised voice argued with a few male voices. The principal was trying to detain their pursuers.

"Rantama," Skyhammer whispered.

Higgins nodded and they crept towards the teachers' quarters, scurrying over pathways and hugging the sides of buildings. One building towered above the rest. The Relic research lab. Instead of a low roof all the way around, the back was cut open to allow for over-sized Relics. The ceiling was at least four times Skyhammer's height and the whole lab was the size of four or five houses, windows lacerating the roof to allow light in. An air of excitement and quiet busy-ness pervaded. Each Relic was raised on a shoulder-high platform, researchers moving with purpose around each one.

Skyhammer loved the lab almost as much as he loved the library. He had spent hours there assisting the researchers. In his secret heart, whenever he touched a Relic, he hoped to feel a spark of power, a change inside him that would mean that he possessed magic powers like everyone else. So although he loved the place, each time a new Relic came and went, a tiny slash of disappointment razored his heart. Who knew how many more Relics with the ability to give him magic powers were left out there?

Higgins had to prod him past the building, so strong was his desire to go in and see what new Relics had arrived.

An S-shaped path, bounded by hedges taller than Skyhammer, gated the entrance to the teachers' quarters. Each door opened onto a central courtyard, houses positioned like a circlet of pearls surrounding grass, a few benches and sweet-smelling bushes, only broken by the hedge entrance.

Steps into the first turn, the hedge's fragrance overwhelmed Skyhammer with memories. A giggling Spark pulling him into the next bend and wrapping her arms around him for a long kiss. She'd disappeared a week later. He'd burst into the principal's office when he found out she had gone, sure she had been kidnapped. Ms. Floss had reassured him that Spark had left of her own volition and she had not given a forwarding address or a reason. He wanted to go after her but had no clue which direction she would go. The pain of missing her became a constant ache.

After she left, as he began spending more time with Higgins, he discovered that Spark's constant negativity had affected him more than he realized. He had ignored her put-downs and biting comments about magic-wielders because he was so grateful to be with someone who understood him so completely. Higgins sympathized of course but only Spark had experienced the same degree of hurt and rejection due to a lack of magic power. They shared a past of ostracism and ridicule and a future searching for a Relic that would bestow on them the magic powers given to every other human, Aridizan, Flyer, Katipo and Nasuchu at birth. How could she have divided herself from him so easily? Surely if she'd felt anything for him she would have told him she was leaving or at least why?

The sight of Rantama's familiar doorway across the courtyard curved a smile into Skyhammer's lips, despite his fear of pursuit. The Byndari decorated his door with the shiniest shells and rocks he could find or those students gave him. The wooden doors of the other teachers were dull in contrast.

Skyhammer knocked and the door opened a few seconds later.

"Rantama is pleased to see you!" The Byndari grinned. "Especially since you are rumoured to be dead!" He noticed Higgins and then examined their faces as they stumbled through his doorway. "What's going on?"

"We're being pursued. Hopefully they didn't see us come

here although since they know you're a friend, it makes sense
that they'd look here next." Skyhammer entered Rantama's
sitting room. A couple of over-stuffed couches were positioned
in a V-shape to take advantage of the view over the courtyard.
Each professor's house was the same layout: a large sitting room
overlooked the courtyard, a small kitchen, a toilet room and a
bedroom took up the other two thirds of the circular house.
Crowded bookshelves, many of them familiar to Skyhammer by
way of extensive borrowing, hid most of the walls. Knitted items
- blankets, pillows, toys and rugs - covered everything else.

Skyhammer looked around. "We need to hide, Rantama. Is
there anywhere we can?"

"Under the bed, dear boy, come right this way."

A true friend, Skyhammer thought as they followed
Rantama to the bedroom. He hadn't even hesitated.

The bedroom was as messy and covered with knitted objects
as the other room had been. Rantama shoved their bags in a
corner and piled blankets on top to hide them while Higgins
and Skyhammer squeezed under the bed. Rantama stuffed rugs
and blankets under with them so they were well and truly
hidden.

Fists pounded on the door. "Open up, Rantama," called a
voice similar to the one at Ms. Floss's office. "We need to ask
you some questions!"

"Coming," Rantama sang out.

Skyhammer heard the door open and the sound of three or
four people entering the hall.

"Ah, Flavius, what can Rantama do for you? Would you like a
drink? Do sit down."

"We don't have time for a drink, Rantama. Have you seen
Skyhammer?"

"Skyhammer? Not for, oh, a few years. He is Relic hunting,
you know." Pride filled Rantama's voice. "Was Relic hunting. He
and Higgins died in the Crystal Lines, Rantama heard." Now his
voice was filled with sadness.

"No, he's at the Academy right now."

"He's alive? That's great news!" Rantama replied in a happy
tone. "He has not been to see Rantama. If he was here he would
come and visit."

"We need to find him, Rantama. We believe that he's the

Retrograph Sorcerer and a number of people have questions for him."

"He is the Keeper, isn't he?" Rantama said. "You may be right! Rantama will let you know if he comes. The King's changed Retrograph showed a Byndari being killed as well, you know. Very upsetting. Very upsetting indeed."

"We appreciate your help. For your safety, we'll post a guard at the entrance to the teacher's quarters. It's getting dark, so be careful."

"Thank you, thank you, kind Flavius. Good luck with your search." Rantama shut the door.

Higgins and Skyhammer didn't move until they heard Rantama entering the room again. Skyhammer hadn't realized Rantama was such a skilled actor.

"Rantama has shut the curtains in every room. You may come out now." He began to remove piles of knitting from under the bed, freeing Skyhammer and Higgins.

"Rantama, it's lovely to see you but we've been on the run for two days. Mind if I just wash up and go to bed?" Higgins asked.

"Of course, dear girl. Let Rantama show you where everything is. Rantama will join you in a minute, Skyhammer." The Byndari bustled off to the small washroom.

Skyhammer wandered into the sitting room and stood in front of the bookcase, running his fingers over their spines. He hadn't done much reading over the past few years. Books were heavy, as well as hard to come by outside of Quasianti.

"What would you like to drink?" Rantama boomed from his kitchen. "Have a seat. Rantama's got fizzy liquids and a milk. Oops, no, milk has gone off. Should stop keeping that really. Pineapple juice."

In an attempt to be more human-like, the Byndari kept drinks and snacks that humans could eat, despite the fact that he could not ingest anything other than salt.

"Juice please, Rantama. Thank you." Skyhammer sank into the sofa's fat cushions. He felt guilty he hadn't contacted Rantama since he'd left.

"Rantama's heard all about your adventures. He's proud of you." The Byndari set Skyhammer's drink on the small triangular table between the arms of the two couches.

"I'm sorry I never-" Skyhammer began.

Rantama waved a hand. "Water under the bridge, as they

say. We're here now, together." He picked up a skein of wool and began winding it into a ball. "So, Keeper. Humans are looking for you. Is what they believe true?"

Nausea filled the pit of Skyhammer's stomach. Rantama thought *he* was threatening the King and the ceremony?

The Byndari peered at Skyhammer then wheezed with laughter, bending forward. "You didn't think that Rantama thought you . . . ha!"

Skyhammer glared at Rantama then couldn't help smiling. He'd forgotten about the Byndari's occasional inappropriate jokes. "Everyone else does. Why not you?" He shrugged.

Rantama raised a seaweed eyebrow. "Never," he said firmly. "Rantama heard that in Four Hills, yesterday, an accountant, Rantama thinks it was, killed a fisherman simply because the fisherman knew something that the accountant thought could only be discovered if someone had seen his Retrographs." He slipped the neatly wound ball of wool under the couch.

Shocked, Skyhammer sat up straight. "But they think it's me! Don't they? If they start suspecting each other. . ." He put his head in his hands.

"Fascinating, isn't it, how attached humans are to their Retrographs. But there is also the good news. How we Byndari have found a Relic!" Rantama smiled proudly. "Found is of course subjective but we were the first ones to see it. Rantama has copies of the drawing here. Did you see them already?" He got up and went into the bedroom before Skyhammer could answer. He laid them out on the table in front of the couches, first pushing back a small bowl filled with white miniature statues out of the way.

Skyhammer slid forward to get a better view of the drawings, excited to be able to record them again. But would the Retrograph Sorcerer turn this set over as well? "How did you get your own copies?" He traced the pictures with his finger.

Rantama smiled. "Each Byndari got a copy soon after they were made. We all assisted in deciphering the relief on the wall. We are pleased that magic will be spread across Pingala."

"Yeah, it's great," Skyhammer said, finger still following the lines of the drawing. "So who figured out what it meant?"

"A Byndari called Almazi. She had a background in social and human art history."

"Had?" Skyhammer looked up.

"Yes, well." Rantama frowned. "Almazi disintegrated while exploring some way outside of our home territory. Possibly an animal got her. A great loss to Byndari culture."

"I'm sorry to hear that." Skyhammer realized Rantama wouldn't have heard about Hermit's death. He told his friend what they had found at Murk Lake.

Rantama was silent for a while then sighed. "Another fine Byndari lost so soon." He plastered a smile on his face. "But enough about Byndari. Why are you back at the Academy?"

Skyhammer stretched one arm along the back of the couch. "I'm investigating the Retrograph changes as per the King's orders. And my own interest." He paused. "Maybe investigating is the wrong word. Hunting down the Retrograph Sorcerer, with express instructions to bring her back to the King."

"Her?"

He shrugged. "A guess. We think that only a woman would have the balls to break a piece of the Retrograph Vault and remove it." A chuckle. "Just kidding. We have no idea who it was."

Rantama's jaw had dropped. It looked quite comical since he didn't have a mouth or jaw, just a slash surrounded by twig lips. He was almost too shocked to speak. "What happened to the Vault?"

"I went in there. Somebody, the Sorcerer, has broken off a piece of it and removed it from the Vault."

"How do you know it was taken out?"

Skyhammer's eyebrows lifted. "As opposed to?"

Rantama shrugged. "Thrown into the cavern?"

"Hmph. I didn't consider that."

"And this is why research on the Retrograph Vault has stagnated." Rantama picked up a small salt statue of a butterfly from the bowl on the table and licked it. "No human dares to disturb the sacred Retrograph Vault. Do you know how often Rantama has tried to encourage the Keeper to experiment on the Vault?"

Skyhammer shook his head.

"Except you of course, you weren't around long enough for me to harass you."

Skyhammer laughed, a little embarrassed.

"And another thing. How do you know it was a woman?"

"I was just--"

"There are three orifices on a human female's body and two on a male's."

"I know!"

"Well, a man or a woman could take a piece out of there."

"But how could that Sorcerer then change our Retrographs?" Skyhammer was silent a moment, then told Rantama about the drawings, the magic slates and the knives.

Rantama listened with a small frown on his face.

"What do you think?" Skyhammer asked, eager to hear the opinion of a non-human.

For a long time, Rantama didn't answer. Just when Skyhammer thought that Rantama hadn't heard his question, the Byndari sighed loudly. "Rantama's first instinct is that someone is threatening to stop the ceremony, destroy magic and kill the King. But then Rantama is assuming a lot of things. But at first glance, that's what it seems to be."

"We think that as well. If this Sorcerer can change Retrographs then who knows what else he could do."

"Who's we?"

"Higgins, Ms. Floss and I."

"You've told Ms. Floss?"

"We thought she might have some insight."

"What does she think?" Rantama looked down at the drawings on the table.

"The same as you." Skyhammer spread his arms in a gesture of bewilderment. "We just have no idea. The Sorcerer could be anyone, anywhere."

"Now wait just a minute. If we say it's most likely the Sorcerer is a human-"

"Because only humans have Retrographs-"

"Exactly. So. Humans can only do magic in the Royal Circle. We assume that the Sorcerer is using magic to make the changes. Since you didn't find anyone in the Retrograph Vault. Thus-"

"The Sorcerer must be in the Royal Circle," Skyhammer exclaimed. A doleful look crossed his face. "Rantama, there are 1.5 million humans in Floatilla alone. How can we find the Sorcerer in that?"

Rantama's shoulders sank. "Good point. But we have nothing

else. At least if you're in the Royal Circle when something comes up, you're right there."

"I guess."

They sat in silence for a few minutes.

"Let us help you find the Retrograph Sorcerer. There are Byndari in every capital city and in most villages in most countries. If there is a whisper of a rumour about this Retrograph Sorcerer, we will know of it. If you get any more information on him or her though, make sure you let us know right away."

"Absolutely. Thank you. That's a weight off my mind, having Byndari eyes and ears in every city."

Someone rapped on Rantama's door. Skyhammer bolted to the bedroom, threw a blanket over Higgins then rolled under the bed.

Rantama opened the door. "Professor Bumble! What can Rantama do for you?" Two sets of feet began walking towards the sitting room.

His empty juice glass. Skyhammer's heart jumped in fear. If the professor entered the sitting room, he would know Rantama had a visitor. They were about to be discovered!

"Just letting you know the guard's been taken off the teachers' quarters." The footsteps halted. "Skyhammer and Higgins seem to have left the Academy grounds."

"What a shame, Professor! Thank you for letting Rantama know. Good night!"

The door closed.

* * *

Skyhammer woke up in Rantama's bed knowing that he didn't want to go back to Four Hills. Without the Retrograph Sorcerer, it was failure, just going back because he had no other option.

Leaning back against the headboard, Higgins snoring beside him, he opened his Whorl. The scent of frying bacon wafted under the door. Would the pages be turned over again? He held his breath.

One drawing was flipped.

"Poof," Skyhammer whispered.

"Nnngg?" Higgins mumbled, then rolled over, eyes shut.

In every Retrograph that included the sixth page, it was turned over. None of the other five pages was touched.

But there was another new change. A change that, at first glance, looked like it had nothing to do with magic or the ceremony.

Chapter 13

Countdown to ceremony: 13 days

Skyhammer shook his head in disbelief. In one Retrograph, Rantama's sitting room had been de-cluttered, as though the school cleaners had been hired to spruce up the room. Every bookshelf was tidy, books organized from tallest to shortest. Every single piece of knitting was piled up neatly, blankets in one pile, pillows in another, toys in a third, biggest on the bottom, smallest on top. It looked like a different room.

Those changes, although startling, were not what truly unnerved Skyhammer. Seeing his own body manipulated was what scared him. Because, in the same Retrograph, Skyhammer's left hand now covered Rantama's mouth and his right hand held a book.

"Like puppets on a string," he murmured. Familiar though, in an odd way, this Retrograph. The changes. The book was entitled *Chronicles of Feorag*. He'd read it. Couldn't remember the plot though. And he certainly hadn't touched it last night.

He let out a huge sigh.

"More changes?" Higgins was watching him.

Skyhammer described the changes to her.

"You don't remember what the book was about?" she asked, sitting up and beginning to get dressed.

Skyhammer swung his legs over the side of the bed and pulled on his clothes. "No clue. But since the book's in the other room, I'll just have a look at it."

As they entered the sitting room, Rantama called from the kitchen, "Eggs, bacon, toast and juice! Hope you're hungry!"

"You shouldn't have gone to the trouble for us," Higgins protested.

"Nonsense. Rantama loves any opportunity to cook. And you'll need strength to reach Four Hills. It's a long walk."

"We have horses," Skyhammer said.

"You do?"

"We left them in the woods tied on long leads when we got in the canal boat to come here." Skyhammer sat down at the tiny kitchen table.

Rantama looked at Higgins, who shrugged.

"We can only pray that nothing ate them," she said. "He was desperate to take the boat here." She buttered a piece of toast.

"Mem'ries," Skyhammer said through a mouthful of egg and toast.

Rantama took off his apron and sat at the table with them. "Rantama slipped out this morning to talk with Ms. Floss." He smiled at them both. "She said to pass on the message that Spelunk had returned from Hermit's house and it looks like Hermit was killed approximately three years ago. He definitely didn't die from natural causes."

Skyhammer nodded.

"He must have seen the Retrograph Sorcerer go into the Vault and was killed so that he would keep quiet about it," Higgins declared.

"Rantama agrees, dear."

"But if the Retrograph Sorcerer went in the Vault three years ago and has been able to see and change Retrographs that whole time, why did he wait until now to show his power?" Skyhammer wondered aloud.

"Simple," Higgins replied. "The Wall. The Retrograph changes only deal with the Wall and that wasn't found until a few months ago."

"Rantama, my Retrographs have been changed," Skyhammer said.

The Byndari d. "Again? What changed?"

Skyhammer recounted the changes.

Rantama sat, silent and thoughtful, staring down at the table. "Let's go into the sitting room. If you're done?" Higgins and Skyhammer nodded.

Not for the first time, Skyhammer wished that Byndari had facial expressions beyond smiling and frowning so that he could get some clue as to what his friend was thinking. "What do you think?" he asked finally, as he sat down on Rantama's couch.

The Byndari pulled the drawing in question out from under his bowl of salt statues and positioned it in front of them. "Almost impossible to say. Rantama might hazard a guess that the Sorcerer thinks that humans having widespread magic powers is a danger to the world." He shrugged. "What else did you say was different?" He yanked a bag out from beneath the table, withdrew a needle and a ball of yarn and started crocheting a granny square.

"My hand covering your mouth." Skyhammer wanted to say it meant that maybe he shouldn't be listening to the Byndari or maybe they were lying about something. It felt wrong to say that to his Byndari friend though, so he held his tongue. The Byndari were helping the humans and the other species.

"Perhaps the Byndari are saying something that humans do not want to hear," Rantama suggested. "We *are* advocating practically a truce between Nasuchu and the other species. If this Sorcerer is political in some way, it may not be in his or her best interests for the ceremony to go ahead. Maybe they are anarchists. Or he could be the leader of some group planning to destroy the King or Floatilla."

"Do you really think there are people out there wanting to do that? If the King was destroyed then magic would be gone and this Sorcerer couldn't do his magic."

"Unless they already don't have to perform magic in the Circle," Rantama said.

"Aaagh. Don't make my job any harder, please! The last thing I need right now is a Sorcerer who can perform magic outside the Royal Circle." Skyhammer frowned. "I don't even want to think about that."

"What is certain is that you have to find this Sorcerer before the ceremony." Rantama picked up a new strand of wool with his needle.

"I know."

"He-"

"How do you know it's a he?" Skyhammer's eyebrows raised.

"For convenience sake, let's say it's a he. Rantama thinks that either the Sorcerer is going to affect the ceremony somehow or the Sorcerer knows that something is going to happen at the ceremony. Either way, we need to find this person."

"Which brings us right back to the fact that we have no idea who it is," Higgins interjected.

Rantama crocheted away, round and round his square.

Skyhammer cleared his throat. "Have you heard of a book called the *Chronicles of Feorag*?"

Rantama didn't look up. "It's on the shelf over there where

you left it."

Skyhammer's head jerked up in surprise. "Of course." He stood up and crossed over to the bookshelf in the corner of the sitting room.

Higgins and Rantama followed him.

"Not that one! By the window. Third from the top. Why do you ask?" Rantama's voice was casual. "You and Spark hated that book."

Skyhammer pulled the book off the shelf, his hand trembling. There it was. The connection. The niggling idea had begged for acknowledgement, but he had ignored it. Couldn't any longer though.

Spark. Only she and Rantama, of course, had any connection to that book and to Skyhammer. He knew Rantama wasn't the Retrograph Sorcerer. That left only Spark. And it fit in with the rest of the changed Retrograph - every item organized and tidy. Covering Rantama's mouth, presumably because he was lying about something. Connecting that with their heated arguments about the book and its unreliable narrator. The three of them had discussed the dangers to society of withholding the truth, among other themes from the book. He'd never talked about *Chronicles of Feorag* with anyone other than Spark and Rantama.

"Well?" Rantama rested his crocheting on his lap.

If Spark was trying to communicate through his Retrographs, if she had magic, if she was the other Keeper . . . Skyhammer couldn't take it in. He stumbled back to the couch.

"What is wrong?" Rantama stood up, crochet square falling to the floor.

Higgins sat beside him. "Are you okay?"

"I know who it is."

His two friends looked at him, waiting.

"Spark."

"What?" Rantama sat down and leaned forward. "How do you know?"

Skyhammer took a deep breath. "This book was placed prominently in the changed Retrograph. When you reminded me about Spark and I reading this and discussing it with you . . ." He trailed off.

"The unreliable narrator." Rantama picked up his crocheting and twisted his needle through the yarn, growing the square. "If we accept that Spark is the Sorcerer," he set his needle and yarn on the table and looked directly at Skyhammer, "then, logically, we must accept that she -"

"Has magic powers," Skyhammer finished.

Higgins gasped.

"Rantama was going to say that she's a murderer," Rantama said, frowning.

"And she's a Keeper-" Skyhammer paused. "What?"

"She killed Hermit to keep him from telling others that she had been in the Retrograph Vault."

"We don't know that for sure." Spark wouldn't murder someone. Would she?

"This makes it even more important to find her." Rantama stood up, then sat down again. "Where is that last letter Rantama had from her?" He reached into a wicker basket at the end of the couch and scrabbled through some paper.

Skyhammer watched him. Rantama hadn't lingered on the message in the Retrograph. He'd just moved on to Spark. And he'd blamed her for Hermit's death. Perhaps it was understandable. But Skyhammer got a feeling that Rantama was avoiding the actual message. "What do you think the changes mean then?"

Rantama's voice was muffled by the couch and rustling papers. "We can wait and see. Nothing good for the Ceremony. Only Spark can tell us."

"Why wouldn't she just send us a message? Send the King a message? Send me a message? She knows how to contact us. Why would she contact us through our Retrographs?" And what was she doing sending Rantama a letter? He yearned to see it, knowing her hand had touched it.

"She always did like to show off her knowledge a bit. Maybe she thinks it's proof. Maybe she's somewhere that a message would be too slow."

"Let's hope not," Skyhammer said with passion. "I want her within a couple days walk ideally." He stood up and went to the window, peering outside through a crack between the curtain and the window frame.

Rantama sat up. "Rantama can't find that letter. Doesn't matter, there was no way to trace it anyhow. And it was a few years old."

"Maybe she doesn't want us to find her." Skyhammer stared out the window, grass, trees, wind, so normal, unchanging. But everything had changed; Spark had magic powers. Spark was a Keeper, Spark had contacted him. Spark, Spark, Spark. Yes, it was all conjecture but it fit the changes in the Retrograph. And he had no other clues to go on.

His eyes closed as he thought of her and then the ache, the sadness rolled in. She had disappeared without explanations. She had torn his love apart like bear with a fish and let his bones flutter to the ground. He set his jaw. He would not let it happen again. She was manipulating him somehow, he was sure of it. He couldn't trust her.

He had to find her, to see her, to hear from her lips why she left. No, he thought, to hear why she was changing the Retrographs. Why him? She could see everything he did and everything the King did. She knew him better than she knew the King and he was the Keeper after all. Maybe she wanted him to find her. But, the little voice inside him replied, she would've sent a message through normal channels in that case. If she didn't want to be found, then he had to be very careful. Since she could see every move he made through his Retrographs, he'd have to sneak up on her. Already she must know that they had discovered something, just from watching his Retrographs of the past hour. She'd know that he'd told Rantama. She must have expected that though; Rantama was a good friend. Maybe she wanted Skyhammer to figure it out, hoping that he'd trust her message more.

He looked over at the Byndari. Rantama was watching him, a frown on his face. As soon as he noticed Skyhammer looking at him, he smiled.

"As Rantama mentioned yesterday, the Byndari can help you find her. Rantama will go to town tomorrow and let the Byndari know that there may be danger to the ceremony. And to look out for Spark."

Skyhammer nodded and returned *Chronicles of Feorag* to the shelf. "Higgins and I will return to Four Hills and contact the King with the news. Maybe we can find a forwarding address or something."

"She never contacted you?" Rantama asked.

Skyhammer looked down at the drawings still spread on the

table. "She didn't say goodbye, she didn't say anything." She told me she loved me. A lie. "I just want to find her and complete the ceremony." And learn how she got magic powers, he thought. And find out why she left.

"Rantama understands." The Byndari sounded distracted. "We just want to get home," he muttered.

"I beg your pardon?" Poor fellow, Skyhammer thought. Finding out that one of his ex-students may be a murderer as well as holding something against the Byndari. No wonder he wants to go home.

"Hmm? You'd better get going." Rantama stood up. "Ms. Floss said she was calling an all-staff and students meeting which should start shortly. You'll be able to get off the grounds without being seen."

"Thank you." Skyhammer stood up and clasped the Byndari's hand. A true friend.

Higgins gave Rantama a gentle hug and a soft smile. "We appreciate the risk you took in hiding us. If we hear anything at all, we'll let you know."

* * *

Gathering their things took less than five minutes. Skyhammer and Higgins left Rantama's house only after they were certain the meeting was in session. They headed in the opposite direction.

Inhaling the fresh morning air after the staleness of Rantama's house, Skyhammer's spirits lifted. He had direction and answers. More questions as well but at least they were making progress.

Higgins stopped in front of a small building off to one side from the others.

"What?" Skyhammer looked it. "Who was here? Oh!"

Higgins' eyes met his and she nodded. "She might know where Spark is."

"Were they such good friends?"

"You know they were," she scoffed.

They started walking again.

"Maybe friend is the wrong word," Skyhammer said, thinking back. "She trusted Counsellor Hanamun. After a period of time. I guess when you are forced to spend that much time with someone-"

"And that someone is a school counsellor who is adept at gaining trust -" Higgins added.

"- then it develops naturally." Skyhammer watched a flock of geese take off from the lake.

"She never told you what she did to have to see the counsellor so often, did she?"

"I didn't want to pry. I did ask once but she ignored me. And somehow, I think I was happier not knowing."

"So where is Counsellor Hanamun living now?" As Higgins walked on the dock, it rocked.

"As far as I know, once she was dismissed from the Academy, she moved back to the Fungal Forest." Skyhammer threw his pack into the canal boat furthest from shore.

"It's out of our way but worth a look. You should definitely talk to her." Higgins stepped into the boat.

Skyhammer untied the rope and slid into the boat. "Me? You should talk to her." He pushed them away from the dock.

"Why would I talk to her? You knew her and you knew Spark."

"You saw her as well. She's more sympathetic to women anyway. I figured that you could tell her you were worried about me, thinking about Spark all the time, talking in my sleep or something."

"You think about Spark all the time? Gosh, I never would have guessed." Higgins rowed across the lake towards the lock. "But . . ."

"You saw her a few times too, didn't you?" Skyhammer looked hard at Higgins. "What is it?"

"Everyone had to see her. I didn't really like her, that's all."

"Yes you did!" Skyhammer said indignantly. "I remember you telling me that you enjoyed spending time with her. There was a time when you went to visit her a few times a week, above and beyond what was required. You said you two were friends as well."

"I guess so. It was a long time ago." Higgins rowed like a madwoman.

"They're not going to see us."

"I know."

"Then why are you rowing like that?"

"We don't have time to waste."

Skyhammer sat back. "You don't want to talk about it. Fine. But you should know that whenever you're ready, I'll be listening."

Her chin jerked in a nod.

Chapter 14

Countdown to ceremony: 11 days

The Katipo were lucky that their country was bounded by such tall mountains, Skyhammer grumbled. They didn't need an army to protect their citizens from the Nasuchu. At least, thanks to a narrow pass, he and Higgins hadn't needed to climb over the mountains to get into the Fungal Forest, home of the Katipo.

And really, he thought as he looked from the top of the small rise where he, the horses and Higgins were standing, who would want such an unwelcoming country anyway? No species had ever invaded the Fungal Forest, as it was hospitable only to the Katipo. Only the Katipo could eat the fungi that grew there and their magic power controlled the spiders that provided safe lodging from the creatures that dwelt in the myriad swamps and bogs. Katipo kept to themselves.

Higgins didn't know exactly where in the Fungal Forest Counsellor Hanamun lived. They'd have to ask once they got to the capital, Ambersilk. The trip back across Quasianti had used up a precious couple of days but Higgins appeared to be sure that Counsellor Hanamun would know where Spark was.

Since the horses had survived the last time they were tied up in a forest, Skyhammer and Higgins risked it again. An open patch of grass on the edge of the tree line and a small stream provided food and water while the trees provided shelter. Skyhammer rubbed his horse's nose one last time, then he and Higgins headed into the valley.

The Katipo had put in a form of road to their capital city, Ambersilk. The first part was simply stone steps going down into the valley of the Fungal Forest. At the valley's bottom, swamp and bog started. Further in, the swamp was laced with pools of coffee-coloured water, dotted with random splashes where the strange creatures that swum in the depths came up for air. Tree-sized mushrooms and other fungi unique to the Fungal Forest grew upon the swamp plants and bog moss. Skyhammer had heard many speculations about what exactly was underneath the valley that could cause so many mushrooms of incredible size to flourish. For while swamps are supposed to be shallow places, not one person had ever found the bottom of the swamp, or at least lived to tell the tale.

Skyhammer and Higgins stood together on the last stone at the swamp's edge. To their left and right, valley walls stretched off into the distance, steep crags far above wreathed in cloud. They could not see the other end of the valley. Mushrooms of every shape, size and colour spread out before them but the dominant colours were purple and blue. It was said that the Katipo Royal Circle covered the whole valley.

A spike had been driven at waist height into the wall behind the stone on which they stood. Tied to the spike was one end of an ebony rope. The rest of the rope stretched off into the swamp. Looped around the black rope was a second rope attached to the back of a three-person rope-haul water craft. It reminded Skyhammer of how his neighbour used to tie up her dog so the animal could run up and down but not get out of the yard.

"You've been here before, right?" Higgins asked as she settled into one of the passenger seats.

"Nope." Skyhammer sat at the boat's prow. The hauler's bench had straps and a bucket seat. Footpads perched on an angle against the front for bracing. He pulled on the pair of thick gloves he found under the seat, and wrapped both his hands around the ebony rope above his head, as far ahead of the boat as he could reach. "Ready?"

"I guess."

A strong tug, his feet braced on the front of the boat and they were shooting across the water. He was happy the back of the seat was padded, as each time he let go of the line, he fell back into the seat.

He didn't say aloud anything about the rumours he had heard. They were just rumours, but still, kidnapping humans and other species? Mind manipulation? A zoo of species for the Katipo? Every Katipo he'd asked about it had denied it. A little too fervently for his liking.

"I thought you'd been everywhere. Skyhammer, the famous Relic hunter who has explored every corner of Pingala!" she proclaimed with a grin.

"Never heard about any Relics in this swamp." Skyhammer

worked up a nice hauling rhythm. "Whew, what did you eat at the Academy? Rocks and cakes?"

"I'm not the one who had trouble doing up my trousers this morning."

"Pure muscle, my friend." He kept his eyes on the ebony line above his head, hands grasping and releasing at a steady pace. The boat's looped rope trailed slackly along the line. He caught glimpses of mushroom trunks. They were reaching the edge of the forest.

"What if someone comes the other way?" Higgins wondered aloud.

"I'm sure the clever Katipo have accounted for that. Strange that we haven't seen anyone else, though. I thought at least there'd be traders heading in or out of the capital with spider silk cloth."

"Perhaps everyone is preparing for the ceremony."

"Huh," Skyhammer grunted as they slid under the canopy of mushrooms. As the fungi blocked out the sun's rays, the ebony rope shone with an amber luminescence. "Hmph. That's unexpected."

A light breeze carried the distinctive scent of mushroom. Most of the mushroom caps started far above their heads. Each cap had a different pattern and mixture of colours but somehow none clashed. A couple of mushrooms were shorter. From under one of low-growing mushrooms, a small, shiny head peeked out, bright blue eyes watching the boat pass. It was too dark for Skyhammer to see any further details of the creature.

"Rope's attached to a tree," Higgins said to him in a low, excited voice. Indeed, the rope slipped around one side of a mushroom trunk then headed off to the left.

Higgins trailed her fingers along the trunk as they went around it.

"What's it feel like?" Skyhammer asked.

"Like baby fuzz," she replied, smiling. "Warm."

The boat slipped deeper and deeper into the Fungal Forest, the abrupt turns leaving Skyhammer feeling dangerously lost as the mushrooms became even more tightly packed together. The quiet was starting to freak him out.

"We're here," Higgins whispered.

"These Katipo should choose a new route if they want visitors," he muttered. Then he saw what was ahead of them and forgot to breathe.

He'd never felt much inclination to visit the Katipo capital and so hadn't really wondered why humans called it Ambersilk. Now of course, it made complete sense. The 'street', if the gossamer-looking web could be called by so crass a word, stretched taut between trunks of mushrooms, like horizontal sailcloth. This created a huge cloth platform, about five feet above the swamp's surface, attached to mushroom trunks. The city was made entirely of spider silk and glowed softly with amber light. Houses and buildings, or what Skyhammer supposed were houses and buildings, were attached to the trunks and the undersides of mushroom caps. They were also spun from the glowing amber silk. He cocked his head as an airy music filled his ears.

Higgins pointed to her right. A screen of horizontal strings ran between two trunks. A Katipo flitted up and down, tugging a string now at the top, now at the bottom. The music came from the wind passing through the vibrating strings.

"Looks like exhausting work," Skyhammer whispered. The Katipo did not look tired though, instead the creature was dancing joyfully between the strings, as though the music carried it up and down.

The ebony rope led them to the edge of the silk platform. They clambered onto the platform, which was springy under their feet. Skyhammer looked around, unsure of where to go. Didn't seem to be any Katipo nearby.

"Ahem."

Skyhammer did an about-face.

"You are looking for a Katipo?" A serious male Katipo stared up at Skyhammer as he climbed onto the platform from another boat. An enormous spider sprang onto the platform of Ambersilk a few feet behind the Katipo. Skyhammer saw its eyes watching him. How had the Katipo arrived undetected?

Katipo were bright red, their skin layer sheer, their blood visible through the skin. Despite their prowess with silk weaving and quality, they didn't wear any clothes. Skyhammer had never touched one although he longed to run his fingers over their strange skin. Up close, they shone as though a film of oil covered their body. He had seen them fight; they were tough. And very solitary; usually the Katipo and his or her spider travelled alone. Not big talkers either. He'd tried to start up a conversation with one female Katipo he'd seen around a few times in the uncharted territories but as soon as the conversation moved past the weather, she'd said goodnight. He wasn't sure if he'd found her attractive or not. The skin colour and sheen were a bit too close to weird for him. A bit short too. He came back to the present moment to find Higgins looking at him, eyebrows raised and the Katipo smiling.

"Hanamun," he mumbled.

"We have no one of that name here." The Katipo turned away.

Higgins stepped forward. "Wait."

The Katipo paused.

"She was a counsellor at the Relic Hunting Academy. The human one," she added.

The Katipo turned back, eyes closed. "Ah," he sighed, opening his eyes again. "My name is Dufu. I will take you part of the way to Hanamun's home."

"Why only part of the way?" Skyhammer asked.

"Skyhammer!" Higgins admonished him. "Dufu is probably very busy." She bowed to the Katipo. "We appreciate your time."

"Why is no one else around, Dufu?" Skyhammer asked as they followed the Katipo across Ambersilk.

"There are many Katipo, as you call us, around. They are sleeping in their chambers."

"Oh. Naptime." Skyhammer nodded. "I get it." But how did Dufu know we were going to be here, he wondered. We saw no one else. Except that string dancer.

"I am the welcoming committee. Along with-" The Katipo spat out some word that Skyhammer did not understand.

"I beg your pardon?"

"My spider." Dufu spat out the word again.

To Skyhammer, the name sounded as though the Katipo had gargled, then spat out, some tea. He glanced back. The spider trailed behind them in silence. One swipe of one of those eight giant legs and they would be drowning in the swamp. Some welcoming committee.

"We're travelling across the main square of the city you call Ambersilk," Dufu explained as they walked along the silk cloth streets. "This is the only city in which other species are allowed. Fortunately, Hanamun lives just past the outskirts of Ambersilk.

I only need to take you part of the way because the rest of the route is direct and accessible by boat. Don't get out of the boat. There are some denizens of the forest that lurk in the waters and are always hungry."

"We didn't see anything dangerous on the way in," Higgins said.

"Really? You didn't see square blue eyes under a mushroom cap?"

"Oh yes, now that you mention it, we did. How did you know?" Higgins sounded suspicious.

"That creature is about the size of three boats put together and is one big muscle with many teeth."

Skyhammer shivered, hoping they wouldn't see anymore of them.

"They know not to interfere with the boats but once you are off the silk or the boat you are fair game for them." His lips spread in a smile that didn't reach his eyes.

Gazing up at the homes attached to the mushroom trunks, Skyhammer was startled to see a pair of pair of huge eyes staring back at him from the bottom of the mushroom cap. A spider had spun its web across the bottom of the cap and Skyhammer could see that the silk home for a Katipo also had a spider web in the mushroom cap.

Skyhammer tried to peer ahead through the fungi but could see no end in sight to the silk road. He trudged after Dufu.

* * *

After an hour's walk, Dufu, his spider, Higgins and Skyhammer reached the outskirts of Ambersilk. During the walk, Higgins and Dufu had chatted while Skyhammer stared at the silk road just ahead of his feet. His eyes half-closed, the dim amber light inside the Fungal Forest lulling him almost into sleep. When he reached the edge of Ambersilk's terrain, he was so exhausted he almost walked off the silk platform and into the murky swamp below.

Higgins grabbed his arm and jerked him back. "Let's eat something before the next part of our journey, okay?"

He collapsed onto the platform. The amber light from the platform seeped into his brain, making it heavy and so hard to get up. Higgins murmured to somebody; he should know the name but he was so tired he had to close his eyes.

Higgins shook him awake a few hours later. At least, he thought it was a few hours. This dark place of no sunlight and weird sounds did not allow for an accurate measurement of the time. He felt better than before although his brain was still a bit fuzzy. Dufu and the spider were nowhere in sight.

"What happened?"

Higgins looked at him with concern. "You dropped to the ground like a ton of bricks and fell asleep. It was odd. Dufu said that sometimes the darkness has that effect on humans." She shrugged. "I kept watch. Didn't see much of anything but heard lots of scurrying insects and splishing about in the water. Loaded our stuff on the boat." She tossed a package in his direction. "Eat this. Dufu said it'd be another couple hours slog through the water to Hanamun's." Higgins' voice contained a strange catch.

"What is it?" He scrutinized her. Cross-legged, she stared out across the water as though trying to burn a hole through the luminescent rope that led to Hanamun's.

"Nothing," she muttered. "Are you done yet?"

"I haven't even opened the package. What's wrong with you?" he insisted. She was usually more frank and open about things that were bothering her.

Higgins turned towards him and he could just make out tears pooling in the bottom of her eyes. This place must be affecting both of them. He slid next to her and wrapped his arms around her shoulders. "Please tell me what's wrong," he whispered. "Is it Polygon?"

She gave a wet sniff, then wiped her nose on his shoulder. "I don't want to see her again." In a low voice, so low that Skyhammer thought he hadn't heard her correctly.

"Why not? I thought you were friends."

Higgins moved away and dried her eyes on her sleeve. She sighed. "Let's get in the boat and I'll tell you."

"Let me eat this first. No, start your story while I'm eating. Sounds like a long one."

"I'll haul this time." Higgins lowered herself into the boat, then turned it around so Skyhammer could slip in. She reoriented the boat to the silk rope, yanked on it and they were off.

Skyhammer started on his bread and cheese. "So?" he mumbled around a hunk of hard orange cheddar.

"She was dismissed at the beginning of our third year, remember?"

It was obvious she didn't want to dive in to the story immediately. Skyhammer let her meander on, as though she was talking to herself.

"We were really good friends. Well, as good friends as you can be with someone in a position of authority. I felt like," she took a deep breath, "she was an older sister. We talked about love, relationships and school and after school. She was always reluctant to talk about the Fungal Forest." She paused, staring at a brown mushroom trunk. "You know her spider died, right?"

"What?" Skyhammer swallowed a huge chunk of bread before his throat was ready and had a little coughing fit. "I'm fine, I'm fine," he said when he could speak again. "No! I had no idea. Why didn't you tell me?" He knew very little about the Katipo but he did know that spiders were almost a Katipo's second brain. Katipo magic power controlled the spiders, with the ability to see through their eyes and communicate with them. Every Katipo grew up with a companion spider. They were more than pets; they were friends, siblings almost. With such a strong connection, most Katipo lost the will to live if their spider died.

She shrugged. "Never came up, I guess. I don't have to tell you everything, you know." She grinned at him.

"I tell you everything," he said in a sulky voice. Then he remembered he hadn't told her about the Aridizan's death.

"That's your choice." She hauled the boat in silence for a while.

Skyhammer wondered what else she had never told him. He snorted to himself. There was always more with Higgins. Perhaps that was why he could spend a ton of time with her and not get bored or angry - there was always more to discover. Not that she was secretive. She was just deep. Which sounded cheesy, he admitted, but fit the bill.

"So she told me that she wandered around Pingala a bit, visiting different cities. She couldn't stay in the Fungal Forest where she saw other spiders all the time. It hurt too much. At first. She finally stopped travelling after she convinced Ms. Floss to give her a job. She developed the counselling position over time. I can't remember at what position she started. Anyway, she had been there for a long time. She and I became friends. But she was always a little crazy, right?"

Skyhammer nodded. She was the only Katipo on campus and came across as wacky sometimes, like dancing alone in the quadrangle with no music. And she would never sit next to certain people at the dinner table. Rantama was one of them, he recalled. But she really did listen and help people work through their problems. He himself had benefited from her counsel when he first arrived at the Academy.

"So you remember she got a little more crazy near the end, locking herself in her room, not seeing anyone, not eating. . ." She trailed off, deep in thought, then resumed. "Just before that, I went to visit her. And she. . ."

Skyhammer watched pain, betrayal and confusion flash across Higgins' face.

Chapter 15

Countdown to ceremony: 11 days

An insect buzzed in a purple mushroom cap far above them. A damp fungus smell permeated the air. Skyhammer felt a rivulet of sweat run down his ribs from his armpits.

Higgins took a deep breath. "Hanamun . . . tried to kiss me."

His eyebrows leapt to his hairline. "I beg your pardon?"

She avoided his eyes. In a louder voice: "She tried to kiss me. And when I pushed her away," she stopped. "I did push her away."

Anger wrestled with jealousy and protectiveness in Skyhammer's heart. Sadness too, that Higgins had never felt comfortable enough to talk about this with him. She must have felt so betrayed by her friend. And so alone.

"I wanted to tell you. But," she turned around to gaze into Skyhammer's eyes. "I didn't want it to reflect badly on her. I knew she was having some problems and if I told you, it would make her seem like an evil person. She just loved me." Higgins started hauling again. "She loved me and asked me to run away with her."

Skyhammer's heart was pounding. "You didn't though."

"Obviously!" she exclaimed. "I didn't love her like that." She paused. "I told her I couldn't leave school and my friends for some wacky theory she had. . ."

"Which theory was that?"

She focused on the rope. "Oh, nothing really."

"It couldn't have been nothing if the Academy had to dismiss her for it." He inched forward on his seat.

Higgins stared into the darkness. "I promised her I would never tell anyone."

"It's just me. I promise I won't tell anyone either," he wheedled.

Her eyes blazed at him over her shoulder. "I gave my word. Stop pestering me!"

He was taken aback by her fire. "Alright. Just tell me one thing."

"What's that?"

"If knowing this secret would save my life or yours, would you tell someone?"

She gazed at him with clear, open eyes. One deliberate shake of her head.

"Huh." He began folding the wrapping of the bread and cheese in half, then in half again, then in half again. He knew this about Higgins. She was, well, she was principled. But to hear it from her own mouth. That she would rather die than betray her word to a friend. No, that wasn't what disturbed him. That she would let him die, before betraying her promise. She would rather he was dead than tell someone about some stupid thing that happened in the past. Anger surged in his chest.

Higgins was still looking at him, a knowing expression on her face. She put her hand on his knee. "That circumstance will never come up, my friend," she said. "Don't think about it."

"So then what happened?" His voice was normal, thank the gods.

Her hands resumed their rhythmic pulling. "I never saw her again. I couldn't go back there, you know? And she was dismissed a couple days later." She hauled the boat around a mushroom trunk, heading in a new direction, following the silk rope.

"How did that make you feel?" Skyhammer dipped his fingertips in the murky water then yanked them up again when he remembered the eyes they'd seen.

Higgins considered for a moment. "Relieved."

He nodded.

"I didn't want to deal with her again. I felt betrayed. She was my friend and she tried to come on to me. I was young; she was ancient. Now I'm a little angry about it but then I was sad and confused."

Skyhammer tried to remember Higgins during that period. Had he even noticed that she was upset? She was good at hiding her feelings, that's for sure. Or was he just so wrapped up in Spark that he didn't even notice? He shifted on the hard seat. Spark was also sad when Counsellor Hanamun was dismissed. Upset and hurt that the counsellor hadn't said goodbye or told her she was leaving. He was so busy trying to comfort the woman who would leave him a few weeks later that he totally ignored the pain of the woman who'd stayed by his side since they met. He shook his head. The choices we make.

"What are we going to ask her?" He should talk to her, he thought. Spare Higgins the pain. But maybe she needed to talk about it with the counsellor. Get some closure. "Should we tell her the truth?"

"No!" Higgins said. "Don't mention anything about the Byndari or the Retrographs or any of that. Just say that we are trying to locate Spark on behalf of the King."

"Surely," Skyhammer protested, "she'll know that we were sent to figure out who's changing the Retrographs."

"She's so far out of the way here, she probably knows nothing about what's happening in the rest of the world," Higgins replied. "Let's find out first. If she does know, then we'll say we're looking for Spark because you'd like to get some closure with her. Maybe finding her and trying to start your life together again."

"But if Spark doesn't want to and she knows where Spark is, then she won't tell me, in order to protect Spark."

"Just don't worry about it, okay?" she said, a note of impatience in her voice. "I'll talk to her. You can wait outside in the boat or something."

"I don't feel comfortable with that, really," he announced. "What if she's dangerous? She'll probably have gotten crazier-"

Higgins waved an arm at him and he shushed. Another smaller silk platform was just ahead, surrounding one mushroom trunk and held taut by three others. A luminescent home gleamed at the top of the trunk. The silk rope led right to the platform's edge. They had arrived at Counsellor Hanamun's home.

* * *

"There's no one here!" From the base of the trunk, Skyhammer stared up at the amber dwelling. How the heck did the Katipo climb up there? "Wait. I saw movement! Hello?"

Higgins stood on the platform near the boat as though afraid to come closer. She had probably been thinking about meeting the counsellor again but never expected it would happen.

Although he saw the material of the dwelling expand and contract as though there was something walking on the floor, he heard no response.

"Hello?" he called again. The dwelling was shaped like a doughnut that had been slid up the mushroom trunk until it got stuck. He walked around the trunk but still couldn't see any way to get up to it. "Counsellor Hanamun?"

A slit opened in the bottom of the amber dwelling right above Skyhammer's head and a black shape hurtled through.

"Higgins, uh," he began, backing away .

The shape landed where he had been standing a few seconds before and swivelled to face him. An insect the size of a cow. Black armoured body. Sharp pincers snapped at him.

Skyhammer drew his sword. Insects were the most difficult opponents since their bodies were covered in armour. Where was Hanamun? Had this insect killed her?

The insect scuttled forward, its multifaceted eyes pinned on him. As it stretched a pincher towards him, he swiped at it but missed. The creature moved fast. He knew the edge of the silk platform was nearby so he began to circle back to where Higgins still was.

"Higgins?" he screamed. "An insect!"

He thought he heard a chuckle. She would know he meant a big scary insect, right? Not a small scary insect. He backed into one of the three mushroom trunks holding the silk taut.

The insect kept coming. Some type of killer beetle.

Why did the Katipo have such huge creepy crawlies in their country, he wondered. "Higgins!" He continued jabbing at it with his sword. Now he danced to the left, swinging and stabbing, until the beetle was backed up against the trunk. Finally, Higgins' rapier danced next to his.

Outnumbered, the beetle turned to climb up the mushroom, its carapace protecting its enormous back.

As the beetle ascended, Skyhammer saw an opening. He rushed forward, raising his sword for a death thrust. A second before his sword tip stabbed the beetle, it scuttled up the trunk. His swing missed the insect entirely. Instead, he chopped through the silk cloth attached to the trunk.

Higgins and Skyhammer dropped straight into the swamp, tangled in the woven cloth, which was rapidly disappearing into the foul water.

Skyhammer gripped his sword hilt, eyes squeezed shut. He'd never find his weapon again if he dropped it in the swamp. He didn't sink very deep so it was easy to swim to the surface then sheath the sword. Higgins had done the same thing. They dog-paddled for a minute, getting their breath back.

Skyhammer felt something brush by his leg. "Oh gods. I just felt something go by my leg."

"Let's get back in the boat." Higgins began swimming to where the boat was still attached to the silk rope.

Skyhammer followed close behind, trying to keep his body as close to the surface as possible. He kept glancing around and during one of these frantic glances, he noticed a pair of eyes and some teeth headed their way.

"Teeth at three o'clock," he shouted.

Higgins was close to the boat.

"You can make it!" he shouted. If she could get in then she would have a better chance of helping him.

The teeth and snout darted between Higgins and boat. She back-paddled furiously towards Skyhammer, the creature following.

"We'll have to fight it," she screamed to him.

A gentle movement brushed across Skyhammer's leg. His heart turned to jelly. He looked down, even though the water was so clouded he knew he couldn't see. Eyes glinted right next to him, just under the surface. A moment later, the long body of a fat snake coiled around him and squeezed.

"Higgins, help!" he yelled with his last breath.

He saw her turn toward him. The serpentine embrace crushed his arms in tight. He looked at Higgins; the world began to darken, like ink spreading across his eyeballs. The toothy creature reared up, sharp teeth and gaping mouth lunged towards Higgins - the world went mercifully black.

* * *

He didn't know if it was hours or seconds later. He opened his eyes and inhaled a huge breath. He was being towed on his back. "Higgins?" he croaked.

His body stopped moving. He twisted over and trod water. She was glaring at him, face streaked with dirty water and red with emotion.

"You scared me!" She shook his shoulder.

"What happened?"

She shrugged. "We were too big and scary for them?" Her voice shook a little. "I don't know. All I know is that they both disappeared and nothing has bothered us in the intervening ten minutes." She started swimming towards the boat again. "Makes me a little nervous. Maybe something bigger is coming."

Skyhammer splashed after her. He felt exhausted again; each of his limbs a bucket of lead. He hated this country. When he looked back where his slash had dumped them in the water, the insect clung to the mushroom trunk, watching them. Weird. It seemed so focused and intelligent.

Higgins helped him into the boat and then they both collapsed on the bottom.

He must have slept again. Or maybe he was dreaming. He thought he heard a voice.

"Higgins and Skyhammer."

His eyes sprang open and he was looking right at Hanamun. Same glossy red skin and kind smile. He sat up and nudged Higgins.

"Whazzat?" she mumbled, sitting up and rubbing her eyes.

He gestured to the Katipo who was standing on a boat next to theirs.

"Where did you come from?" Higgins asked her.

"When I learned you were in trouble with the creatures, I came right away."

"You stopped them," Skyhammer said. It was a statement.

Hanamun turned her gaze to him. "I did."

His brain was fuzzy but, "They're not spiders."

She inclined her head. "Correct."

It meant something, he was sure, but he was so tired that he couldn't make the connection.

"My boat will tow you to my real home. You can just lay back and rest, both of you. I'll let you know when we arrive. Eat this first." She handed a mushroom to each of them, Higgins' blue, Skyhammer's pink.

His stomach growled as he stuffed the fungus in his mouth. It tasted like oats.

Higgins swallowed her mushroom then curled up and closed her eyes.

"I should stay up," Skyhammer mumbled as he lay back but his lids dropped of their own will.

* * *

Skyhammer felt himself being lifted from the boat and carried. He tried to open his eyes. Everything was black. Voices drifted as if through a fog.

"Will he be safe here?"

"They'll keep an eye on him. We'll just sit over here."

"How have you been?"

"Lonely. But safe."

One of the voices was Higgins'. Why was he so tired? His limbs felt heavy but his mind was alert. He tried to speak but couldn't move his jaw.

"Why are you here?"

A long pause.

"What have you heard from the outside world recently?"

"I know the Byndari found a Relic." Derisive laughter. "And I know about the humans' changed Retrographs. That's why you're here, of course."

Silence.

"I'm glad you're doing well here. And are safe."

"My traps work well, I learned today. At your expense. I'm sorry about that."

"We want to contact Spark."

Rustling, like someone shifted.

"Why?"

"Skyhammer wants closure."

"What about the Retrographs?"

"She may be able to help us find the Retrograph Sorcerer."

"How would she do that?"

Higgins sighed. "It's a long story."

Water slapped against something, a mushroom trunk perhaps. His ear must be against the silk platform. The water sounded close.

"I have time."

"We don't."

"I don't know where she is."

Skyhammer felt a hand brush across his forehead and hair.

Higgins spoke in a firm, quiet voice. "Hanamun. You trusted me with a secret once. And the other thing was, difficult. But we were friends. Of a sort. You trusted me. Please. Trust me again."

Skyhammer's body bounced as someone walked a few paces

on the silk platform.

"I need to know why. You can trust me. I promise. I've gotten better. Now that I'm here. Away from, them. They won't come here, I don't think."

Higgins inhaled a deep breath. "You do appear to be more relaxed." A pause, then, "We think Spark is the Retrograph Sorcerer and is changing the Retrographs to warn us about something." She described Skyhammer' changed Retrographs. "It's something to do with the ceremony or the Byndari-"

"The Byndari?" Hanamun interrupted.

Higgins snorted. "Maybe you were right about them. But we need to talk to Spark to know for sure."

Skyhammer heard a skittering noise above him, like claws on rock. He felt anxious but still couldn't move or make a noise.

"I'm a bit worried about him," Higgins said.

"He'll be fine."

Waiting, anticipation filled the air.

"You owe me." Higgins voice was curt. "For what you, for *that*." Her voice had a slight edge of anger. Of pain.

"That's not fair."

If his ears could prick, they would. They were talking about that secret that Higgins had never shared with him. A whisper of jealousy, then guilt. It didn't sound like a pleasant secret.

"I don't care. I, we, need to know where Spark is."

"If she can see your Retrographs," said Hanamun, "then she has great power now."

"Yes. But Skyhammer's paying for it. They believe since he's the Keeper, he must've changed the Retrographs. And that he wants to sabotage the ceremony because he doesn't have magic power. They're trying to kill him. We have to find her. I promise," Higgins' voice cracked. "We won't let any harm come to her."

Hanamun whispered a word.

Skyhammer couldn't quite hear it. He felt sleepy again. And then his brain was falling away, off a precipice into darkness.

* * *

"How could you do that?"

Higgins sounded indignant, Skyhammer decided. Angry too.

Although reluctant to open his eyes, he figured some poor person must need protecting from the wrath of Higgins. He sat up, thankful his head was clear again.

They were still at Counsellor Hanamun's real home in the Fungal Forest. Higgins faced Hanamun, her hands on her hips.

Hanamun raised her chin. "It was for his own good. He didn't need to hear our conversation and he was half-asleep already. The fungus simply made his sleep deeper and the nutrients in it restored him." The counsellor shrugged.

It was time to intervene. "What happened?" Best if Higgins and Hanamun didn't know quite yet that he had heard them speaking.

Higgins turned around and in an instant was down on her knees next to him. "Are you okay? Do you feel alright?"

"I'm fine. I was just sleeping, right?" He stood up, then stretched his hands high above his head.

Hanamun stepped forward and Higgins put a hand out in warning. "Don't come near us. Just take us out of here."

"I was trying to help." Hanamun spread her hands out, palms up.

Higgins opened her mouth.

Skyhammer, seeing Higgins readying a torrent of angry words, put a hand on her shoulder. "Hanamun, thank you for your time and help. Please tow our boat back to Ambersilk. Now." He directed Higgins into the boat, then sat down and waited.

Hanamun tied their boat to hers then stood in the prow, watching Higgins.

"She's making me nervous," Skyhammer whispered. A water creature of some sort was towing Hanamun's boat along with theirs but Skyhammer didn't want to think about the creature's size and strength. How were they tamed?

Higgins didn't reply, just continued locking eyes with the Katipo.

When they reached Ambersilk, Higgins put on her backpack without a word and headed towards the boat landing on the other side of Ambersilk.

He sighed. Another hauling extravaganza before they got back to Quasianti. His back and arms already ached in remembrance.

Hanamun spoke to Skyhammer. "Don't think badly of her. She made the only choice she could."

"Higgins?" He was confused.

"No. Spark. When you see her...be gentle. Be patient."
Skyhammer's eyebrows drew together. "We'll see."
"And Skyhammer."
"What?"
"Beware the Byndari. They are not what they seem."
Before he could ask what she meant, her boat had disappeared into the dark forest of mushroom trunks.

Chapter 16

Countdown to ceremony: 8 days

"We have to move faster." Higgins tore a pine cone to bits as they rode towards the border of Quasianti.

Spark resided in HriHriKari, the Aridizan's capital city, Hanamun had told Higgins. They still had to cross the Deadlands and Flyer country then enter HriHriKari. After that, they had to find Spark, who had already avoided detection for years.

Then there was the issue of getting her back to Quasianti: not just to Four Hills, but all the way to the Kingmaker Tower. Skyhammer refused to let his anxiety surface. He yearned to talk to Spark. To know how she had acquired magic powers. Could he get them as well, the same way? Had she found another mesh glove? Or worse, had the Retrograph Vault been able to bestow magic powers all this time and he'd just never known? A flash of desperation hit him.

"Maybe the eclipse is actually a couple of days later than predicted so we have some extra days before the ceremony." The joke didn't sound as funny aloud as it had in his head.

Higgins rose up in her stirrups, peering ahead. "We'll have to go through the Deadlands by ourselves and not join a caravan. They're too slow."

"Is there not some other way to communicate with her?" Skyhammer burst out. "It seems ridiculous to travel all the way to HriHriKari and back. We just need to talk to her." His horse neighed as he yanked the reins in frustration. "Sorry. Sorry, horse."

A flock of tiny brown birds disappeared into the foliage at the path's side.

"Flyers!" Higgins called out. "We could ask the King to send a Flyer messenger to HriHriKari-"

"Yes, now would be a great time. Our popularity is at its height in Four Hills. Great idea."

"Don't hear you coming up with anything."

Skyhammer rode on in sullen silence. He observed a reflection of the horses, Higgins and himself in a puddle bounded by tree roots. Ripples spread as they rode past. "I've got an idea!" He stopped his horse and faced Higgins.

"She can see what we are doing," he confirmed.

"Yes."

"We can communicate with her through the Retrographs!"

"But if she could, wouldn't she just write us a message?"

Skyhammer waved her suggestion away. "Maybe she can't affect the Retrographs that way. Who knows what the rules are?"

"That's kind of strange."

"This whole thing is strange." He opened his Whorl and peered at a Retrograph. "Look. From what I can tell, she can move items or people but not change them. We can write questions or statements on a piece of paper. For yes, or true, she puts an object at the beginning of the sentence-"

"And if it's no or false, she puts the object at the end of the sentence." Higgins nodded. "One problem. We need paint and a big piece of paper."

"Or we could write on the ground. With stones and sticks."

"We're in the middle of a forest. Not a lot of space. And kind of hard to see. Time consuming as well. No, we need paper."

Flicking through his Retrographs, Skyhammer found one showing a map of Quasianti. "We're near Kulik Town." He closed his Whorl. "We can get some there."

"And who just reminded me of our popularity with humans right now? Sauntering into Kulik could be dangerous."

Skyhammer stared at the puddle, thinking. Then he grinned and began rooting around in his pack. A moment later, he yanked out a long white shirt. "Disguises!"

"Disguises? Those are our best clothes. We wear them for the King or Relic collectors only."

"Exactly. Humans will be looking for dirty and tired Relic hunters, not Lord Whatsit and his sister, Lady Whosit."

"I guess." She twitched the reins. "Most people haven't seen us in our finery, true."

He stuffed the shirt back in his pack. "Let's get to the outskirts of Kulik before we change."

Their horses' clopping hooves combined with birdsong to create a soothing rhythm.

"Why do you think Spark went to the Aridizan capital?" Skyhammer mused. "HriHriKari isn't that big. It's in the desert, for goodness sake. She hates the heat."

"Maybe that's why. No one would think to look for her there."

"But no one was looking for her."

Higgins rolled her eyes. "Yeah, no one important I guess."

He coloured. "Except me of course. But I didn't even try that hard, did I?" He had felt guilty for not trying harder, he realized. Why? Because once Spark was gone he felt free? He had been lonely sometimes and missed her but he had felt . . . unshackled. For the first time in a year or so. He hardened his heart. She had left him. He was mad about that at the time. Still was. Looking down, he noticed that his thumb was rubbing along his fingertips. He flexed his fingers. He had to stop thinking about the glove. Perhaps she had found a way to get magic for herself only. For surely if there was a way to give him magic, she would've tried to contact and tell him about it. Would he have looked for her if their positions were reversed?

They came to a fork in the forest pathway. Higgins went left and Skyhammer cantered along behind her, then caught up to fall in beside her.

"What should we say in the message?" There were so many questions he wanted to ask. Did you kill Hermit? Why? How did you get in the Retrograph Vault? When did you know you were a Keeper? Why didn't you say something to me-

"We should say we know she's trying to warn us about something but we can't understand what. And then we tell her the method we worked out for communicating and write down our questions."

"How about if we ask her to tell us where she is and then we can go talk to her?"

Higgins brushed a leaf off her shoulder. "We know where she is."

"Do you think Hanamun would lie?"

"No." She shook her head with certainty. "She wouldn't lie to me."

So Hanamun would drug Higgins' friend but not lie to her? He decided not to respond to that remark. "Okay. So we know Spark's in the Aridizan capital. We're supposed to bring her back to the King."

Higgins watched a bluejay dart among the tree branches. "But maybe, if we can convince the King that she is helping him and isn't going to sabotage the ceremony, we don't have to bring her back."

"That may be a little difficult since last time she communicated to the King through his Retrograph, she put a sword through his chest."

"Yep."

"Then we need to know exactly what she's trying to tell us. We should write out a few sentences saying what we think she's trying to tell us and ask her to confirm."

A rabbit fled down the path in front of Higgins' horse.

"What if she doesn't answer?"

"We have just enough time to get to HriHriKari, grab Spark and get back to the Tower for the ceremony. Cutting it close but we could do it." Skyhammer snapped off a huckleberry branch and popped berries in his mouth as he rode.

"Do we tell the King where we're going?"

Skyhammer laughed. "And what human would be willing to send that message for us? Nope, we're on our own until we capture the Retrograph Sorcerer and the ceremony finishes successfully."

"We're wasting time, then. Shall we gallop?" A mischievous smile crossed Higgins' face.

Grinning, Skyhammer nodded. Higgins leaned forward, knees deeply bent and bounced ahead. Skyhammer jolted on his horse behind her. He was bigger and taller. That's why he had trouble galloping. It wasn't because he wasn't in as good a shape as Higgins. And, he thought as he looked at her pert bum bouncing along in front of him, she did have a very pleasing shape. He shook his head to get rid of the thought. Had he just been attracted to Higgins? No, no, he reassured himself, he was just admiring nature's booty, uh, beauty. Higgins was like a sister to him. And that was how she thought of him. Like a brother.

The winding forest path they followed finally joined up with a main road leading to Kulik. They halted, unseen, in the trees lining the road. Wagons, horses, donkeys and crowds of people were travelling towards the town.

Skyhammer felt a twinge of guilt as they tied to horses up again. There were wolves in these forests. But he didn't need the hassle of horse-minding while in Kulik.

Blue dress trousers, a long white shirt, and a dark blue jacket with silver embroidery replaced Skyhammer's usual all-black Relic hunter uniform. A wide-brimmed hat pulled low, plus a fake black moustache, completed his outfit.

A glance at Higgins took his breath away. Thigh-high boots barely met the bottom of a short red skirt and form-fitting black top. Her neck, wrists, ears and fingers tinkled with jewellery. Red ringlets curled over her shoulders. A black eye patch covered her left eye and a black cape hid her rapier.

"Sister? Lady?" He lifted an eyebrow. To meet the King she normally wore more clothes. She must have decided to forgo another layer of clothes. Or this must be what she wore to parties in Floatilla.

"Sisters are boring. Mistresses are fun." She flicked her fingers at her bag. "Carry that, darling. Let's go."

Clamping his slack jaws together, he stepped onto the road a few paces behind her.

Higgins hailed one of the children capering around a wagon. "What's going on?"

The girl stared a moment in awe, then found her voice. "The fair, my lady. Kulik is having its annual water fair. Come on, it's fun!" She scampered off.

"Ever heard of it?" Higgins asked.

"Nope. It's a fairly small town though so I'm not really surprised. They often have their own celebrations. The crowds mean people won't pay too much attention to us."

The road was becoming clogged with people and animals but Higgins and Skyhammer wound their way through. Since Kulik was outside the Royal Circle, no one would be expecting any magic. Humans walked and talked with one hand raised, automatically flicking through their Retrographs as they chatted.

Kulik, like most forest towns, had an enormous wooden wall around it. Dangerous bears and wolves roamed the woods. As well, it was close to Katipo country. Most border towns were still mistrustful of other species, even though humans were now at peace with every species except the Nasuchu.

The wooden wall enclosed communal grazing land - the bears and wolves weren't after humans of course, they were after the townspeople's goats and sheep. Also enclosed were the homes of the townsfolk, shops, inns and pleasure houses; it was a self-contained community. Not huge, like Four Hills, but a good size.

They'd be putting on a good party for the folks that came from smaller settlements spread through the forest, Skyhammer thought. The scent of roasted meat reminded him of how long it had been since he'd eaten anything but mushrooms or berries. Too long. He promised himself a lamb kebab once they'd sent their message through his Retrograph.

An enormous cleared area between the wall and the forest, typically empty, was now covered with tents, wagons, animals and people. A few Byndari wandered about, as did a couple of Aridizans and Katipo. But the majority of the crowd was human.

Just outside the north town gate, Skyhammer and Higgins paused to join the crowd looking at a huge fountain. Some highly skilled engineer had created an amazing system using pulleys, levers, fountains and waterfalls. A series of tiny animals such as whales, fish, turtles and otters floated up and down the fountain. Made from wood and wire, the whole contraption was twice the height of Skyhammer and about three times as long. A low fence ringed it to keep out people fancying a swim.

Skyhammer admired it as he continued through the gate, which led into the residential section of town. Towns tended to be laid out similarly so Skyhammer guessed the shops would be in the south part. He and Higgins strode down the main street. Everyone smiled at them and no one seemed to recognize him. He began to relax. People were dressed up for the celebration anyway, so he and Higgins blended in.

The buildings, all wooden, were quite simple on the outside, nothing elaborate. Most were two or three stories high. The glass windows were covered in paper. Most home or shop owners had gone to a lot of trouble to make intricate and colourful designs of animals or people or geometric shapes.

As they travelled south through the town, the buildings became more commercial. At first, just a few shops were scattered among the residences and then it was all shops. Except for a large green park at the center of town, none of the residences had lawns for children to play on. Potted plants crowded front stoops, window sills, every square inch of sunlit space possible. Skyhammer found that a bit odd. No individual spaces for people except indoors. Perhaps it forced people to interact more. The townsfolk appeared welcoming and chatty.

The road branched off to encircle the central park. They traversed a footpath that cut across the middle of the park, observing with pleasure the crowds of children, teens and adults lounging or squirting water at each other or canoodling under the shade of the trees that ringed the park.

Commercial and industrial districts fully took over on the other side of the park. Big wide doors allowed passers-by to peer in and watch the carpenter or the baker at their work. Skyhammer shuddered to think what would happen if there was a fire here. The town would be ash in an instant.

Higgins stopped another child, a young man this time, and asked him for directions to a paper shop. The kid wore grubby shorts and a collared shirt. Dirt streaked his bare feet.

"I'll take you!" he said, staring open-mouthed at Higgins.

"It's not necessary but we really appreciate it," Higgins said, smiling.

"It's Waterfest and we want to welcome all our visitors to Kulik and make sure everyone has a good time," the kid recited.

"What's your name?" Skyhammer asked.

The kid started, as if noticing Skyhammer for the first time. He stared at the Relic hunter for a moment. "I'm Daniel." He paused. "The shop is this way." He led the way through some darker back streets that cut between the west and south roads.

Distracted by a street performer, he and Higgins dawdled a few steps behind their guide, who had just turned a corner. They quickened their pace to catch up. When they stepped around the corner after him, he was gone. People packed the street but Daniel had disappeared.

Chapter 17

Countdown to ceremony: 8 days

A flash of anxiety twisted Skyhammer's stomach. Had Daniel recognized them? What if he told an adult and they were attacked again? He looked at Higgins. She seemed unconcerned.

"Let's keep walking." She slid her arm through his.

Halfway down the street Skyhammer saw a sign hanging off a building, a few scrolls sketched on the wood.

"There." He pointed.

They crossed the street and entered the cool darkness of the paper shop.

Skyhammer blinked as his eyes got used to the darkness. He looked around. The store was very small in depth but the ceiling soared three stories high. A counter ran in front of him, slicing the room in two, leaving a small space for customers to stand. On the walls behind the counter hung long strips of paper of every imaginable colour and texture, a stunning paper mosaic. The only light came from the two windows on either side of the door, their paper covering filled with letters and numerals of all shapes and sizes.

A door in the right wall opened and a well-groomed man bustled through. "How can I help you?"

Higgins stepped forward. "We're looking for some paper."

The man frowned "Sorry, we don't sell that here. You'll have to go down the block." At the surprised expression on Higgins' and Skyhammer's faces, the man guffawed. "Ha, ha! Just kidding! You've come to right place! Pulp's Paper Emporium has everything for your paper needs." He stroked his chin. "Now, what did you need? Something to send to a mother? A scented sheet for a lover? A businesslike missive for your business partner? A new window for the marriage bedroom?" He leered at Higgins. "I am Mr. Pulp, the proprietor of the finest paper establishment in Kulik."

"We need your cheapest paper, Mr. Pulp." Higgins contemplated the wall of paper as she spoke.

She ignored the leer with grace, Skyhammer noted. He wanted to punch it off the little peacock's face himself.

An offended look crossed the man's features. He opened his mouth, then snapped it closed. "Our paper is all high quality," he stuttered.

"The King himself has given us a task to complete and your paper is a key component in completing it." Higgins leaned across the counter. "If your paper helps us be successful in our mission, Pulp's Paper Emporium could become very well-known indeed."

Mr. Pulp rubbed his hands together. "Because of the course the King would want to know where the paper came from!" His voice rose with excitement. "So you need some cheap paper. Just something that can be written on by a normal writing implement."

Skyhammer stepped forward. "We'll need a brush and paint. We want to make sure it's highly visible. The one who will read it, uh, doesn't have great . . . eyesight."

Higgins nodded. "Can you procure a brush and paint for us as well? And we need paper that takes paint well. Just black paint will do. And not too big a brush."

The proprietor nodded eagerly. "Yes, yes. My gods, the King! Just give me a minute. . ." He bustled out the door. "Donna! I need help with this order. Now!" The door swung shut behind him and they were left in the relative silence of the cool shop.

A few seconds later, the door opened again.

"Who did you say you were?" Mr. Pulp, hands on his hips this time, regarded them with suspicion. "You say you are on a mission from the King. Do you have papers to that effect?"

The door squeaked. A feminine face, eyes narrowed, peered through the crack. Skyhammer sighed. Of course. His wife had popped Mr. Pulp's rosy dream of fame and asked him to prove these people were who they said they were. He stepped forward, placing one hand on his sword hilt and one on the counter.

"Mr. Pulp. Do you know about the Retrograph Sorcerer?"

"Yes," the store's proprietor said. "*My* Retrographs have been tampered with." He shivered in disgust, then tilted his head to one side and looked at Skyhammer. He gulped as recognition dawned.

Skyhammer smiled.

"The Keeper," Mr. Pulp choked. "Benjamin Skyhammer."

"That's me. Now, the King has kindly asked us to find this

Retrograph Sorcerer. We are in the midst of doing that but we need some paper. Do you know anyone, Mr. Pulp, anyone at all," he leaned over the counter until their faces were inches apart, "that might be able to help us?"

Mr. Pulp stepped back and wrinkled his nose.

Higgins placed a hand on the counter and hopped lightly over, landing next to Mr. Pulp. He shrank under her fierce glare.

"I have the perfect paper for you. Donna!"

His wife came through the door.

"This is my most excellent partner, Donna. Donna this is the Keeper of the Retrograph Vault, and of course," he turned to Higgins, "this must be Higgins."

Skyhammer kept his hand on the hilt of his sword. "Mr. Pulp, there may be people who are certain that I am the Retrograph Sorcerer. I assure you it is not true." He rattled his sword. "If word ever gets out of our visit here, I will personally come back with my weapon in hand."

Mr. Pulp inclined his head.

"Charmed, I'm sure." Donna did not smile. Instead, she fetched a stepladder from the wall opposite the door, then picked up a long pole with a hook at the end. She thrust the hook high into the upper reaches of the room, caught something, and then pulled. The mosaic of paper covering the back wall swung away, revealing two columns of thin drawers.

Mr. Pulp climbed another ladder. His arms snaked above his head and he stood on his toes to pull out one of the drawers. He lowered it down to his wife who placed it on the counter.

In length and width, the drawer approximated the size of a desk but was about five inches deep. Higgins and Skyhammer crowded around it with Mr. and Mrs. Pulp.

Gray and lumpy sheets of paper lay inside.

"Perfect!" Higgins exclaimed. "You're sure they'll take the paint well? Leave well-defined lines?"

Mr. Pulp nodded.

"And you can get us some paint and brushes?"

Mr. Pulp nodded to his wife, who left and returned with a bag of brushes and a few small pots of paint.

"What do we owe you?" Higgins felt in her jacket for her bag of coins.

"No charge." It took the businessman some effort to say

those words. His wife glared at him. "No charge for servants of the King."

Higgins laid a few coins on the counter, at least worth three quarters of the price of the paper, paint and brushes. "Consider this a gift then. Thanks from the King and his . . . minions." She grinned.

Donna started to roll the paper for them.

"Not necessary." Higgins held up her hand.

The Pulps stared at her.

"We'll use your counter. Sit down in the corner over there where we can see you. Please."

"But we have a business to run!" the proprietor protested as Skyhammer locked the door. "And there will more customers for the festival. We can't afford to close for . . . however long you wanted us to close. How long?"

"An hour, Mr Pulp, that's all. Maybe less. The sooner you let us do our job, the sooner we're out of here." Skyhammer got the paintbrush and pots out and set them on the counter. Mr. and Mrs. Pulp retreated to the corner.

"What are we going to say?" he asked.

"Exactly what we discussed before." Higgins unscrewed a lid.

"Well, you should write because my handwriting is atrocious."

"Fine." Higgins already had a brush and pot in her hands. "Could you hold the paper steady? Big letters will take a few sheets."

Skyhammer held the corners of the paper down with his fingers and Higgins got to work. He read aloud as she painted.

Spark. We know you're changing the Retrographs and trying to tell us something. We don't understand your message. Please communicate with us another way or tell us where you are so we can come speak with you.

If you can't tell us where you are, please put this paint pot at the beginning of a sentence to indicate yes and at the end to indicate no in to answer our questions.

She filled two pages with questions about the Wall, the Byndari, the ceremony, the Retrographs.

Skyhammer continued reading as she painted.

Does the danger come from the Wall? Does the danger come from the Byndari? Is the King in danger? Is the Retrograph Vault in danger? Did you kill Hermit -

"Whoa!" Skyhammer cried. "Are you sure you should be putting that question in there? What if she gets pissed off?"

"It's a part of the whole mystery. She can say no if she wants. Hopefully she didn't kill him."

"I don't think that question is relevant," Skyhammer protested.

"Well, too late," Higgins snapped. "I wrote it down already."

Skyhammer didn't read any more of the questions aloud.

When she was done, Higgins held up each page in order so Skyhammer could clearly observe each one. When he had recorded the six pages as Retrographs, she rolled them up and stuck them in her bag. An extra paint pot and brush went in as well. She looked at Skyhammer. "Well, let's go."

"Thanks, Mr. and Mrs. Pulp," Skyhammer called as he closed the door. "Remember, we were never here."

* * *

East of the swathe of forest that swept through Quasianti, the plains began. Miles and miles of tall green grass sprinkled with blue and yellow flowers. Skyhammer felt like dancing. It was so good to be out in the sunshine again. No fungus, no tree branches, no Floatilla. No fussy clothes. Just the wind and the light. He inhaled deeply. "Thank the gods." He patted the sweaty neck of his horse.

Higgins twitched her reins, frowning. "She still hasn't contacted us."

"It was a long shot anyway." Skyhammer had checked his Retrographs obsessively since they left Kulik. No reply from Spark.

"I was thinking that we'd go as far north as we could. The crossing will be shorter."

"Yeah, that's the thinnest part of Nasuchu country. We'll have to follow the border on the other side to get back to the trader road."

Higgins thought for a minute then said, "We'll have to spend at least one night in the Deadlands, right?"

"We could just keep walking. But then we'd be so tired that if Nasuchu attacked, we wouldn't be able to fight them off." Skyhammer trailed his hands through grass that was almost tall enough to hide the horses .

"What do you mean, if?" she joked. Her bottom lip was red from gnawing.

She looked really nervous, Skyhammer decided. That was unusual. "We've fought these guys before, tons of times. We'll be fine." Lucky for them, Nasuchu country was a relatively thin isthmus at this point. He figured it would take them sixteen hours of hiking to get through. More time lost in travelling, which was unfortunate. But the horses couldn't fit between some of the boulders and definitely couldn't clamber between the ground and the boulder tops.

"Who knows what they've learned since then?" Higgins' voice quavered. "We could encounter any warrior band that has eaten any race and learned new tactics."

"We can handle them," he said firmly. "Don't think about it right now."

"There'll be humans on the trader route. We'll need a ride through Flyer country if we want to make good time. What if no one will give us a ride?"

Sighing, Skyhammer faced Higgins. Where was all this negativity coming from? "I know. But they're traders. They choose to spend most of their time away from Floatilla. They're sensible. Stop worrying!" He rode on.

* * *

Only a shallow stream separated the grey boulders of the Deadlands from the grassy plains of Quasianti.

Higgins and Skyhammer squatted to refill their water bottles. No patrols were in view. The King's Guard who protected the region had permission to shoot on sight.

All species feared the Nasuchu. They captured and ate the bodies of other creatures. Their species' magic power meant that they acquired all the skills and memories of any creature they ate. Luckily, they could only do this within their Royal Circle.

No living person had seen their capital, if they had one. The Nasuchu were said to come from human stock, aeons ago. Grey-skinned and hairless, they were otherwise the same size and shape as humans. They were very long-lived, supposedly, and had few children.

The Deadlands consisted of huge grey boulders the same

colour as the Nasuchu's skin. No moss or plants grew anywhere. Narrow passageways wound through the boulders and it was possible to travel on top of them as well, if you were sure-footed.

Unfortunately, the only way to reach the Flyer and Aridizan countries lay through the Deadlands.

"We'd better get going, partner. The border patrols could be coming by soon. It's better they don't see us." Skyhammer stepped across the stream. They had set the horses free in the plains and he missed his already.

The one thing that made travel through the Deadlands possible was the Nasuchu's aversion to fire.

Higgins had made an art of firechain fighting; she was as good as the professional firechain guards that accompanied the trade wagons and protected the road. The trade road was built wooden on tracks across the top of the boulders and was forever being attacked and damaged by the Nasuchu. But the Kings and Queens of the Flyer, Aridizan and human countries worked together to ensure its continued maintenance.

Skyhammer wondered why Higgins seemed so frightened. She could fight off the Nasuchu. Skyhammer was not quite as skilled but he had no problem fighting with firechains too. He was confident that as long as they could get them lit in time, they would be able to fight off a band of Nasuchu.

The hunters, always females, travelled in packs of five while the men stayed at home and raised the kids. The males prepared the kills that the women brought back . . . and now Skyhammer recalled that the Nasuchu had taken Higgins' brother when she was just a child. He felt guilty for forgetting such an important part of her history. But they had travelled through Nasuchu lands before. Why was she afraid this time?

He thought back. For previous crossings, they had joined large groups of traders so that Higgins was distracted protecting the people within the group. She had always been on the alert but since there had been professional guards with them, they hadn't had to fight much. She had felt safe in such a big group.

He sighed. This was the first time that they had crossed alone. It was almost certain they would be attacked.

"Hey!"

Higgins had just stepped over the stream when the shout came. Skyhammer glanced to the north. A human border patrol. Galloping straight for them, arrows nocked and ready.

Chapter 18

Countdown to ceremony: 7 days

"Run!" Skyhammer shouted and they dashed across the short stretch of open land on the Nasuchu side. An arrow whistled by and then they were safe in the shade and protection of the enormous boulders.

The shouting continued. "Come on out, Nasuchu cowards!" Skyhammer rolled his eyes.

"They were dressed like humans," one guard exclaimed.

"Did you see a body?" the second guard asked.

"No," the first guard replied. "Damn it, if the Nasuchu are disguising themselves as human they must be getting desperate."

"Or cleverer," the other muttered. "We should let the King know."

"Agreed. Move out!"

How aggravating. The Nasuchu border guards were sure to have heard that exchange; sound travelled far in the Deadlands. Now they'd be alert for intruders. Great.

Daylight was fading. They had a quick bite to eat and prepared for the crossing.

First, they slipped assassin's boots over their shoes. The supple leather deadened the tap of their soles.

Next, the firechains. Skyhammer withdrew the two separate lengths of light chain first then the spiky balls attached to the ends. The balls were made of metal covered with small slits for air. He opened them and stuffed oil-soaked cloth inside.

He grinned. They'd burn hot and long. He brought out his firestone. One strike of the stone against the metal and a spark would erupt to light the cloth. He placed it in his tunic, handy.

Higgins was ready too. At her signal, they started walking. As agreed, they did not speak. Skyhammer, looking down an almost straight passageway between the boulders, saw the dark height of the Flyer country trees far off in the distance.

* * *

Skyhammer and Higgins heard the Nasuchu before they saw them.

A low laugh.

They froze. In front of them was the biggest boulder yet and Skyhammer knew they'd have to go around it. However, he discerned a flicker of light from the far side. They crept around until they could see what was going on.

The boulder was a cave lit by a wall of nekrowite glowing in the firelight. Skyhammer inhaled in quiet amazement. Nekrowite was the most sought-after jewel in the world. The stones burned with the colours of sunset when polished - purples, oranges, pinks, yellows. They cost more than Relics.

It was also the most reviled jewel because of its origins. Nekrowite was, supposedly, the centuries-old excrement of Nasuchu. Its colours, so bold and stunning, were the combination of remnants of Nasuchu magic and undigested body parts.

The Nasuchu had covered the entire cave wall with nekrowite and the fire's reflection lit the faces of a family at dinner. Four Nasuchu knelt around a table, their heads bowed, long arms by their sides. Dishes covered the table and in each dish was a different body part. One bowl was filled with fingers, all kinds of fingers - baboon, Katipo, human, Aridizan. Skyhammer and Higgins watched in horror as the Nasuchu raised their heads at the same time and then one took up a utensil and proceeded to serve the others, all chatting in the guttural Nasuchu language.

Skyhammer had no idea what they were saying, but the looks of happiness on the creatures' faces as they munched a toe, slipped a human eyeball on a fellow diner's plate, or slurped down some intestines was at once a reminder that these barbarous food items were their family dinner. They ate with elegance, wiping their mouths after each bite and taking small sips of red liquid from goblets made of nekrowite. Skyhammer shuddered - the goblets probably contained blood drained from the bodies.

The plates and bowls were also made of nekrowite but the utensils looked to be carved from bone. Skyhammer wondered if they had made the plates and bowls; he had never heard of the Nasuchu making anything. They killed humans and ate humans and that was as much as most people wanted to know about them.

Higgins and Skyhammer watched the Nasuchu laugh and smile and look with affection upon each other. After a while, Higgins pulled back and tugged Skyhammer's arm. They backed away and crept off.

When they had found a defensible place between boulders, they took turns getting some sleep.

* * *

They had only slept a few hours, then started to walk again. When the sky grew light enough, Skyhammer boosted Higgins on top of a boulder to check their progress. The trees were only a few hours away now.

Skyhammer's legs ached. Eyes were watching him; he could feel them. For a few minutes, he thought about how to communicate this to Higgins. He waited until they had come to a place where they could make a stand, then stopped walking.

He turned around to face Higgins. With the fingers of one hand, he tapped his eyes, then he released his firechain. She nodded; she had clearly had the same feeling. They both stood, alert, with their backs to an enormous boulder and therefore didn't notice the Nasuchu on top.

"Aaaiiii!" was the first thing they heard as a Nasuchu warrior leapt from above and twisted in the air to land facing them, spear in hand.

Skyhammer and Higgins ducked and rolled in opposite directions. The spear clattered against the boulder where they had just been. The warrior must have been pretty confident in her attack if she'd yelled like that. His lips folded into a smile. The Nasuchu didn't know what she was up against.

Skyhammer rolled to a standing position, grabbed the fire stone from his pocket and struck it against the two balls at the ends of his firechains. They lit. He twirled them in simple circles to keep them alight. He turned to see how Higgins was doing just as a spear flew past where his left ribs had been a moment before.

Higgins had disappeared.

"Higgins?" he yelled. The Nasuchu warrior woman advanced on him, hands held up in a defensive position.

"Here," Higgins screamed back. She had been smart enough

to dart around the back of a boulder while she was lighting her firechains.

He knew there would be four more warriors nearby. The first woman halted just beyond the reach of his firechains, chest heaving. She was naked from the waist down. A band of cloth covered her breasts and she wore a small backpack. Her eyes darted from him to her fallen spear and back again. He straddled her spear then sensed a movement on the boulders above him.

He darted forward, swinging the chains out and up in an arc, and then yanking them back towards the middle. The warrior stumbled back but misjudged the length of the chains. The spiked balls snagged on both her shoulders. The force of the swing sent the warrior face first into the ground at Skyhammer's feet.

He yanked the spiked balls out of her back. No time to see if she was dead but he was sure no one could survive that. He leapt over her body, shortening the chains so he could manoeuvre in the narrow passageways between the towering rocks, then headed to his right. Shadows of the warriors above flitted on the ground as he ran, always managing to keep up with him. He presumed they must have only one spear each if they hadn't thrown anything yet. He either had to entice them down to the ground, or go up and fight them up top. The fires in the spheres had reduced to a smoulder.

He stopped running and stood with his back to one of the boulders, listening. The two warriors above also halted. He guessed the other two warriors must be in pursuit of Higgins.

The Nasuchu women conversed in their harsh language. Only one seemed to be on top of Skyhammer's boulder. The sides of the large stone bulged above Skyhammer's head so the one on top probably couldn't see him. The second warrior leapt to another rock.

Skyhammer smiled. They were searching for him. They wouldn't come down and lose the height advantage unless he gave them a good reason. He glided around the other side. Aha! A large open area surrounded by five boulders; that would do. Like a cat, he slunk between the rocks until the two warriors were across the circle from him, looking the other way. Then he stepped out, swinging his firechains. Flames grew inside the spiked balls.

Now the warriors faced him. They were about his own age, battle-hardened and lithe. Their grey skin made them look sickly but they both had bright blue eyes. Grinning, they raised their spears.

Skyhammer swung the chains faster and faster while the warriors watched. Flames darted out the holes until the spheres were balls of fire. They were certain they had him, Skyhammer thought. He was indeed a sitting duck, from their point of view.

The warriors nodded to each other and at that moment, Skyhammer released his chains. The fiery balls, chains streaming out behind them like a tadpole, flew through the air, each one taking a warrior right in the stomach and hurling her back over the boulder and into the passageway below. Skyhammer wasted no time in getting his sword out and racing over to where the Nasuchu had fallen. He came upon the first one writhing in pain, slashed her throat and retrieved his firechain. He did the same for the second then sheathed his sword.

He looked around. Nearby were three odd-sized boulders. He ran at the smallest one, leapt up on the side, then leapt to the medium rock without losing his momentum and leapt on top of the largest one. Where was Higgins?

Shading his eyes, he looked in all directions. Towards the trees, he saw a figure leaping off a rock. That must be where she was. Like a mountain lion, he ran across the boulders.

When he arrived in the area where he had seen the figure jump down, he halted and listened. To his left, something grunted. He dropped to his belly and slithered to look over the edge of the rock.

Higgins had slain one warrior in the open area between boulders and while another pursued her.

Skyhammer wanted to call out but didn't want to distract her. He watched for an opportunity to help.

Higgins ran without making a sound. Skyhammer saw the Nasuchu stop, and turn around, waiting. Higgins raced around a boulder and almost impaled herself on the waiting Nasuchu's spear! She twisted to the side at the last moment but the spear tip still managed to cut her across the belly. Her tunic turned red. Skyhammer's heart clenched in fear.

Chapter 19

Countdown to ceremony: 6 days

Blood soaking her ripped shirt, Higgins faced the warrior, who now wore a smug smile. The Nasuchu lunged at Higgins. Skyhammer's partner stepped backwards and parried with her remaining firechain to block the spear. The warrior shifted the spear to her other hand and again advanced on Higgins with hatred in her eyes. She looked very similar to the other girl Higgins had killed. Skyhammer wondered if they were sisters.

The warrior cast her spear at Higgins' chest. As the Nasuchu threw her weapon, Higgins flung the firechain and ducked the hurtling spear. The warrior kept moving forward, following her spear. The flaming sphere crashed into her chest. The chain wrapped around her body, drawing the ball tighter and tighter into her until its spikes protruded from her back.

The warrior toppled forward, dead. Higgins collapsed.

"Higgins!" He jumped off the rock.

She looked up, a weary smile on her face.

"Nice moves." Skyhammer spied her backpack a few feet away and brought it to her. He rummaged for a flask of water and they sat in the boulder's shade, together, silent.

"Let's have a look at that wound," he said after she'd sipped some water. She was paler than usual.

Higgins lifted her shirt. Skyhammer sighed in relief. The wound across her belly was shallow.

"Just a scratch." Higgins directed him to her medical kit and patched herself up. Then she leaned back against the boulder and closed her eyes. "I had such horrible thoughts while fighting these things," she whispered.

Skyhammer waited.

"I was so happy to kill them. I hated that feeling, yet I revelled in getting revenge for my brother. And then." Her voice caught. "Then I was thinking what if he was inside one of them and I was killing him again? And I almost stopped. What if the things they eat live again within the Nasuchu? Who am I to kill them?"

Skyhammer cleared his throat. "You were protecting yourself."

She lifted her head and looked straight at him. "I was saying, for Joseph, for Joseph, over and over. What if he heard me inside them and tried to communicate and I just killed him?" She dropped her head again.

He didn't know what to say so he slid next to her and put his arms around her. When she had cried herself out, he released her.

She sat up and cupped his face in her palms. "Thank you, my friend."

He looked into her eyes and his heart swelled with love and happiness. His best friend was beautiful. And safe. She wouldn't break their gaze. He didn't want to look away. She moved her face forward, lips pursing. . . A cloud covered the sun, the world darkened and the moment passed.

They both sat back, grinning at each other.

"We'd better get going." Skyhammer jumped up and held his hand out to pull Higgins up. She grasped it and he pulled her up, closer to him than was necessary. She smiled and dropped his hand. His heart was pounding. What was happening to him? His skin tingled with excitement.

"Come on, partner. Let's get the hell out of this nightmarish place." She put on her backpack.

"Okay, Phoebe."

"Pah!" She snorted. "You'll never guess." She started walking.

"Stinky? Janine? Philippa? Betty? Gordon?" he whispered as he followed her through the winding passageways, the trees of Flyer country ahead beckoning.

She shook her head, a soft smile on her lips.

* * *

Boulders nudged up against the bulbous tree roots of Flyer country.

At the border of the Deadlands, they had turned south-east, hopping across the rocks parallel to the tree line until they reached the trading route again. They saw no more Nasuchu. The road across the Deadlands for traders was made of wood, supported by the boulders.

Majestic. Always the first word that came to Skyhammer's

mind at the sight of Rainbowcloud. A stupid name for a country, he thought. But apt. Brown tree trunks, smooth and branchless, shot up a few hundred feet then burst into foliage for another hundred feet. Lush, multi-hued leaves created a rainbow cloud clustered at the treetops. The bark was slippery; the merest damage to a trunk brought an investigating Flyer and the intruder would be picked off with an arrow. The Flyers had a symbiotic relationship with their trees but their actual magic power was unknown.

The smooth roots that bulged above ground were at least twenty feet high, then the trunks proper started. As they approached the road, Skyhammer could make out Aridizans doing repairs and patrolling. It must be the Aridizans' Upkeep Year. That meant next year the road maintenance was the humans' responsibility, he recalled.

At the edge of the Deadlands, where the trader road ended, was a large platform. A system of weights and pulleys raised a large lift up and down, carrying wagons, animals, cargo and passengers to the wooden highway four hundred feet above.

The busy platform fell silent when Higgins and Skyhammer leapt onto it from a nearby boulder. He looked around. A lift had just gone and there was one wagon trundling into the Deadlands and four more waiting for the next ride up. The wagon drivers were always human but their passengers could be Katipo, Aridizan, human or animal.

The wagon drivers, their families, their passengers and the contingent of Aridizan guards protecting the platform stared at them, eyes wide. Retrograph Whorls vanished. No one ever crossed anywhere other than the trader route. If they did, they didn't live to tell the tale.

Applause. The wagoneer next in line for the lift stood, clapping his hands. "I don't know how you did it but I bet it's a great story. If you and your lady are looking for a ride to Hightown, I'll take you for the price of the tale."

Skyhammer and Higgins exchanged a look. The wagoneer either didn't recognize him or didn't care. They had no other option really. Didn't seem as if any other offers were forthcoming. Skyhammer nodded and they climbed up on the man's wagon. The wagoneer turned around to make sure they were nestled safely amongst his potato sacks. Aridizans loved potatoes.

Conversations resumed around them; Retrographs were opened and examined. A wagon drove off the lift and into the Nasuchu lands. It was their turn. Their wagon drove on; the Aridizans made some final adjustments and with a lurch, they were off and up.

Lifting smooth and steady, backs against the wagoneer's seat, they could see all the way back to Quasianti. Skyhammer breathed deep, slow breaths, and reminded himself not to look down.

Like layers of a cake, the different lands stretched away in front of them. The lumpy grey sea of the Deadlands closest. The dark green of Quasianti's forest next to the black-brown Fungal Forest. Mountains. A glint of ocean. And a black spot far, far on the horizon. Floatilla. Skyhammer mentally shook his fist at it.

"I know you," the wagoneer said, twisting around. He was chubby and hairy with large black eyes.

Skyhammer tensed. His hand crept to the hilt of his sword. If he had to kill the wagoneer, at least they could steal his wagon.

"You're Higgins!" He laughed a great belly laugh as both Higgins' and Skyhammer's jaws dropped. "See," he said with a nod to Skyhammer. "I pays attention to the pretty ladies, not the fearsome warriors."

"But you're doubly clever, sir," Higgins replied, "As in this woman you have found both great beauty and a fearsome warrior." She flashed a smile.

The wagoneer stared a moment then laughed again, slapping his knee. "Well met, Higgins. I'm Spokes. Is this your sidekick, Skyhammer?"

Skyhammer smiled tightly while Higgins chuckled.

"Indeed he is, Spokes. Now, how about I tell you that tale?" She hopped over onto the seat beside the wagoneer.

Skyhammer glanced up. They were still a few minutes away from the upper platform. He indulged in a long sweep of the gorgeous vista and noticed some movement near the border of the Deadlands. He couldn't quite see details but it looked like a large crowd of Nasuchu had gathered on the border. The largest gathering that he'd ever seen, about fifteen of them together. Something, not a Nasuchu, was in the middle of the group but he couldn't tell what species or type of creature it was. An escort? Who would the Nasuchu be escorting? They ate allies!

The lift jerked and Skyhammer grabbed onto the side of the wagon, looking up. When he looked back down, the group had disappeared. Must have been a prisoner.

The platform at branch level was surprisingly empty. Although, if folks were heading back to the Royal Circle in preparation for the ceremony and subsequent celebration, as Skyhammer guessed, then this was probably to be expected. His stomach clenched in nervousness. The ceremony was only six days away and he still had not captured the Retrograph Sorcerer. What if he was wrong about the Sorcerer being Spark?

Two Aridizans locked the lift in place then Spokes clucked to his donkey. The wagon rolled onto the wooden track that meandered through the tree branches.

It was like floating through a rainbow, Skyhammer thought as he watched the leaves overhead. Each leaf on each branch was a different colour. In contrast, the birds were all dull shades of brown but they twittered like cheerful ladies at the market.

Higgins plucked a pink leaf off a branch as they passed, chatting to Spokes the whole time. Skyhammer snoozed on the sacks in the warm rays of sunlight.

A shout roused him. Spokes had stopped his wagon and was chatting to a wagoneer going in the opposite direction.

Higgins slipped down beside him. She rubbed her jaw. "I think I've talked more this past hour than in the last week!"

Skyhammer told her about the Nasuchu escort he had observed.

"They could've brought down some big animal," she suggested. "Maybe a bison from the plains of Quasianti."

He frowned. "It didn't look like they were carrying it. And why would they bring it all the way over here?"

She shrugged then hopped back into the front as the wagon began to move again.

* * *

As they approached Hightown, the trader town in Rainbowcloud, small wooden buildings began to pop up amongst the branches on either side of the highway. Bridges connected the buildings to platforms and each other. A roar like the sea - the sound of the wind in the leaves mingled with hundreds of voices - preceded their first glimpse of the Flyer's concession to a trader town.

The road opened onto a large circular platform. At the opposite side from Skyhammer's wagon was the exit road to HriHriKari, the capital of Aridizan country. To the left and right, ramps led up to the higher platforms. The next level was wagon parking. The level above contained inns, food stalls and gathering places. If visitors weren't official residents running a stall or an inn, they were only allowed to stay one night.

Spokes parked his wagon on the second level. "Sure you can't stay the night, Higgins?" he said in a wistful voice.

Skyhammer rolled his eyes as he jumped off the wagon. "Thanks for the ride, Spokes. Higgins?" He waited.

Higgins hugged the hairy old wagoneer. "A pleasure. We'll meet again."

"Safe travels." Spokes saluted her, grinning. He drove away.

She leapt down to Skyhammer's side. Noise from the wagon's wheels masked his voice. "What did Spokes say about me?"

She snorted. "Nothing."

"About me being the Retrograph Sorcerer I mean." Impatient.

"Nothing, I said." Higgins put on her backpack. "He did say good luck capturing the Retrograph Sorcerer though."

Skyhammer heaved a sigh of relief. There were still some sensible humans in the world. Now all they had to do was find another nice wagoneer to give them a ride out of Hightown. He didn't think much of their chances.

Staircases flanked the wagon ramps and took them to the shopping and sleeping level. A wave of spiced and cooked meat scents assailed him as he ascended. Skyhammer's nose was used to the fresh smell of the trees and the dry dusty wind of the Deadlands; a nasal assault had never been so welcome, he thought, smacking his lips together.

"Let's grab a bite before we ride out of this place." Higgins ambled over to a bison burger stall.

Skyhammer watched her. Chatting with that old guy had revived her spirits, he was pleased to note.

He wandered along the stalls and paused at one selling lamb kebabs. As he waited for his food, he scanned the crowded tables. The food stalls stood in a cluster in the center of the platform. Tables and benches ringed the outside, with views over the edge. Skyhammer kept away from the edge. He had glanced over before, once, on Higgins' dare. It was like looking into a brown abyss. He refused to do it ever again. The inns were out on separate platforms, reached only by precarious bridges. He hoped they would meet someone on the main platform who would give them a ride so he didn't have to cross a bridge.

Higgins was making her way back to him, bison burger in hand. As he watched her approach, a person in a tall bright green hat passed her going the other way.

He knew that hat!

He took off after the man and his hat, kebabs forgotten.

Chapter 20

Countdown to ceremony: 6 days

It was hard to move as the platform was thronged with people but the hat was highly visible. As he reached Higgins, her smile dropped.

"What's going on?" she asked, concerned.

"Saw Jessup! Follow me!" He was already a few feet past her. She struggled to keep up in the crowds.

Skyhammer kept his eye on Jessup's very distinctive hat. Tall and bright green, with three blue bands around it. He caught a glimpse of salt-and-pepper hair and grinned.

After glancing over his shoulder to make sure Higgins was still with him, he lengthened his stride and wove his way through the crowd. The place was packed. The stalls had long lines of hungry customers waiting and crowds filled the spaces between the benches and tables.

Jessup turned to the right between an ale shack and a candy stall. The bridge he crossed was deserted.

Skyhammer passed a sign at the start of the bridge saying "Inn of Nor Egrets." He glanced back again. Higgins was pushing her way through the crowds, glaring at him. He took a deep breath then dashed across the narrow bridge, eyes on the inn ahead, hands shielding his view to the left and right. The bridge connected to a balcony in front of the inn. The balcony went around the back to the right, a sign saying "Deliveries" on the fence with an arrow pointing left. Jessup was nowhere to be seen. Skyhammer sat down on the bench outside the inn and waited for Higgins to catch up.

"What's Jessup doing here?" she puffed as she came up. "Isn't he still Relic-hunting?" She sat down beside Skyhammer. "I dropped my burger for this."

"He's a wagoneer now," Skyhammer said with a satisfied smile.

"I presume we're going to request a ride with him?"

"If he's still in the business." The smile dropped away. What if he too thought Skyhammer was planning to sabotage the ceremony? What if he refused to give them a ride and instead trapped them here in Hightown? The only way in or out of Hightown were the trader wagon roads.

Higgins stood up. "Let's get on with it then. Time's ticking." She rapped on the door.

A small boy dressed in a raggedy suit too big for him opened the door.

"Yes?" He looked up at her. "How can I help you?"

Skyhammer stepped up beside her. "I'm looking for Jessup. Could you tell him that Benjamin Skyhammer is here to see him?"

"Would you like to come in and wait?" The boy opened the door wider and gestured for them to come through.

Skyhammer and Higgins followed the boy through the first door on the left. An airy room with windows looked out into the treetops and onto the front porch. The room had couches, chairs and low tables grouped in cosy formations in the four corners. Etchings of the Fungal Forest decorated the walls.

Skyhammer was drawn to one etching in particular that covered the whole wall to the right of the door. The huge piece of copper had been etched and soldered with bits of gold and silver to get just the right shading of Ambersilk. Overcome by memories of the Fungal Forest, Skyhammer realized the artist had captured the place perfectly.

The door opened behind them. They stiffened, hands going to their sword hilts as they turned around. The man in the tall green hat entered, smiling.

"Jessup!" Skyhammer exclaimed in delight. "Wonderful to see you." He and Jessup met in the middle of the room and shook hands, grinning at each other.

"No one will believe me when I say that I scared the living daylights out of our two most fearsome Relic hunters because they were looking at a piece of art!" Jessup said. He crossed the room to a side table laid with glasses, decanters, cups, a teapot and bottles. "Would you like a cup of something to calm your nerves? Tea? Wine? Surely even the greatest of Relic hunters occasionally partake in a little whiskey or relaxing cup of tea?"

Higgins was staring open-mouthed at Jessup. In addition to his colourful hat, he wore bright red velvet pants, very tight, a canary yellow blouse tucked into his pants, and black boots. He wore it all with ease, like a tropical flower wore its petals. Even the hat fit in. His sword was slung across his back in a white velvet scabbard.

"Jessup. Let me introduce you to Higgins."

She had crossed the room to shake Jessup's hand before Skyhammer had finished the sentence. "Finally! Skyhammer's told me so much about you." She stepped back a few steps.

Jessup smiled. "Not what you were expecting?"

"Not so much." She came closer, cautiously. "I guess I expected someone a little more, uh, rugged?" She smiled and it lit up her face such that Jessup was gaping now.

Skyhammer hid a smile. The oldest Relic hunter on the planet was rarely surprised but Higgins's smile was pretty fantastic.

Jessup bowed. "Milady, it is a pleasure to meet you. Welcome to my little investment."

"This is yours?" Skyhammer asked.

Jessup served some tea then gestured for them to sit on the couch. He perched on the edge of a chair.

"Yes, well, when I retired from Relic hunting, having had enough of being 'rugged'," he said with a nod to Higgins, "I had enough money to last me three lifetimes but nowhere to call home. And frankly, I didn't want a 'home', but I did want somewhere that I was welcome to stay any time. So I bought and built a few places. One in each capital roughly. It's worked out well. I have my wagon for travelling and making the odd bit of money, for still being a part of society, I suppose, and then I have my inns and houses if I want to take a break from that. And of course, the inns make money as well. I'm pretty happy with the life I've chosen, all told." He leaned back in his chair, playing with a tassel on its arm.

"Do you miss Relic hunting?" Higgins asked.

Skyhammer glanced out the window into the beautiful multi-coloured foliage. Through breaks in the leaves, he could also see birds and Flyers soaring above the treetops.

After a short pause, Jessup said, "Nope. I don't miss it. I was a Relic hunter for a long time and it's good to have a change, to have stability and not be afraid for my life at least once a month."

"That does sound nice," Higgins admitted.

Skyhammer glared at her and she smiled back at him. "Don't worry, I'm not quitting. Yet. Not until we get this latest mystery, er, Relic found."

Jessup looked at them both with interest. "Mystery Relic? Or just mystery?"

Skyhammer shrugged. "Both. The King has asked us to find some information on the Retrograph Sorcerer."

"Ah, yes." Jessup gave Skyhammer a long searching look. "My Retrographs have been changed as well. Within the last couple of hours too."

So Spark wouldn't reply to their message in his Retrograph but she was still changing strangers' Retrographs? Maybe it wasn't Spark after all. He had to know for sure though.

Higgins went to the window and stared out, one hand on her belly.

"We really need to get to HriHriKari as fast as possible. Do you have a wagon leaving soon?" Skyhammer looked intently at his friend.

Jessup spread his arms wide. "For you, we can leave right away and chat on the journey. I'm intrigued by this Retrograph Sorcerer." He shuddered, a look of repulsion crossing his face. "I'd appreciate the chance to pick your brain. And we can chat about the Relic the Byndari found as well." He stood up. "Wait here. I'll go and arrange things and we'll be off."

"The King wants us at the ceremony. We don't have much time," Skyhammer called after him. "I'd be grateful if we could leave as soon as possible."

"Consider it done. I'll be back in a few minutes." Jessup set down his glass and left.

"What did you do to get him to be so good to you?" Higgins asked without turning from the window.

"I helped him capture a Relic and gave him all the credit for it. It was at a low point in his career and he's never forgotten it. He's a good man." Skyhammer helped himself to a glass of wine. "He did that etching you know."

"Really?!"

"That's all his own art up there."

Facing the huge piece of art on the wall again, she reached up and touched a corner of the cold metal then dropped her hand. "He did that?"

"Yes, I did." Jessup bounded back into the room. "Took me a damn long time and I will probably never get the energy up to do it again but the view that I got it from has an amazing story to go along with it! I'll tell you on the journey. Come on, my friends!" Jessup beckoned to them. They grabbed their packs and followed him out of the inn to the wagon parking platform.

His wagon and pony were as colourful as his clothes.

* * *

Jessup's bright eyes darted every which way, greeting acquaintances with a wave of his arm, all the while words tumbling out, stories, tales of his Relic hunting days and tales of his life now as a wagoneer visiting the capital cities. He was always saving the world, saving the girl, saving the Relic from the baddies - just in time!

After two hours, Skyhammer's head was spinning. Three more hours to go, he groaned. Maybe he could convince Higgins to sit up here with the wagoneer. At least Jessup hadn't asked him any questions about the Retrograph Sorcerer. He wasn't ready to talk about it to him. What was Spark doing? He'd checked his Retrographs every fifteen minutes. No changes. Was she aware they were on their way to track her down? Had she seen him almost kiss Higgins? He avoided thinking about that whole situation. It both excited and scared him silly.

"I'm not feeling very well," Higgins said, about an hour later. He had convinced her to sit up at the front with them but she had been pretty quiet.

"Lay down in the back," Jessup suggested. "There's a mattress and blanket." He stopped the wagon so she could climb over the back of the seat and into the wagon bed. There were a few shouts of anger from the wagons behind. Most wagons didn't stop, as there was nowhere to turn around and no reason to stop. A halt could back up traffic for ages since there were no passing lanes.

Skyhammer helped her over the seat, made sure she was comfortable, then nodded to Jessup to continue. Jessup continued chattering away and Skyhammer listened with half an ear. Higgins never got sick. Maybe she had eaten something. But they ate the same things so Skyhammer should have been sick as well. And Jessup had been eating the same things too and he was fine. Maybe it was a female thing. That was probably it.

"-Spark?" Jessup said, turning to Skyhammer.

"What?" Skyhammer started in surprise. "What did you say?"

Jessup gave him a sidelong glance. "Spark? When you first started hunting, you were talking about her all the time, about finding her and gaining magic powers. You didn't find magic but did you ever find her?"

"No," Skyhammer muttered, looking at the line of wagons ahead. "I never did. I changed my mind. If she wants to hide away, then why should I chase after her? She wasn't interested."

"I see. Anyway, as I was saying, I was surrounded by a ring of wolves the size of houses . . ."

Skyhammer tuned out again. Jessup didn't used to talk this much. And why had he brought up Spark? Did he suspect something? Skyhammer tried to remember if Jessup knew any Byndari. Maybe he should listen to the stories more and figure out what the guy had been doing recently. He might have some information about the Byndari.

"So." Skyhammer interrupted the monologue. "What do you think about the Byndari finding the wall?"

Jessup's eyes lit up. "Now that is huge news! Everyone is excited about being able to use magic anywhere on the planet. Some folks are worried about the other species getting planet-wide magic too though. People are a little nervous. And the Nasuchu, I mean really, how did the Byndari convince the Nasuchu not to eat them, in the first place and second, to agree to do the ceremony at all? Some people think the Nasuchu are just pretending to agree and that they won't go through with it."

Skyhammer shook his head. "I don't think they can eat Byndari because Byndari have no skin or flesh. Also, they too want planet-wide magic. They wouldn't jeopardize that I think."

"Skyh-," Higgins called in a weak voice.

He turned and scrambled over the seat into the wagon bed, then knelt beside her. "What is it? How can I help?" He pulled the cover down. Large red spots covered her neck and her skin was cloud white.

"I'm getting worse, Skyhammer. I need help. Help me." Her eyes were shut tight and she was breathing deep measured breaths.

"Where does it hurt?" he asked.

"I'm cold and itchy. My head hurts. I don't know." Her head dropped back. She was unconscious!

He shook her, called her name. Nothing roused her. He clambered back over the seat and spoke to Jessup. "She needs a doctor. Fast. I have no idea what's wrong or how she got sick. We eat the same things, for god's sake. It couldn't be food." He knew he was rambling but couldn't stop. "We've been with you the whole time. We have to get her out of here and back to the human province as soon as possible. Turn around." He made as if to snatch the reins from Jessup's hands.

"Calm down," Jessup said. "We'll get her emergency medical attention right away. We're stuck in the wagon train until we get to the turnaround point and head back. I know an excellent doctor in Hightown."

"What if only magic can save her? We have to get her back to Quasianti!"

"How are we going to do that? Think, man!" Jessup gave him a stern look. "We'd have to get to the Deadlands, then through the Deadlands, then back to Four Hills. It'll take a few days at least. We can keep her here and have my doctor on call at all times. She's a talented professional. Don't worry."

Skyhammer fretted. "She never gets sick! She hates doctors. How could this happen?" He thought about the past few days. Could it be the spear wound from the Nasuchu? But they didn't use poisoned tips, as far as he knew.

Jessup handed the reins to Skyhammer. "I'm going to pass the word on that we have someone in need of medical attention."

Skyhammer watched in surprise as Jessup ran over to the wagon track heading back to Hightown. He hopped on the nearest wagon and spoke with the driver and passengers. He shook the driver's hand and then ran back to Skyhammer. Skyhammer watched the woman driver point to one of the passengers, her son he supposed, who jumped out and ran ahead a few wagons. He saw how the word would get passed in a short time back to the capital. He'd just have to trust that all the wagoneers would be willing to pass the word.

"They're good people," Jessup said as he hopped back up beside Skyhammer. "We'll get Higgins better, don't worry."

"Is this really the fastest way to do it? It's still going to take a few hours to get back to Hightown. And we're supposed to be back in Four Hills soon. And the wagon's still headed towards HriHriKari!" His thoughts seemed like feathers in the wind.

Jessup put his hands on Skyhammer's shoulders. "The Flyers will send out the emergency services team. They have a contraption like a flying bed that two of them can carry with their feet. They'll send that, we'll all go back and everything will be fine."

Skyhammer scrambled into the wagon bed again. He sat cross-legged beside Higgins, holding her limp hand in his. "You'll be fine Higgins," he whispered, stroking her hand. "You'll be fine."

* * *

The Flyer emergency services team landed in Jessup's wagon bed, jolting Skyhammer awake.

He reached down and brushed Higgins' slack face with his fingers, then stood up. Cold, so cold and pale. More spots had appeared so from the chin down her skin flamed red. She hadn't awakened in the hour that Skyhammer sat by her, whispering to her, telling jokes and stories, and murmuring about their mission.

The tiny Flyer's wings were folding neatly onto her back. The top of her head reached the middle of his thigh but her purple crest made her appear another foot taller.

"Please help her," he pleaded. He had never felt so helpless and scared, even in the Royal Circle. Again, he cursed his lack of magic. Not that it would've worked here anyway. But maybe he could've protected her somehow...

"We will help her," trilled the Flyer. Her musical voice soothed him. Three other Flyers, all female, walked in pace with the wagon.

The Flyer female stepped to the other side of Skyhammer and squatted down.

"My name is Skyhammer. This is Higgins." He wanted the Flyer to know how important Higgins was to him but no words would come.

She didn't answer. One hand cupped Higgins' forehead and a second rested on her neck. "She is very sick. I am Adela. I will take her to Hightown. She must go now. I am the doctor's assistant. I fear she may not make it. She is too cold. Unresponsive. We must leave now." Adela stood up.

Skyhammer inhaled sharply. "What can I do to help?"

Two Flyers flew down to hover over the wagon bed. A human woman jumped out of a hammock hung between the Flyers. "I'm the doctor. Max." She spoke with Adela, swaying a little with the wagon's movement.

Jessup waved from the front. Skyhammer looked from Max to Adela to Jessup.

"We have to get her back to my examination room right away," Max said. "She's in shock. If we don't treat her soon, she could die."

Chapter 21

Countdown to ceremony: 6 days

Die? Higgins? Skyhammer's mind filled with worry. All those times she had protected him and now he could do nothing for her. "What's wrong with her?" Skyhammer moved back as the doctor and her Flyer assistant lifted Higgins into a flying bed. Constructed from a hammock with a board down the middle, the four corners of the material was gripped by the prehensile toes of four Flyers standing in the wagon bed. The Flyers would have to be very skilled indeed to keep their patient flat and stay coordinated. "It may have been from the wound of her belly. We were attacked by Nasuchu while crossing the Deadlands." The more background information the doctor had, the better she could help Higgins.

"I've never seen this kind of sickness before. This inflammation worries me. I've got better instruments back in Hightown and with Adela's help we may be able to do something but we have to get there fast. Come on!" The doctor leapt into another board-less hammock, which now swung between Adela and a second Flyer.

Skyhammer glanced toward Jessup. He was gone from the driver's seat. Skyhammer glimpsed him walking beside the wagon, his arm around the shoulder of a young girl.

Jessup slapped the young girl on the back and she climbed up to the seat of his wagon and caught the pony's reins. Jessup leapt over the sideboard and onto the wagon bed as the doctor's hammock swung next to it.

"I'll go with her. Your mission for the King is too important."

"We have to leave now. Her life is in danger!" Max yelled at them.

Skyhammer stared at Jessup in surprise. "She's my best friend. I can't leave her sick with no one she knows around her."

"She knows me," Jessup said. "If you go you'll never make it to HriHriKari and back to the ceremony in time. Higgins would want you to go on, right?" He looked into Skyhammer's eyes. "There is a hell of a lot of people counting on you to find the Sorcerer and ensure the King does not die and the ceremony is a success. If you think being hunted as the Retrograph Sorcerer yourself is bad now, imagine what it will be like afterwards if the ceremony fails or the King is killed."

Jessup knew! For all his mindless babbling, he had cut straight to the heart of Skyhammer's problem. "But the doc didn't know why she was sick! She may . . . die." The words caught in his throat. Higgins couldn't die. His heart was racing. He couldn't leave Higgins. But the mission had to be completed. He had to find out what Spark was planning, what the Byndari were doing with the wall, why they were not to be trusted. His chin dropped to his chest.

"There's something terrible coming, related to the Byndari. I haven't lost that much of my Relic hunter's instinct for mystery and danger," Jessup said. "We need you to protect magic, protect the ceremony. Go! Sit with the girl. We're almost at the lift. Good luck."

Skyhammer caught his arm. "Tell her I'm sorry."

Jessup pulled away. "Whatever for? I'll tell her you're bravely battling and completing the mission for her."

Skyhammer shifted from foot to foot. Was he a bad person to be leaving her? Choosing Spark and the possibility of magic powers over the life of his best friend?

"Let's go! One of you has two seconds to get in here or I'm gone!" The doc was signalling to the Flyers to leave.

"Go before I change my mind," Skyhammer said through gritted teeth.

"I promise to take care of her for you, Skyhammer." Jessup's hand gripped his shoulder, then released it as he hopped into the hammock beside Max. "I swear by the fact that you may have saved my life once. Or twice." The Flyers rose, gaining speed, and Jessup called down, "Complete the mission you set out to do."

In silence, Skyhammer watched the Flyers disappear, carrying the body of his best friend. He should be in that hammock, going to Higgins, comforting her and being there for her as she'd been all these years. She had never gotten sick before. How could she do this to him? He needed her. Especially now. This was the most difficult thing he'd ever done...he shook his head, trying to clear his thoughts. This wasn't helping. He clambered back into the front seat.

"Hi," he greeted the girl. He couldn't smile.

She glanced at him but didn't answer. She was probably thinking he was an arsehole for leaving his sick friend behind. His heart dropped.

"I don't care that you don't have magic," she said as she slid away from him. "But don't touch me please. I'm not prejudiced."

Skyhammer snorted and hopped back into the wagon bed. He didn't have the energy to deal with ignorance right now. He wanted to be alone anyway, to come to grips with the contradictions in his own heart. He felt more alone than when Higgins went on vacation. At least then he was 100% sure she'd be coming back. Pulling his legs close to his body, he hugged them into his chest and rested his forehead on his knees. As the rainbow-hued leaves fluttered in the breeze above, his every thought focused on his best friend.

* * *

Skyhammer didn't look back as he galloped away from the lift that had brought him from the branches of the Flyer's home to the ground.

In the wagon, he had brooded for a while, hating himself for leaving Higgins, for being a bad friend. For not realizing until then just how much she meant to him. But he got tired of that, impatient with himself. The choice had been made. To make it up to her, he had to find Spark and discover the real purpose of the ceremony at the Kingmaker Tower.

A few hours of jolting on the back of the horse helped take his mind off Higgins. He'd purchased the animal from enterprising young Aridizans at the bottom of the lift. The terrain, a layer of rock called Bethanri's Shield, was fairly flat. Treacherous however. The constant streams of water that trickled everywhere and the algae that bloomed with the water made the rock slippery. His horse was sure-footed though and he made good time to the border of Aridizan country, speeding on through the night, trusting his steed.

The sun was rising as he reached the Aridizan desert, separated from Flyer country by a huge crack in the ground. At the bottom of the canyon, a river of green slime flowed. Folk tales had it that a huge monster slumbered under the desert and that the green slime was the snot of his runny nose flowing unchecked as he slept.

The Aridizans had built a sturdy bridge across the narrowest part of the canyon and placed border control on the side closest to Rainbowcloud. A youthful Aridizan stepped out of the border cabin to meet him, loose grey robes dancing in the breeze. After climbing a set of stairs that raised the small being to the height of the horse's head, he placed a notebook on the podium between himself and Skyhammer. His hood was down, revealing the wrinkled black skin possessed by all Aridizans. His eyes, hidden by folds of skin, peered down at his notebook.

"Name?"

Aridizans, an organized and logic-oriented race, required that each visitor to their country register with the government upon entry. Skyhammer was hoping that this registration would help him find Spark.

"Benjamin Skyhammer."

The Aridizan's head shot up. A look of revulsion crossed his face. "Welcome to HriHriKari." The words seemed to choke in his throat. "Country of origin?"

"Quasianti."

"Job? Sorry sir, must ask although I already know you are a-"

"Relic hunter." Skyhammer could see that it was painful for the Relic protector to even write the words Relic hunter. All Aridizans were indoctrinated with the Relic-protecting philosophy. Only a few Aridizans were actually out in the field doing the protecting. Those ones were very antagonistic, and Skyhammer had battled them a number of times. Although Aridizans did not approve of the human relic hunting fervour, the two species tolerated each other.

"Length of stay?"

The ceremony started in eight days. He needed four days to return to Quasianti's Kingmaker Tower from HriHriKari. "Three days?"

The Aridizan looked up from his note taking. "That's fine sir, we just need an approximation. Purpose?"

Should he say now that he was looking for someone? What if it got back to Spark? She already knew he was here. If she was still looking at his Retrographs. But she might hide even better if she found out he was asking the Aridizan government for help.

"Relic hunting assignment."

The Aridizan's eyes widened. He was young. "Here?" He swallowed.

Skyhammer wished it were true. "In the desert somewhere. I'll be staying at the university."

After clearing his throat, the border guard stated in a loud voice, "It is my official duty to remind you that you will be accompanied by an Aridizan Relic protector as soon as you leave the city. Any Relics found in Aridizan country are the property of the Aridizan Relic Protectorate. Do you understand?" He scrutinized Skyhammer's expression with narrowed eyes.

Skyhammer nodded. Anything to get through the border and get his hands on Spark.

The guard gestured for him to proceed across the bridge.

* * *

The gate to the actual city of HriHriKari was some distance from the bridge. Skyhammer cantered for another hour across the sand before he reached it.

The Aridizans had planned their city well. With stones cut from the rocky plains across the canyon and glass from the sand and heat of the desert, they had created a sturdy fortress of a city, well able to withstand the storms and blowing sand of the desert.

Inside, order reigned. Visitors and residents were regulated. Aridizans hoarded information like gold. Their most beautiful buildings were not religious but instead the universities and colleges and libraries; they worshipped knowledge.

Skyhammer had stayed at the university before. It was cheap and food in the commons room was plentiful. Best of all, it was close to the Relic hunters' office. The Aridizans tolerated a Relic hunting office only because the Academy had an agreement with the Relic protectors to leave in place any Relic found in their country, Endless Sands. In return, humans got to claim Relics and research them, but only in the field. Most Relic hunters that entered Endless Sands did not graduate from the Academy and disregarded the Academy's agreement.

He had realized after the bridge that he now was really on his own. The only system he could access was that of the Relic hunters. Any contacts of Higgins' were out of the question. Her people were unknown to him and if they were human, not likely to want contact with an Untouchable. He had two nights maximum to find Spark and head back to Quasianti in time for the ceremony. He felt a surge of energy as he realized that he could be seeing Higgins in three nights. She would be fine, he tried to reassure himself. Laughing, teasing him as usual. Then he opened his Whorl to a Retrograph of her white face and inflamed neck. Her stillness. His heart contracted in pain.

At the city gate, he sold the horse for less than half of what he paid. The Aridizans were not only mercenary but also subtly unwelcoming to Relic hunters. Cool stone streets enticed his wandering feet. Buildings overhung the streets so they were almost tunnel-like, providing a large amount of shade. HriHriKari had been designed so that the wind was funnelled through the shaded streets, cooling everything.

It was late morning so the farmers were still out selling their goods. The city had been built around a few oases and large areas were farmland, enough to support the whole population. Most roofs had gardens as well. Every square inch of space that could grow a plant, did.

The cool shade was refreshing after the long hours on the horse. It didn't take him long to walk to the university grounds. It took him even less time to check in to the dormitories.

The back wall of his room was the outer wall of the city but it still had a huge window. The glass was a handspan thick so he couldn't see out of it very well but it let in glorious light. A table and chair completed the furniture. He tossed his backpack on the floor and lay on the bed, boots hanging off the end. He checked his Retrograph Whorl.

Spark had not responded to their message or communication system but . . . he sat up. A couple of Retrographs had changed!

Chapter 22

Countdown to ceremony: 5 days

A Retrograph after the Nasuchu fight. Blood and gore splattered the grey rocks around Skyhammer. The boulder behind him had been lifted and balanced on another one.

Almost as though Spark was showing off. Or just being silly. What was she thinking? Was this her response to their message?

The earth underneath the boulder was different from the uniform greyness of the Deadlands. The ground was opaque with a tinge of green. As though he was looking through a dirty window onto a field of grass. He wondered how many Relics were under the sea of boulders in the Deadlands. Maybe that was her point?

He flicked ahead to another Retrograph. This was the one of Higgins looking at the enormous etching of the Fungal Forest on the wall in Jessup's inn in Hightown. Higgins had been moved to the side and the etching had been removed from the wall and placed near the window.

On the wall where the etching had hung was a dark patch of wood where the sunlight had not touched the wall for years.

Skyhammer punched a pillow in frustration. What did it mean? In both changed Retrographs, objects were moved and the areas beneath were exposed. He flicked between the Retrographs again, straining to see a connection between the rock, the etching and the ceremony. Or maybe it was the countries. Beneath the Deadlands and behind the Fungal Forest was what? He wished Higgins were here. She would've made a connection. Fear for her closed up his throat. What if she died? He struggled to conquer the fear and concentrate on deciding what to do next. What would Higgins advise?

After closing his Whorl, he stood up and stretched. He rubbed his eyes and paced around the room. He had no one to talk to, no one he could trust here. Jessup had been babbling about the Retrograph changes. People were more openly accusing each other of changing Retrographs or being able to see each other's Retrographs. Tension was rising. Jessup had told him the police were called out a lot in recent months to handle the increased number of violent arguments about Retrographs.

At least there were fewer humans in HriHriKari. If only he could talk to Higgins or get some idea of how she was doing! Then he could focus better. He stopped and stared out the window. Okay Skyhammer, what would Higgins do if she was here, he asked himself. What would she say about the two new changes? He let out a dark chuckle. It was simple. She'd think he was stupid for not realizing they were related to the previous changes.

He put his palm against the warm glass and leaned his forehead on his palm. What did they mean? He pushed himself away from the window. His brain hurt. He needed food. He needed Higgins. And sleep. He couldn't remember the last time he'd gotten a full night's sleep. He walked to the door. He couldn't have Higgins or sleep but he did know where to get food. Then, belly full, he'd go Spark hunting.

* * *

As he neared the door to the HriHriKari Relic hunting office, Skyhammer recalled that the receptionist was a beautiful human female who had graduated from the academy last year. He whipped out a handkerchief and wiped his face, putting aside thoughts of Higgins. The receptionist would be able to contact the Aridizan officials on his behalf. Spark would be watching him even more closely now that he was in HriHriKari.

He strode through the door and then froze. Behind the reception desk was a grizzled older man flicking through his Retrographs. The young woman was gone. Skyhammer resumed his walk with a little less confidence and stepped up to the desk.

"I'm Skyhammer."

"I know who you are," the old man said, returning his eyes to his Whorl. "What do you want?"

"Is the receptionist here? Sarah, I believe her name is."

"Sarah became a Relic hunter last month and is out on a job," the man said. "I've replaced her. What do you want?"

"I need to find somebody in town through the Aridizans' official records. She came to HriHriKari a few years ago. I need you to contact the officials on my behalf."

"Whoa, what is this all about?" The receptionist gave him a suspicious look.

"The changed Retrographs. I need you to find - don't write anything down, she can see it!" he burst out as the man reached for a writing implement.

The receptionist froze.

"Pick up something else as though you are being watched and-"

"Are you crazy? There is no one else in the office. Look around!" the man exclaimed.

"She can see us through our Retrographs."

The man recoiled in horror. "The Sorcerer is here? Watching us?" He closed his Whorl with a terrified jerk of his hand.

"Just keep looking at my face and don't do anything to let her know that we know she's watching us," Skyhammer said. "Whatever we see, she sees. You're under orders from the King not to repeat this information." He prayed this small lie wouldn't come back to bite him in the butt. "I'm running out of time and need to find this woman. Since you've been in contact with me, she's watching your Retrographs too. She may be able to send someone to kill you if she suspects that you're after her as well, so be very careful."

A look of shock and fear appeared on the man's face. Then he grinned. "Why should I believe you?"

Skyhammer shrugged. "You know about the Retrograph Sorcerer. You know I'm the Keeper of the Retrograph Vault. I figure you're smart enough to make the connection." He smiled. It wouldn't do to annoy the only person in HriHriKari that could help him.

The receptionist sighed. "Okay, Skyhammer. I know you do have the King's ear. What exactly do you need to know?"

"I need to find out the names and whereabouts of all human females who have arrived in the city since the end of 6006 and before the middle of 6007. She's still in this city." He gnawed his lip thoughtfully. "That should narrow it down. Most females come in and study but don't stay. I hope."

"The only humans who come here are Relic hunters and students. Maybe the odd tourist. Could she be a Relic hunter?"

"No, definitely not. She'll be in hiding somewhere. She may have committed a crime in Quasianti."

The receptionist sucked in a sharp breath. "What'd she do?"

"She's wanted in connection with the death of a Byndari."

The man's eyes widened.

"But don't tell the Aridizan officials that. They might alert her somehow." He leaned in closer. "Please tell them to keep this investigation under wraps and especially not to tell any humans. Or Byndari. Just me."

The man nodded. "I'm Guzzle, by the way." The receptionist stuck out his hand.

Skyhammer shook it. "I'll make sure the King is aware of your contribution to the investigation, Guzzle. You have my word."

"I have a question. If this human female is watching us through our Retrographs-."

"Most definitely," Skyhammer assured him.

"Then she will see us chatting and me going straight to the Aridizan officials. I think she'll realize that you sent me to them."

Skyhammer nodded. "You're right. Why am I wasting time sending you? I should just go myself." He leaned his elbows on the counter and cradled his head in his hands. He felt exhausted. His thoughts were moving like sludge in a sewer.

He felt a hand on his shoulder and looked up into Guzzle's face.

"I'll go anyway. You need to sleep. If the Sorcerer learns we're after her, we'll just have to move faster."

Skyhammer was about to protest but he realized Guzzle was right. He could sleep while Guzzle was visiting the officials. He nodded. "Guzzle. If," he hesitated. Should he tell him? Would it scare Guzzle off or spur him on? "The Retrograph Sorcerer threatened the King and the ceremony. If the officials need encouragement to help us, that should do it." He swayed. He was reminded of his time in the Fungal Forest. So tired.

"I have a cot in the back for emergencies," Guzzle said, leading him behind the counter to a cot set up in the Relic hunting supplies room. "I'll be back in a couple of hours."

Skyhammer fell onto the cot fully clothed. His last thoughts were of Higgins.

* * *

A long metal object dug into Skyhammer's right hip. He wriggled forward then remembered where he was and sat bolt upright. He pulled his sword around until it felt comfortable again. He poked his head out of the door of the office. It was mid-afternoon. Where was Guzzle? He couldn't leave until the man came back.

He pottered around in the supplies room for another hour before he heard the office door open.

"Skyhammer?" Guzzle's voice came through, tentative.

Skyhammer dashed into the reception area. "So? What took you so long?"

"Let me sit down, man." Guzzle flopped into his chair. "You know those officials like their long lunches. By the time I had found the right person to speak to, they had all closed their offices for lunch. I had to wait." He rubbed his belly. "I'm starving. Let me get something to eat." He stood up. "But while I'm doing that, have a look at these documents." He indicated the papers he had tossed onto his desk.

Skyhammer slipped into his chair while Guzzle rummaged in the supplies room. Skyhammer spread the documents across the desk. The first was a list of names.

"That one took a while to write out, let me tell you!" Guzzle emerged from the back, munching on a piece of fruit. "So while she was doing that, I got a cartographer to draw that out." He indicated the other four pieces of paper.

Skyhammer laid them out in a square. A map of the whole city, drawn with skill. One hundred stars were marked out on the map, one in almost every section of the city. Names were written by each one.

Guzzle swallowed and belched. "Those're the locations of each human woman. Lots, eh?" He popped a knob of cheese in his mouth.

Skyhammer's heart sank. So many! He only had two days! Well, one day now since this one was almost over.

"We'd better get started, eh?"

"We?" Skyhammer looked at the receptionist. "You've been an enormous help. There is no need. Higgins and I," He stopped. "I mean," he went on, "I can take care of this. You have work to do here and I've taken up enough of your time. . ."

"Piffle!" Guzzle leaned in close enough that his cheesy breath blew up Skyhammer's nose. "This sorcerer needs to be captured as soon as possible. It involves all the races. My wife and kids are in Four Hills. I'm here. If we could do magic anywhere and they could come here, then life would be about perfect. Nothing else is happening; all the other Relic hunters are out. Nothing for me to do now. I want to help you. I want to help the King." He stood up straight and proud. "I am still a citizen of Quasianti and damn proud to be a human."

Skyhammer regarded him for a moment, then smiled. "We've got a lot of area to cover. Let's get to it." His heart soared. Guzzle wasn't Higgins but he needed brawn not brains, for the near future at any rate.

* * *

The plan had been hatched. Guzzle locked up the Relic office.

"Send me a message if any human females try to leave the city," Skyhammer ordered. There was only one way in and one way out of the city - the front gate.

Nodding, Guzzle asked, "How will I know you've found her?"

"I'll come to the gate. Don't leave it until I do."

"No problem. I've got a buddy who's a guard there. I'll pay him an extra-long visit. They've got spare cots." He saluted. "Good luck."

Skyhammer shook his hand. "Thank you."

Guzzle left.

Now it was almost midnight and he had been walking around town since four o'clock. For the last two hours, none of the people had opened their doors to Skyhammer's knock. Those doors wouldn't open until the sun rose, he guessed. But with the list of names growing ever bigger and longer in his head, Skyhammer had not wanted to give up. He needed to see each woman to make sure she wasn't Spark and that wasn't going to happen now.

He rubbed his eyes. He had one more day in HriHriKari. If he hadn't found Spark, hadn't discovered who was planning to kill the King and sabotage the ceremony, then he would never get magic powers. He refused to believe it was Spark's own plan. She would want him to have magic; he knew that even after all this time apart. And the idea that it might be the Byndari didn't sit well with him. They had told all the species about the ceremony. Why would they sabotage it? He went back to his room and slept like the dead until sunrise.

The following day he went from door to door to door to door. On occasion, he was directed to a shop or office where the lady of the house was working. By the time the sun set the second evening, he still had ten more women to see. He groaned. It was impossible to see them all before he left. Hanamun must have lied to protect Spark. No message from Guzzle. So Spark was still here. Would he have to leave before finding her? The King said to find the Sorcerer or not to bother coming back.

In the main plaza of HriHriKari, he slumped on a bench, frustrated. All around him, Aridizans were setting up stalls to sell food and cheap trinkets at the night market. Higgins loved markets; he missed her.

He had the feeling that Spark had somehow played him for a fool. But he had to find her. At least if he missed the ceremony, he would have the Sorcerer in hand and could prevent her from affecting its outcome.

Skyhammer stood up, failure hanging over his head like a black cloud. He wouldn't be there for the ceremony and he quite possibly wouldn't have found the Retrograph Sorcerer. Maybe it was better to fail here where nobody knew. Higgins would be so disappointed. Was she all right? He closed his eyes and imagined his vision sailing out across the desert, into Hightown and into a little room where he could see Higgins laughing with Jessup, walking around, cured. He opened his eyes to the chaos of the night market and uncertainty. Surely he would be able to feel it if she died. Surely, no matter how far apart they were, he would feel that loss. He pictured her: teasing smile, red hair, big hips, cute pot-belly. How had he not noticed her growing in his heart? Life without her was - unimaginable.

You don't know for sure, he told himself. Just deal with the matter at hand. He looked around. Tendrils of smoke from cooking fires curled in front of the lamps hanging from the corners of food stalls. He wasn't hungry. He wanted reassurance that life was working out as it should. On the other side of the street, tucked between two stalls, a female Aridizan sat hunched over a round table. As he watched, the Aridizan looked up and met his eyes. A crystal ball glittered on the table. He crossed the street.

Chapter 23

Countdown to ceremony: 4 days

Skyhammer sat down across from the Aridizan. She was ancient, a crone. Skyhammer had not thought that Aridizan skin could get more wrinkly than it already was. Her robes were wine-red.

"What do you wish to know, man?" she said, leaning across the table. She put her hands around the crystal ball. Skyhammer shuddered. Her fingernails were long and sharp. Could Aridizan magic be telling the future? Or the present?

"I wish to know if my friend is alive or dead." Why did he ask that? Saying it aloud made it more real somehow. He should have asked about Spark instead. He stood up. "Forget it."

"Sit down." The Aridizan's voice demanded obedience. He sat. "You are no idle fortune seeker, man. I can see that your friend is someone of great importance to you. Maybe even more important than you realize. And your quest." She paused, watching his face.

He wondered what she saw. How did she know about his quest?

"Your quest could change the world." Her voice lowered so that Skyhammer had to lean in closer to hear what she was saying. "You don't need my speculations and guesswork. You need the real one."

"Real one?" he whispered. "Real what?"

"The Eye." Her gaze bore into his very soul. "She knows everything, she views everyone. She can tell you about your friend. She can tell you your chances for completing your quest."

"The Eye? Really?" He snorted in scepticism. Most likely, the Eye was just another, more expensive Aridizan fortune teller. But something niggled at him, words in the fortune teller's phrasing. "What did you mean, "she views everyone"?" he asked.

The Aridizan's cloak drooped over the table as she brought her ancient face closer. "Rumours only, you understand, my young human friend." Skyhammer tilted his right ear closer to her mouth. "The Eye has a special eye. Kept in a black box. It can view people's lives!"

He recoiled so fast that he was sure the chair had imprinted a welt across his back. A special eye in a black box. An eye used to view daily life. He knew someone with a black box. "Spark," he breathed. The fortune teller had admitted it was just a rumour though. At this point, he couldn't afford to dismiss any clues. He had to leave HriHriKari tomorrow. With Spark.

"How do I see her?"

"No one ever sees her," the Aridizan said, smiling. "Never has anyone seen her. She has a servant, a tongue-less boy called Mute. You ask him your questions and she relays her answer to you through him. She is a shadow on the wind. Her powers connect time and place. She can tell you about your friend and your quest."

"Where do I find Mute then?"

"He waits near the dragon fountain in the south-east plaza."

Skyhammer threw a few coins on the table. "Many thanks, milady," he shouted as he dashed through the crowd. Would Mute be there now? With only a few hours left to find her, his urgency grew and he ran faster than ever before. He had found Spark.

* * *

Skyhammer skidded to a stop next to the dragon fountain. The plaza flagstones gleamed silver in the moonlight. At each corner was a different fountain. In addition to the dragon stood a unicorn, a mammoth and a bumblebee. Skyhammer had never seen any of these animals. They lived on another continent but he had yet to travel there. There were so many Relics to find on this continent that he'd be an old man before he got to another one. He had dreams however, of riding a dragon, taming a unicorn. He wasn't sure what he'd do with a bumblebee.

The statue of each creature had water spraying out of its mouth and cascading down to a central pool. A few benches were scattered around the plaza. Skyhammer went to sit on one with a good view of the dragon fountain.

Despite his best efforts he soon nodded off, chin on his chest.

Footfalls woke him. He jumped up. How could he have fallen asleep? He didn't have time to waste snoozing! Still dark, so he hadn't slept long. A Byndari sat down on a bench across the pool from him. Skyhammer glanced at the dragon fountain. A boy sat cross-legged on the edge of the pool. Mute? Skyhammer walked over to stand in front of the boy.

"Are you Mute?" he whispered, squinting at the boy in the moonlight. He was barefoot, with light-coloured hair, dressed in dark pants and a short sleeved shirt.

The boy nodded.

"I have questions for The Eye. But I want to see her. Can you take me to her?"

Mute lifted a flat board from the shadow of his chest. A piece of chalk appeared in his left hand. He wrote on the board for Skyhammer to read: "I take your questions but not you. Is forbidden. You stay here until I back or my mistress very displeased. Punish you. Like she punish me." The boy opened his mouth. No tongue, only a ragged hunk of flesh. "You have money?"

"I must see her!" Skyhammer's voice rose.

Mute shoved the board closer to Skyhammer's face and jabbed at it with his finger. He shook his head for emphasis.

That warning was so like Spark, always dire consequences for disobeying her. Skyhammer considered. The boy would have to go back to The Eye's hideout. Skyhammer would just follow.

"I have money and I'll wait here." He told Mute his two questions, then sat on the edge of the fountain. "When will you return?"

"One hour," the boy scribbled. "First show me coin."

Skyhammer opened his money bag and let Mute peer inside. Satisfied, the boy walked away.

As soon as Mute had rounded a corner, Skyhammer ran after him. He flew past the Byndari on the bench, who half-rose up, arm outstretched. Skyhammer noticed the movement but pushed it to the back of his mind. He had to focus on following Mute.

When he came to the corner where Mute had turned, he paused and peeked around it. The kid was a block down the road, walking at an even but not hurried pace. Spark's place couldn't be far. Skyhammer slipped into the shadows of the buildings and crept after the boy.

A couple of times, Mute turned around, as if he could sense he was being followed. Skyhammer stayed hidden.

Doubt began to infiltrate Skyhammer's mind. He had no

proof The Eye was Spark. Why was he so fixated? He could be entering the last ten women's houses now, breaking in to see them even though they were asleep. Creepy. He shook his head. The details were too close to the truth if Spark was a second Keeper and had changed the Retrographs. And something, his intuition he supposed, motivated him.

Skyhammer paused at the end of an alley that opened out into a residential neighbourhood quite close to the university. Mute had darted across the road and up to the front door of an apartment building. He glanced around, then slipped inside. Skyhammer raced across the road and up to the entrance. He set his ear to the door. Footsteps on a staircase, going up. He waited until the footsteps were gone. As he turned the handle and opened the door, he thanked his lucky stars that HriHriKari had such a low crime rate that Aridizans rarely locked their doors. The door closed with a soft snick. He paused in the dark. Moon beams came through the windows, lighting the stairs in front of him and a door to his right.

Anticipation of seeing Spark and finding out Higgins' condition lifted his heart. A floorboard creaked above him, and he started climbing.

Crouching at the top of the sixth flight of stairs, Skyhammer tried to slow his heartbeat down and catch his breath. There was only one room on this top floor. Light flickered from under the door and as his breathing slowed, he thought he heard the sound of a scuffle. Shadows danced under the doorway. Yes, there was fighting in there. He thought of the young boy and then of Spark. He couldn't lose her, not when he was so close to seeing her again.

Loosening his sword in its sheath, he crept up beside the door. He put his hand on the handle, turned it and shoved the door open, sheltering his body with the wall. A strange sight greeted him through the doorway.

Three still forms. Two were Byndari and one was the boy. The boy was stock-still, a book in hand, on the opposite side of the room. As the Byndari half-turned to the open door, the boy unfroze and hurled the book he was holding at one of the Byndari, who exploded on contact into sand, shells and millions of tiny amoebas. The second Byndari turned around lightning quick and threw a dagger at the boy. At the last second, the boy moved to the left, but the dagger cut through his baggy clothes and pinned him by his shirt to the wall.

Skyhammer's jaw dropped in amazement. He had never seen a Byndari be violent or move as fast as that one. The Byndari turned to face Skyhammer.

"What are you doing?" he shouted at the Byndari. "Where's Spark?"

The Byndari said nothing, just watched Skyhammer while producing another dagger from somewhere behind him. A Byndari wearing clothes? Skyhammer's mind was having a hard time grasping this. He did realize that the Byndari was out to kill him and he'd better do something before both he and the boy were dead.

Out of the corner of his eye, he could see Mute struggling to slip out of his shirt. Skyhammer would have to keep the Byndari's attention on himself if he wanted to save the boy. He pulled out his sword as the Byndari raised his arm to throw the knife. Skyhammer threw himself to the left behind a pillow-laden chair and heard a clatter in the hall as the dagger flew through the open doorway. Squatting, he pushed the chair across the floor towards the Byndari and stood up. The Byndari had another dagger in hand already.

Skyhammer hurled his sword at the Byndari and flung himself over the chair. The creature dodged the sword but it distracted him just long enough for Skyhammer to plough right through him splattering sand, amoebas and shells everywhere. Skyhammer jumped up, brushing all the Byndari remnants off his body.

Mute was gone. Skyhammer sighed, picking up his sword. Who were these Byndari? Specially trained fighters but Skyhammer had never heard of the Byndari having a fighting force. They were a peaceful knowledge-loving nation as far as he knew. It seemed he knew nothing.

Spark. He'd worry about the boy later. The room was a mess. Bookshelves on the ground, tables and chairs overturned, oil lamps broken all over the floor. Light spread from one lone candle flickering on the window sill and moonlight streamed through the glass as well. There was an open door on his left leading to another room, a cooking fire, smashed cups and plates. A kitchen. A crack of darkness led to a room on his right.

He drifted towards the dark room. She would be in there. Hiding probably, she was good at that.
"Spark?"

Chapter 24

Countdown to ceremony: 3 days

He poked his head through the crack. No sound, no light. His nose wrinkled. The reek of sewage. "Spark? It's Skyhammer." Another odour, less familiar. Blood. No breath. Maybe Spark had run away and a stranger's body lay bleeding in the room. No. It was she. He knew as he went back to the window to fetch the candle and he knew as he opened the door wider and held the candle out in front of him.

An enormous bed took up most of the room. Mounds of books plugged the small gaps behind and at the foot of the bed. In the center, a pile of blankets. Wood covered the large window on the far side so that no speck of light from the outside world came in.

Skyhammer sucked in a deep breath through his mouth. There was no sign of a struggle. He walked forward and lifted the candle above the bed, desperately wanting to close his eyes, to avoid what he knew in his heart to be there.

What he thought was a mound of blankets was the body of Spark. Obesity had replaced the lithe slenderness. Lifeless holes caged by flesh had replaced flashing black eyes. A girl who used to wander the forest for hours now looked like an old woman who hadn't left the bed in years. She was only nineteen! His heart was a fist in his chest. Spark's head was thrown back, her throat slit. Blood, still sticky, stained the sheets beneath her neck.

He closed her eyelids and cupped her cheek with his palm. In death, she looked peaceful, but her face still held lines of bitterness. She had created some sort of life for herself here but it was not enough to make her happy.

"Spark, I'm so sorry I didn't get here in time to save you," he said aloud. Darkness and silence filled the space around his words. He found it a struggle to speak again. "I'll do my best to discover what you were warning me about." His voice broke. This was not the reunion he had imagined. In his secret heart, he'd been planning to talk her into joining him and Higgins in Relic hunting. Maybe she would have been happy with them. It didn't matter now. He still didn't know what she had been trying to communicate to him. How had she gotten magic powers? Why had the Byndari gone so far as to kill her? For the black box from the Retrograph Vault maybe.

His breath caught in his throat. He glanced back through the door behind him. Stillness. A pile of books next to the bed served as a shelf for the candle holder. He ran his fingers down her right side, reaching under the blankets. "Sorry," he whispered as he knelt on the edge of the bed and leaned over her. "I need the black box." It had to be on this side then. Propping himself up with his left hand, he ran his right over the bed. No black box. He groaned with frustration.

A foot stamped on the floor behind him. Skyhammer spun around, sword at the ready. Mute stood in the doorway to Spark's room gesturing at his board.

Skyhammer moved closer. "Where did you go?"

The boy pointed at his board. "More Byndari come. They killed her. Leave now," Skyhammer read.

He looked at the boy. "We can't leave yet, I have to find the part of the Vault she stole. And I have to find out if she left anything, any information that would tell me why the Byndari killed her."

The boy stamped on the floor again, then wrote on his board: "No time. They in alley now. I have letter to Skyhammer. Go go now!"

A letter? Skyhammer's brow furrowed. Maybe he should stay here and talk to the Byndari, find out what was going on. But if they were just intent on killing him and not interested talking then he was in trouble. One or two dagger fighters he could handle but a whole squad could wipe him out. He took a last look around the room then bent and kissed Spark's cold cheek.

"Goodbye, my love." He probed the bed in a last desperate attempt to find the piece of the Retrograph Vault.

The boy stamped his foot again.

"Okay, okay, I'm coming." Skyhammer followed Mute out of the apartment and down the hall to the top of the stairs. They both froze as a door opened below them. The Byndari!

The boy tugged Skyhammer's hand and ran lightly back along the hall to a window at the end. He pushed open the window and climbed out.

Skyhammer stuck his head through. The back of the

building. A small ledge connected to a ladder going down the wall. Mute was halfway down the ladder already. Skyhammer gulped and closed his eyes in prayer. A tread sounded on the stair.

Eyes flying open, he swung his leg over the sill, onto the ledge. Five or six Byndari were climbing the stairs now. He pulled the window shut then lay flat on the ledge. He poked his head up a little so he could just see through the window.

Two Byndari reached the top of the stairs. They walked around the banister toward Spark's door.

He ducked down. He'd have to swing his body off the ledge and onto the ladder. He slithered a little further along. The ladder seemed none too sturdy. He looked down. Mute was at the bottom, waving frantically. It was now or never. He grabbed a rung of the ladder with both hands then let his body fall off the ledge and swing below him. Then he climbed down the ladder. When he reached the bottom, he looked up. The window was open. Two dark heads leaned out.

He grabbed Mute's hand and they dashed down the alley. They had been seen. He realized the Byndari had probably been following him since he left the Academy. That must have been whom the Nasuchu were escorting. He recalled the Byndari sitting on the plaza's bench.

The boy tugged his hand as he went around a corner. He stopped. The boy pointed the opposite way.

"I have to get my bag from the university," he explained. "We have to hide until . . . until the city gates open in the morning." Damn! How were they going to get past the gates? Unless Guzzle could help them. But the Byndari would be watching them of course.

The boy shook his head.

"Do you know another way out?" Skyhammer grasped Mute's shoulder.

The boy nodded and tugged his hand again.

"But, my bag! Oh, forget it. Let's go. I'll follow you."

Mute took off, glancing over his shoulder every so often to make sure Skyhammer kept up.

It didn't matter that the boy knew another way out of the city, Skyhammer thought as he raced to keep up with Mute. They still had to cross Flyer country, a 1-day journey, and the Deadlands, a 1-day hike, not to mention the journey from the

Deadlands to the Kingmaker Tower, another day at least. If they could buy horses. Ample opportunities for the Byndari to catch them. If they could elude the Byndari, they might just arrive in time for the ceremony, if they didn't stop moving for three days straight.

Only now as he ran, blindly following the boy through the alleys and streets of the moonlit city, did he allow himself to wonder exactly what the Byndari were trying to hide. Spark had hit upon something quite important to them. So important that she was killed for knowing it. Killed for trying it share it with the rest of the world. Something to do with the ceremony, if she was the one who had changed Retrographs. Mute was the key now.

Skyhammer kept his eyes on the boy. He had a letter from Spark. Mute must have heard Skyhammer say his name as he entered Spark's room. Smart kid. Would they ever stop running long enough for him to read it? He was thirsty. And hungry. And he missed Higgins. Now he wouldn't know if she was alive or dead. Okay, he thought, stop dwelling on the past. Focus on the positive. It's just as likely she's alive as is she's dead, and she would be the first to tell him that. Right now, we have to get back to the King. Skyhammer felt even more confused now. The Retrograph Sorcerer, Spark, was dead. So was the ceremony safe? He didn't think so. She was dead because she was attempting to expose the Byndari. They were the real threat. How, Skyhammer still didn't know. He hoped the letter would explain.

The boy stopped. They had run across a park, Skyhammer realized, and were in front of some kind of low building.

"This isn't the city wall," he whispered. "I thought you said you knew how to get us out of the city."

Mute nodded then put his finger in front of his lips. The building had the peaceful, dignified air of a temple. But it was like no temple Skyhammer had ever seen before. It was built from cacti.

The kid led him to the entrance. Skyhammer looked behind them but saw no movement.

Mute put out an arm to bar Skyhammer from entering. There was no door, just a passage leading into darkness. Skyhammer was intrigued to see how entwined the cacti grew. None of their spikes appeared to grow inside. Despite the fear of a Byndari attack, he was very curious about this temple.

"What is this place?" Skyhammer whispered.

Mute dropped his arm and wrote. "Dragon temple. Do not touch *anything* or you die. Everything covered in poison dust. Kills."

Skyhammer's jaw dropped. "Dragons?" he squeaked. Then he clamped his mouth shut. He wondered if the dragon cultists had travelled to the continents rumoured to have dragons.

The boy led him inside as night began to recede.

Skyhammer followed Mute deeper into the darkness of the dragon temple, sand shifting under his feet. The cactus walls were indeed lacking spikes on the inside. They headed to the right in what seemed to Skyhammer to be a very large circle. As his eyes adjusted to the darkness, he noticed that the walls had tiny pinpricks of light at eye and ankle height. The points were small but cast just enough light for him to see the boy ahead of him. He wondered how the cactus emitted light from inside and decided he didn't need to think about it right now.

They walked in silence for a while, passing gaping dark voids off to the left every so often. Skyhammer peered through the door-sized gaps but saw only blackness.

His mind wandered, the faint yellow light putting him into a kind of trance. Had anyone seen them come in here? The Byndari at Spark's place were quick. They could have followed them here and now have them trapped in this temple. It was a little hard to trust such a young boy. The dragons were a myth and no one had any information on them besides rare primitive art on rocks. No one talked about dragons these days. They talked about the Moksha instead. Could they be the same thing? He focused on the boy's heels ahead of him.

Should he trust this boy so much? He did work for Spark after all. Spark, who had been killed, he reminded himself, a wave of sadness washing over him. He had expected her to be beautiful still, to be bitchy and fun like when they were at the Academy. He wondered what else the boy wasn't telling him. How would Mute have found out about this exit? Was he a member of the cult?

The passageway opened up into a room. Now just the ceiling was covered in larger points of light and he could see the whole circular room, which extended about ten feet in diameter. His eyes locked on the centrepiece of the room. A huge egg rested on the sand, as if it had fallen there then tipped over. An iridescent powder covered the egg, adding to the brilliance of the shell. It looked like water, like the blue water of Pingala's warmest seas, a brilliant, soothing, ever-changing hue. Enticing.

The kid jiggled his arm and dragged him around the egg. Skyhammer couldn't tear his eyes away from it. He needed to touch it. If he just reached out his hand and dusted off some of the powder with his sleeve, surely-

The boy shoved him and Skyhammer scowled.

"Don't push me!" he hissed.

Mute pointed at the egg and waggled his finger.

Skyhammer sighed. "If I brush the powder away with my sleeve on one spot," he whispered. Just one touch. One tiny part of his brain screamed NO but the egg filled his mind; he could think of nothing but falling into that warm blueness.

The kid grabbed Skyhammer's hand and dragged him to another dark passage on the opposite side of the egg. Skyhammer allowed himself to be pulled away. He could come back without the kid now that he knew about it; no one was here anyway.

They went through the black gap, Mute pushing Skyhammer ahead of him. They walked about five steps into complete darkness. No points of light here. He yanked Skyhammer to a stop.

Skyhammer faced him the place where he thought Mute stood. A glimmer appeared on his left. The wall pulsed with green light, framing the boy.

Mute stuck his skinny arm into the wall's light, one hand still grasping Skyhammer's hand.

Skyhammer stiffened. Mute's arm had disappeared. His body was going too and dragging Skyhammer along! He baulked. He had no idea what was through there.

A faint clattering arose far behind them. He heard voices calling to one another. The Byndari? Maybe he could hide inside the spiral and kill the Byndari through surprise attacks. He tried to let go but Mute was stronger than he appeared. Skyhammer was pulled into the green light.

It was like going into the Retrograph Vault, Skyhammer discovered, like walking through thick mud. Then he stood on the other side, blinking in the light and gazing around.

"Where are we?" he asked Mute.

Chapter 25

Countdown to ceremony: 3 days

Most striking was the sky. Or lack thereof. It was more like a ceiling, very high above but close enough that Skyhammer could make out bubble-like formations. It looked, he thought, like the Deadlands. But upside down. Or, and now he squinted even more, as if they were under the Deadlands, looking up at the boulders from below.

Still staring up, he asked, "Hey kid, are we under the Deadlands?"

Chalk squeaked across the writing board. Mute marched up to him and held the board above his head with two hands. "My name not kid. My name Mute. Yes under Deadlands." He had underlined the word Mute twice.

"Are we safe?" Skyhammer turned around. A towering granite wall shot up to the ceiling. No door in sight. Although he could make out a faint green shimmering right in front of him. The door was still there. Relieved, he turned around again. A field of purple and blue flowers stretched out over rolling hills away from them. No bushes or trees grew, at least none Skyhammer could see from where he was standing. The door was some kind of portal, like the entrance to the Retrograph Vault.

"We safe," Mute scratched on his board. "They not know how get in unless dragon acolytes. They not."

"So how did you find out about it?" Skyhammer spotted a well-trodden path heading out across the fields.

Mute smiled and shrugged. "Hear a lot. When you not able speak, people assume you stupid and not understand what they talk about or you not tell anyone. Only those that seek The Eye's wisdom . . ." Tears trickled down his cheeks.

"She was your friend too, wasn't she?" Skyhammer squeezed Mute's shoulder.

Mute nodded, sobbing.

"I'm sorry that you had to see her like that."

Mute wiped the tears away, reached into his pockets and pulled out a crumpled piece of paper.

"Spark's letter?"

He nodded.

Skyhammer looked around then walked over to a patch of grass and sat down. Mute squatted a short distance away.

He took a deep breath, steeling himself, then read the letter.

* * *

Dearest Skyhammer,

The Byndari are closing in on me. If you get this letter then I am dead. Please take care of Mute. He is very dear to me. He is bright, as I'm sure you've already discovered.

Skyhammer, I have many regrets to write about but I'm trying to put those behind me. Let me say, however, I was wrong to run away and not tell you anything. I know it hurt you and I would do anything to take back the pain I caused you. I have no excuse, except fear.

When I discovered I could also enter the Retrograph Vault - I was so scared. No female had ever been a Keeper. I couldn't tell anyone. I was afraid that if I told someone, they would take me to the Royal Circle and experiment on me. After hearing your own stories of that experience, I vowed never to let it happen to me.

But hiding my secret from you was getting harder and harder. One day I unhooked a piece of the Retrograph Vault and tried to take it out with me. It worked but Hermit the Byndari saw me. I had to kill him, so he wouldn't tell anyone. Then I ran away.

The black box allowed me to view Retrographs from anyone, anywhere, but only recently did I discover I could move objects around in the Retrographs too - when I saw the Retrographs of the poor people who the Byndari had kidnapped and taken down to their ship deep in an ocean canyon. I saw the horrible things the Byndari did to them.

They are aliens, Skyhammer, not a Pingala species at all. Rantama, he did it too, he hurt those defenceless men and women. I'm sorry to have to tell you that. I know he is your friend.

Watching the torture, I was so shocked that I reached out to touch the woman's Retrograph and actually moved the image of her body.

The Byndari did move the Wall to their ship, briefly. They forced the woman to help them interpret the panels. That's how I saw the Wall before they changed it to display what your drawings show.

The Wall really shows that the ceremony will remove all magic from Pingala.

You're probably wondering why I didn't tell anyone earlier, why I just flipped Wall drawings in Retrographs. But they are everywhere, Skyhammer - the Byndari have ears everywhere. I feared they'd take me too, down to their watery ship, to their cruel instruments.

But they found out anyway and they'll be here, maybe today, maybe tomorrow. Now it's too late for me to do anything. Fear kept me from saving magic.

Despite the pain I caused you, please do one last thing for me. Stop the Byndari. If magic disappears from Pingala, Floatilla will fall. The human race could go extinct. You can't let that happen. I know you won't. Unlike me, you are fearless.

I have always loved you.

Spark.

* * *

Skyhammer rested his chin on his knees. His heart soared. She *had* loved him. She had just been scared. He frowned. She had been scared and Floatilla would crash, the hundreds of thousands of people living there would die, if he didn't stop it. But only three days remained. He jumped up.

"Mute, we need to to get moving. Fast. Do you know where the exit is?" He'd focus on the task at hand and deal with the emotions later.

Mute pointed down the dirt path.

"No, I meant where does the exit out of here go?"

"Somewhere in Quasianti," Mute wrote.

"Excellent then, let's go."

Mute's stomach rumbled loud enough for Skyhammer to hear.

"This is where my pack would've come in handy. Can we eat any of these plants or drink the water? If there is any?" Skyhammer strode off down the path, Mute beside him.

"Not eat or drink here. No water. Plants poisonous."

"It's daylight now. How long will it take to get to the other side?"

Mute shrugged. "A day? Not really sure."

A day without water. They'd be exhausted at the other end. But they had no option. If the Byndari were lurking in the dragon temple, Skyhammer couldn't go back there anyway. The Byndari might even stumble on the entrance to this place. He increased his pace. How was Higgins? Was Jessup taking care of her? She had been so weak and white when he'd left her. He missed her smile, her laugh. She wouldn't have left her pack behind. He sighed.

Time moved like a slug. The scenery never changed. Off to the right and left of the path, the fields just went on and on, no end in sight. It was the same in front and soon the granite wall through which they had arrived disappeared behind them. They were alone in a field of flowers, only the path to lead them through. No wind and no animals. The only sound their footfalls.

So the Byndari were aliens. Even his friend, Rantama. Skyhammer found it hard to reconcile his image of Rantama with that of an alien torturing humans. Rantama the Byndari was a consummate actor. Hadn't Skyhammer figured that out last time he was at the Academy? What information did the Byndari need so badly that they had to torture humans? Or maybe Rantama had been forced by other Byndari. He hoped for that, in his heart.

The presence of magic must be an issue for the Byndari somehow. Skyhammer tried to imagine a world without magic. A world where he would be the equal of any human, accepted as normal. He wanted it, wanted that to happen. Then he thought of Higgins and her joy in magic. He wanted her to be happy. A twinge of discomfort pricked him. A tiny part of him existed that wanted no human to possess magic. Then they could all see what it was like to be magic-less, to be sub-human. He imagined all the humans in Floatilla forced to live on the ground. For a moment, the thought made him feel good. Then he felt appalled - thousands people would have to die for that wish to come true. He couldn't let that happen. Spark's last request must be fulfilled.

About halfway through the day Mute asked him, "How magic work?"

Skyhammer halted. The boy stopped a few steps later and turned back to him, a surprised look on his face.

Mute wouldn't know that Skyhammer had no magic powers, he realized, starting to walk again. If he'd been born and raised in HriHriKari, outside the human Royal Circle, then he would never have seen a human performing magic nor tried it himself. And if he had spent most of his life with Spark, a non-magic human, there would be no reason to discuss magic. He wondered what happened to Mute's parents. How did he end up working with Spark? Skyhammer felt a kinship with the boy; they both had never experienced magic powers. As soon as they reached the Royal Circle however, that would change. Or perhaps not. If he'd never done magic in his life, why would he start? He didn't have a slate so he couldn't perform spells anyway. Hence his question.

"Most humans are born with magic powers," he began. Should he tell the boy about Spark and himself? "As soon as a child's parents believe he or she is mature enough to perform spells, they take their child to a slatist."

Mute's face was rapt.

"The slatist takes some blood from the child and mixes it with glass, creating a slate. Do you know what a slate looks like?"

The boy shook his head.

"It's a rectangle of glass about the size of your palm. Has streaks of blood in it, so it's called blood-glass. You draw a picture with your finger of the change you want to make with your spell, then you blow across the picture-"

Waving his writing board, Mute interrupted. "How you draw on glass?"

"As I understand it, the front of the slate isn't hard glass. When you press down, the blood gathers where your finger touched and outlines the picture."

"Where your slate?"

An initial flutter of anger, then fear. He couldn't risk losing Mute's support. He had no idea how to get out of here. What would the boy do when he learned Skyhammer had no magic powers? He took a deep, controlled inhale. Mute was not like those people raised inside the Royal Circle. And he had lived with Spark.

"I don't have magic powers. Neither did Spark," he hastened to add.

Mute gazed at him, then wrote, "She see our Retrographs. Had magic power."

"That was different. Did she use a slate to see the Retrographs?" Now Skyhammer was curious. He hadn't realized that Mute knew about Spark's power.

"No slate. Black box. Small."

They had stopped walking. Skyhammer watched Mute write.

"She touch box. Retrograph open. Not picture Retrograph. Names came first. See Retrographs of any name."

"Did she know you were watching too?"

Mute made a gurgling sound in the back of his throat, a look of pride on his face. A laugh, Skyhammer realized.

"Not know at first. Hidden. She see my Retrographs. Then know." Skyhammer chuckled.

"See slate in Retrographs only. Spark not talk about magic."

"She was a little bitter," Skyhammer murmured.

"Blow on picture. Make magic?"

He made a concerted effort to remember exactly how Higgins had explained it to him. "When you draw the picture you also hold it in your mind. The change you want your spell to make, I mean. When you blow on the picture, it activates the spell and if your will is strong enough, magic will make the change you imagined."

"Another person not want change?"

"If their mind and magic is stronger than yours then the spell fails."

"Stronger? Who?"

"Different people have different strengths of magic. Sorcerers are the strongest, below them are Wizards, then Mages, who are people like the King's Guard. Most people are Enchanter level but below them are Conjurers with very little magic power. They tend to live outside the Royal Circle. If you have no magic power you are, well, nothing."

"You no magic."

Skyhammer nodded.

"Why?"

He couldn't speak, yet there were so many things he wanted to say. Too much. He settled for a shrug, not opening his mouth lest something come out that a young boy should not hear.

"Why Spark do magic outside Royal Circle?"

This was a smart kid. "I don't know. It's the first time it's happened. You know about Relics right?"

Nodding, Mute scribbled, "Moksha coming back. Need to protect Relics."

A small groan escaped Skyhammer. The kid had been indoctrinated by the Aridizans before he'd met Spark. Or had she come to believe that as well? Perhaps she had learned something about the Moksha during her time in HriHriKari. The Moksha had made and used the Relics, then disappeared off the planet. The kid would learn soon enough that other people thought differently about the Relics' purpose on Pingala.

"Well, the Relics have to be found by someone. The Retrographs are a Relic that humans can use. If Spark was using part of the Retrograph Vault, then she may not have been doing magic, she may have been utilizing a Relic. They can work anywhere on Pingala." He waited for more questions but Mute seemed to have had his fill of new information.

Many hours later, the light began to dim. The end was nowhere in sight. Skyhammer wanted to keep walking through the night but the boy was tired and so was he, to be honest. They couldn't afford to lose any time though. The ceremony started in a couple of days. He had to be there in time to stop it.

"Mute, hold my hand while it's dark," he ordered. "If I ask you a question, squeeze my hand once for yes, twice for no and three times for I don't know. Do you understand?"

Mute caught his hand. One squeeze.

"Great." Skyhammer weaved across the path while it was still light. When he left the path, the ground felt different, more springy. If it got very dark, he'd have to use that as his way to find the path. He was sure it wouldn't get that dark though. The moon would be full in a couple days, at the time of the ceremony in fact, so as it waxed it was quite large and bright. If sunlight could get through whatever material it was that made up the boulders above them, then moonlight most likely could as well.

The ceiling got light again as the moon rose. It was enough to see the path by at least. The moonlight turned the flowers to silver stars dotting a grey plain.

Mute's pace slackened and Skyhammer had to slow so as to not drag him along.

"Would you like me to carry you?" The boy was only about eight years old, Skyhammer guessed. And he was thin. He could carry Mute on his back for a few hours; give the boy a chance to sleep.

Two squeezes.

Oh well. Skyhammer picked the pace up until they were almost back at their daytime rhythm. The sea of flowers seemed never-ending.

Just when he thought he'd fall asleep on his feet, the air around them began to lighten. The sun was returning. Skyhammer breathed a sigh of relief. They must be nearing the end. They had walked for a whole day. In front of them, an hour or so walk away, was another wall, identical to the granite one they had come through.

"Thank the gods," Skyhammer muttered under his breath. "Come on Mute, we're almost there. They've got food and water in Quasianti." He had a thought. "You've been there before right?"

Two squeezes.

"Really? Well, we'll stop by the market since we have to get a carpet and a pilot for it - Moksha's balls." He remembered. The Royal Circle would be gone so magic wouldn't work in Four Hills. The King would have moved to the Kingmaker Tower and the Royal Circle did not reach Four Hills from there. "Double Moksha-balls!"

Mute let go of his hand.

"What?" Skyhammer looked down at him.

"Light now," he scribbled, then scampered ahead of Skyhammer.

Skyhammer grinned. The kid's eyes were lit up with the excitement of a new adventure in Quasianti. He frowned. They'd have to ride horses to the edge of the Circle.

Another sheer granite wall loomed up in front of them. About twenty feet before the wall, the path stopped. Mute was already running his hands over the wall, searching for a door like the dragon temple one. Skyhammer joined him in the search but after thirty minutes, they had found nothing.

"Stop, stop," Skyhammer called. "Let's sit down, take a break and think about this." He started feeling a little panicky. What if the door wasn't here? There was no time to return to HriHriKari and make their way back through Rainbowcloud and the Deadlands.

Mute shook his head and continued running his hands up and down the wall.

Skyhammer backed up until he could see a large part of the wall with Mute at the center. No, not quite the center. Skyhammer squinted. He could see lines running in a pattern on the wall. He walked a few steps closer. The lines arced from the ground on the left to the ground on the right, increasing in size as they moved up the wall. Mute stood to the right of where the centre would be if there was a spiral. Yes, Skyhammer thought, hope growing within him. A spiral graced the wall and the center . . . there.

He ran forward. The center was at about the level of his shoulder. He patted the wall where he thought the middle of the spiral should be. A large rectangle glowed green at his touch.

Mute clapped, the sound raucous in the quiet space.

However, the bottom of the door started at Skyhammer's shoulder height. They would have to jump or lever themselves up somehow.

The ceiling above contained the only boulders. Skyhammer scrutinized the wall, hands on his hips. He should go first anyway, to make sure there was nothing dangerous on the other side. After gripping onto the bottom edge of the doorway with both fingers, he hoisted himself up. He pushed his head and body through the green doorway. The sludge-like substance surrounded him again.

He landed in a semi-dark room, panting. Only the silence of an empty room reached his ears. Safe enough for the moment. After turning around, he dropped to his knees and crawled through the door until he felt the edge of the wall. Then he stuck his head out and looked down. Mute was standing just below him, looking up with such a sad and lonely expression that Skyhammer laughed out loud.

"I wouldn't leave you, kid!" he shouted. "Come on, give me your hands." He pulled Mute up and through the doorway.

Chapter 26

Countdown to ceremony: 2 days

Skyhammer and Mute kept still and quiet on the floor for a couple of minutes, listening. Silence and a faint light came through the open doorway opposite the green door. Skyhammer experienced a sudden fear that this was not in Four Hills. Mute had only said that the path led to Quasianti. They could be anywhere in the country. Time to find out; he stood up and offered his hand to Mute.

"Let's get out of here and see where we are." He hauled open the door and marched out. An empty hallway stretched in front of him, brick walls bare, the opposite end cloaked in darkness. Two doors, one on either side of the hall. He walked to the door on the left. Mute scuttled along behind him.

Skyhammer pushed at the half-open door and peered inside. A window barely lit the room, rain trickling down the glass pane. Bed, chair, desk, everything was covered in a thick layer of dust. No one had been here for a very long time.

Where in Quasianti could this building be? Why had the green door led here? There wasn't a single sign of human habitation. He began to feel anxious but quashed it before Mute could see. "Come on!"

Not bothering with the other door, Skyhammer strode down the hallway. His hand went to his sword hilt. Behind him, Mute's breathing grew audible. As Skyhammer's eyes adjusted to the dark, he thought he could make out the faint outline of a door in the wall ahead.

"Almost there," he murmured over his shoulder. Withdrawing his sword, he advanced, alert.

Thunk. The tip of his sword jammed into wood. It must be the door. Yanking out the sword, he returned it to its scabbard and ran his fingers across the door where a knob would normally be. Nothing. Mute's breath came faster; the boy was scared. Skyhammer tried the left edge of the door. A round handle jutted out. He tugged it, eager to escape the dark and eerie hallway. The door didn't move. He twisted the knob to the right and pulled. The door burst open. Rain and fresh air hit

Skyhammer's face. Even the low, dark clouds couldn't dampen his happiness at being outside again. Mute stuck a hand outside and breathed deeply. They both looked around.

Bare muddy ground surrounded the building, as did a high wall. Skyhammer did a quick circuit around the building. Brick walled them into the yard.

"We'll have to climb it," he told a shivering Mute when he returned. The boy had probably never seen this much rain in his life, if he'd lived in the desert since he was born. Rain on his face felt good but Skyhammer was anxious. They had wasted time finding their way out of the building. It had only taken them a day to walk through but what if it took another two days to walk or ride to the Kingmaker Tower?

The wall rose a foot higher than Skyhammer. He and Mute carried a desk out from a room inside and placed it next to the wall. Mute wrapped his arms around his skinny body. Skyhammer stood on the desk and peered over. The rain was falling harder now but he could see some sort of garden and the back of a house.

"Come on," he said to Mute. "I'll boost you over first." He lifted the boy up until Mute could pull himself to the top of the wall. Then Mute scrambled over and dropped to the ground. Once he was over, Skyhammer hoisted himself up, scraping his belly in the process. He let himself drop to the ground on the other side. If the Byndari came after them by the same route, they would have a hard time getting over that wall without killing themselves. Mute and Skyhammer sidled around the side of the still house.

Skyhammer judged it to be about mid-morning as they stepped into the street in front of the house. He glanced up and down the street, which sloped down to his right and up to his left. Only a few houses were visible; cloud obscured the rest. Were they high up in a mountain somewhere?

"Let's walk up and see who we can find."

Mute nodded. A young girl emerged from the gray cloud to their right, face shining out from under her umbrella. Skyhammer and Mute ran right up to her.

She backed away, raising her basket in the air in front of her like a shield. "What do you want?" Her voice was suspicious.

"We need your help," Skyhammer said. "Please tell us where we are."

"Uh, the corner of-"

"No, no. What city are we in?"

The girl looked at him as though he was the village idiot. "Four Hills of course. This is Port Hill."

Skyhammer slapped his forehead with his hand. "Of course! Floatilla is gone. The King must already be at the Kingmaker Tower and Floatilla went with him. That's why I didn't recognize it, even with the clouds. The light changes everything. I couldn't smell the sea because of the rain!" He paused and turned to Mute, a puzzled expression on his face. "We were only in that place for a day, right?" He turned back to the girl. "How many days till the ceremony?"

The girl looked puzzled. "You mean how many hours? The eclipse will happen in 12 hours."

"What?" Skyhammer stared at the girl in shock. "Twelve hours?" He looked at Mute. "I thought you said it was a shortcut. We've lost about a day and a half in there."

Mute's shoulders drooped. The doors must not only transport people through space but also through time. He wondered why it was different at the Retrograph Vault. He'd never noticed a time difference there. That was something he could think about later.

Skyhammer frowned at the girl. "Could you tell us which direction the market is?" He'd never visited the small market in Port Hill before.

She lowered her basket. "I'm going there now. I could take you." She smiled shyly at Mute.

"We're probably going to run. We're sort of in a hurry." Skyhammer sighed. "Just tell us how to get there."

When the girl had finished giving them directions, Mute gave her a small peck on the cheek. She blushed.

"That means thank you, I guess," Skyhammer said. "You may have just saved the world!" He took off running and waved to the girl as they turned a corner. Mute pounded along behind him. Skyhammer started to recognize more of the streets as they went further into Four Hills.

Fifteen minutes later, they arrived. The market was pretty quiet for a weekday due to the ceremony. They made their way to where animals were sold. Skyhammer thanked the gods he always carried his money in his trousers and not his backpack. He missed its comforting weight on his shoulders.

After a quick haggle with the horse master, he secured a large strong horse with two large saddlebags. As he patted the horse's gleaming shanks, he felt glad he had paid extra for a very healthy one. They had far to go but this fine horse would have no problem carrying them to the edge of the Royal Circle at least. Mute he had already sent off to buy food and water, despite the kid's complaints of sore feet.

When the boy got back, Skyhammer made a cup with his palms next to the horse.

"I'll give you a leg up."

Mute didn't move, just looked up at the horse in fear.

"You've never been on a horse, right?" Skyhammer straightened.

Mute nodded, fixated on the horse's huge mouth.

"They're gentle animals for the most part. He knows I'm the master. I'm good with horses." He stroked the horse's neck. "I promise I won't let you fall and he won't bite you. I'll tell him not to. I speak horse, you know."

Mute's eyes widened.

"Yup. Here." Skyhammer stepped up, rubbed the horse's nose and whispered in its ear. "There, I told Whale that you're a good friend of mine and never to hurt you."

"Whale?" Mute wrote.

"That's right, you're riding a horse called Whale. A whale is a kind of big fish you see but doesn't lay eggs like a fish. . ." As Skyhammer recounted a story about the horse called Whale, he lifted a calmer Mute onto the horse. Skyhammer swung up to sit in front of Mute, then they cantered away.

* * *

The sun drew abreast of the moon. The Kingmaker Tower was still quite a way off. Skyhammer and Mute had passed the Palace and were making their way along the Crystal Lines.

On their left the mountains rose straight up, their peaks ringed with cloud. Skyhammer followed a narrow path along the mountain side and on his right, the cliff dropped straight down to the Crystal Lines. Jagged bits of crystal rose up, death for anyone who fell. They saw no one else on the road, just birds and a couple of mountain goats.

Skyhammer judged it would take them a few hours to pass the Crystal Lines, then another couple of hours to get to a town on the edge of the Royal Circle. From there he planned to hire a carpet and fly to the Kingmaker Tower in time for the ceremony. He began to relax. Mute appeared to be managing all right with the riding although he would be sore when they got off the horse.

Tales of Whale the horse had entertained Mute for the first hour but then the environment became more interesting and he was happy to look at the mountains and Crystal Lines. It must be a little overwhelming for the boy, Skyhammer thought. First time out of HriHriKari and in two days he's crossed under the Deadlands and is on a horse to a Kingmaker Tower on the far side of Quasianti.

"Mute, I really appreciate your help these past few days," he said over his shoulder. "I couldn't have escaped from HriHriKari without you. Spark told me, asked me, to take care of you but I would have done it anyway."

One long, hard squeeze on his arm.

He knew it meant thank you. The boy was all alone in the world now. Like Skyhammer. He wondered how Spark and Mute had met. Spark had done her best to save the world from the Byndari. But she couldn't save herself. Skyhammer lifted one foot out of the stirrup and rotated his ankle. It hurt a little, him not having ridden in a while. He looked down at the Crystal Lines sparkling in the sun. The rain had stopped just before they reached the palace and the crystal was covered in drops of water that amplified the shine. Dangerous beauty. He remembered the curious upside down world he and Higgins had seen in the cavern a few weeks ago. Where was Higgins now? He hoped she would be waiting for him at the Tower. If not . . . he wouldn't think about that. He would imagine her waiting impatiently for him, making snide comments about how slow he was, how disorganized without her.

And she would be right, he thought with an internal chuckle. She made him a better person, made him try harder, made him want to improve himself, to be good enough for her.

Because . . . his heart quivered in his chest . . . because he loved
her. He watched the path ahead, looked at the mountain scrub
brush, looked anywhere but inside himself where this feeling
had been acknowledged. His mind danced around it, coming
back, touching it briefly, then moving away again. It was so big,
so overwhelming a feeling. If he let it take him over he would be
sobbing right there on the horse named Whale.

Higgins had to be at the Tower. He couldn't go on without
telling her how he felt. Fear and happiness roiled in his chest.
He wanted to move faster, to dance and shout, and let all the
energy stream out of him. Instead, he kicked Whale and the
horse heaved into a gallop. Mute let out a moan and held on
tighter to Skyhammer's waist.

Skyhammer grinned as they crested the top of one mountain
and galloped madly across a plain to the next mountain. The
Crystal Lines were disappearing from sight as they moved
deeper into the mountain range.

But did she feel the same way? The horse slowed down to a
canter and Mute sagged, laying his cheek against Skyhammer's
back. If he considered their almost-kiss in the Deadlands a week
ago, the maybe she did care for him. But wouldn't she have said
something? Higgins had never stopped sleeping with the
various men, or women, that they met on their travels. She had
still had feelings for Polygon. Never had she given him any sign
that she cared for him as more than a dear friend. And why
should she, he admitted. The way he only focused on finding
Spark and gaining magic power. He didn't exactly project the
image of a man looking for a relationship. He shook his head
and sighed. As long as she was healthy and happy, and
continued Relic hunting with him, he might eventually have a
chance. But could she love a sub-human, a non-magic person?
Maybe being friends with him was the limit of her relationship
with him. He shifted in the saddle. He wouldn't know for sure
until he talked to her. The horse started galloping again but this
time Skyhammer slowed it down. He needed to save Whale's
energy for the long ride ahead. He needed a clear mind.

Up and down the sides of mountains they climbed, the range
stretching endlessly in front of them. And then. They crested
the top of a particularly high mountain and looked out across
the range. Mute shook Skyhammer's arm.

"I know, I see it too," Skyhammer murmured.

Floatilla. Mute couldn't seem to take his eyes off the floating city, which hung darkly in the sky.

"Most humans live in Floatilla," Skyhammer explained as they rode. "It's a floating city, held up by the collective magic powers of the King's Magician and the residents." His voice trailed off. It hit him again - if he didn't stop the ceremony, all the people in the city would fall onto the teeth of the planet and die. Skyhammer slapped Whale's rump and the horse leapt into a gallop. The ceremony could not be allowed to happen. Once he told the King the real purpose of the ceremony, the King stop the procedure. Skyhammer just had to reach him in time.

The moon's rim approached the sun. In another two hours, Skyhammer judged, the moon would fully eclipse the sun and the ceremony would begin. He had to make it to the edge of the Royal Circle and get on a magic carpet.

They galloped wildly up and down the mountains until they were in Floatilla's shadow. They had seen a few paths leading off to small towns in the valleys between the mountains but until now had not stopped.

CHESHIRE the sign proclaimed, with an arrow pointing west. Skyhammer directed Whale along it. He was certain they were inside the Royal Circle now. Which reminded him, he'd better get Mute set up with a slate when they got home. Where was home? Higgins would love Mute. They could do magic together. If Skyhammer could stop the ceremony in time.

The moon edged onto the sun's disc as they rode up the main street of the town. The front porches and shops were devoid of people. Silence had settled over the place. If he couldn't find someone to spell a carpet for them, then they would never reach the Tower in time. He needed a human who could do magic. And was willing to help them. Which might be the more difficult of the two, he admitted.

"Howdy strangers!" a voice called from the right side of the street. "You're going to be late for the ceremony at that rate!"

Skyhammer couldn't see the speaker. He lifted Mute down off the horse where the boy collapsed onto the grass, rubbing his legs. Skyhammer went up the front steps of the house he thought the voice had come from. A chair rocked in the corner of the porch, a human shape visible under a blanket, a curled-up cat in the lap.

"Are you planning on switching to a carpet now, young man?" The voice did come from the chair and at first Skyhammer thought it was the cat speaking.

Then a head poked up above the blanket. "Well?" Tufts of hair protruded from the old man's nostrils and ears. Bright eyes twinkled in a worn face.

"We're looking for a carpet, sir. Do you have one we could borrow?" Skyhammer asked.

"Nope. All out of carpets, I'm afraid. Every last one was taken by the good townsfolk here. Help yourself to a blanket or something equivalent though. Got one in our bedroom upstairs in fact."

Mute sat on the steps below and rested his head against the banister.

Skyhammer shifted from foot to foot. "Sir, neither of us can do magic. Would you be willing to spell the blanket for us to get us to the Tower as fast as possible? I am the Keeper of the Retrograph Vault and I have important news for the King about the ceremony."

The old man laughed loud and long.

"Can't do magic?" he spluttered when he could talk. "Neither of you? You're Skyhammer then. This must be your son. My eyesight is not what it was. But I'm afraid I can't help you. My slate broke yesterday and no one had time to fix it as they were all going to the ceremony." He stopped chuckling. "And there is no one but me left in town. You'll have to get back on your horse and start riding. Maybe you'll get there by midnight."

Skyhammer slumped into a wicker chair on the porch. "No. I have to get there before the full eclipse!" He put his head in his hands and closed his eyes.

A light touch on his trouser leg. He opened his eyes. Mute had come to sit beside him, leaning against his legs. He patted Skyhammer's knee and watched him, love and concern in his eyes. Skyhammer sighed. He had truly failed. The ceremony would continue and everyone in Floatilla would crash to their deaths. But he had to try.

He stood up. "The only thing to do is get back on the horse," he said heavily. A thought occurred to him. "Is there another town near here?"

The old man shook his head. "We're the last town before the Tower. You'd better get riding, boy. You got far to go!" He cackled as they walked down the steps and back to Whale who was munching on the grass.

Skyhammer put both his hands on Mute's shoulders. "Mute, you know I have to get to the ceremony before it starts. It would be easier," he paused and swallowed, "easier if it was just me on Whale. We can go faster without your extra weight."

Mute shook his head, faster and faster and then wrenched himself away from Skyhammer. Chalk screeched across his writing board. "Not staying here without you. Will drag behind holding Whale's tail. Will not let you go!" He threw the chalk on the ground and crossed his arms over his chest, glaring at Skyhammer.

"Fine, fine," Skyhammer said, hands open in appeal. He didn't know how to deal with a tantrum. "Let's go."

When they both sat atop the horse, they headed out of town without further words to the old man. Skyhammer looked at the path that wound its way up the side of the mountain and took a deep breath. A tired horse, an aggrieved boy and a failure crossing the valley, too late. All he could do was keep on keeping on.

The moon crept across the sun's face.

"Skyhammer!" The shout fell from high above them.

Chapter 27

Countdown to ceremony: 1 hour

Skyhammer tilted his head back, almost knocking Mute on the forehead. Fortunately, the boy had leaned back to look at the same time.

"I know that voice."

Mute gripped Skyhammer's biceps, uncertain.

"I know that voice!" Skyhammer grinned and leapt off the horse, bringing Mute down as well. "Higgins! Higgins!" He jumped up and down and screamed and ran around in a circle.

The white and brown blob in the sky resolved into a hammock hanging from a cloud of Flyers. He ran towards them. Higgins slipped out of the hammock.

A smile lit her face as Skyhammer got closer. "I can't believe I'm rescuing you again, you silly man-" she began. "Oof!"

He raced up to her and lifted her up, hugging her to his chest. He never wanted to let her go. He smelled her hair, her neck and then realized she was batting him away and saying something. He put her down.

"What was *that* all about?" Her face was red.

Skyhammer stepped back to look at her. No sign of her illness, just a healthy glow and a red face because he'd squashed her.

"Higgins." He took her hand.

She went a deeper red and made as if to pull her hand from his.

"I have to say this now because-" He stopped and looked around, then shook his head. Not an appropriate place for what you have to say, his brain screamed at him. The Flyers and Mute watched them with curious eyes. And if he left right now, there was still a chance to save the people in Floatilla and Pingala's magic power. The sky darkened.

He dropped her hand. "Rescue me? I was simply waiting for you. You're late, by the way. This is Mute. Mute, Higgins." He walked over to the Flyers. "Can you take us three to the Tower? The Byndari tricked us - the ceremony will destroy Pingala's magic power, not increase it as they said. We have to get there and stop the ceremony." He looked up at Floatilla. "If magic is destroyed, Floatilla will fall and all those people will die."

The Flyers glanced at each other, horrified expressions on all their faces. With lightning speed they created a three-person hammock. Skyhammer, Mute and Higgins nestled in, Skyhammer lying in the middle where he couldn't see the ground. A few seconds later, they were airborne.

"So you found Spark."

Did he imagine the catch in Higgins' voice? He smiled, taking her hand again and this time kissing it. A bewildered look crossed her face.

"Are you okay?" she asked.

"Me? I'm great." He beamed. "So?"

"So what?"

"Your illness! What happened?"

"The Nasuchu." She told him in a few quick words about the poison found in her spear wound and how the Flyers had made an emergency trip to the Fungal Forest for a cure. "I owe them my life."

Then I owe them as well, Skyhammer thought, gripping her hand even tighter. He was so busy telling Higgins about his adventures that he didn't even feel scared by the height. When he reached the point in his story where he had found Spark dead, Higgins caught her breath and closed her eyes.

"That poor woman," she murmured. Skyhammer nodded. After a moment of silence, he continued telling her about the letter and finished recounting the tale.

"How did you get them to carry you here? They don't even carry their Queen anywhere," Skyhammer asked.

Higgins' eyes widened and she glanced up at the Flyers above. "If magic is gone. . ."

"What?"

She had learned a lot about the Flyer species while she was in Rainbowcloud, Higgins told him. "The Flyers need magic to reproduce. Their eggs are fertilized by the tree sap and it's magic that keeps the Flyers and the trees . . ." She swallowed.

"Like Floatilla." He nodded. The Flyer species would not survive. If Floatilla fell, at least there would be those few humans who didn't live in Floatilla to carry on the human species.

They sat in silence together for a while. Skyhammer wondered what magic properties the Aridizan, Nasuchu and Katipo species had that would affect their survival if he didn't stop the ceremony in time. The sky grew darker as the moon slid another step across the sun's face.

"Hey." Higgins' eyes narrowed. "What was the hand-kissing malarkey back there?"

"My dear Amanda," he said raising one eyebrow and putting his arm around her.

"Wrong again," she whispered.

He pulled her in close. "I've learned some things while you've been . . . away." A flash of pain crossed his face as he recalled how close he had come to losing her. "I've learned how important you are to me, for one." He dropped kiss on her hair.

Higgins laughed. "Oh! You've learned you love me at last."

Skyhammer's jaw dropped. "Must you always be two steps ahead of me?" he stammered.

"It's so easy," she said, chuckling, then cackled and wriggled with laughter as he tickled her in revenge. "But seriously, Spark had been in your heart for a long time. I've been waiting."

He dropped a kiss on her cheek. "Why didn't you just say?"

Higgins shrugged. "You had to get over Spark yourself. I wasn't going to force you to choose between us. And there was your magic problem."

"Problem?"

She gave him a sceptical look. "You know what I mean."

Cupping both her hands in his, he whispered, "Magic be damned. You love me as I am and even more importantly, I think I like me as I am."

Her lips felt even softer than he had imagined.

"We've arrived, Lady Higgins!" a Flyer called down to them.

Skyhammer and Higgins separated and sat up straight.

Only a sickle of sunlight lit the Kingmaker Tower below.

* * *

Countdown to ceremony: 3 minutes

Skyhammer climbed out of the hammock and stared up at the Kingmaker Tower. The pink-veined marble tower jutted up into the sky as though to pierce the heart of Floatilla looming high overhead. He shivered. It was uncomfortably close to the truth. He noticed the crowds of people on the flat plain. Jagged white peaks rose around the Tower, marching off into the distance. This high into the mountains, not many plants thrived. A ring of soldiers held the crowds back from the Tower. The Flyers had landed inside the ring.

He only had a few minutes left. If he didn't make it - he had to make it; three minutes was not enough to evacuate Floatilla and where would all the people go anyway? He had to succeed.

"Go." Higgins kissed him again, hard. "We'll be right behind you." She took Mute's hand. "Go!"

"Don't let any Byndari in." He touched her face and Mute's head briefly then took off for the small doorway at the bottom of the Tower. Before entering, he gazed up one last time. Cheering and waving black and orange flags, the residents of Floatilla waited for their King to perform the ceremony and extend magic across Pingala.

Inside, a staircase went up. No windows or balconies opened the Tower to the elements. He took the stairs two at a time. Finally, the staircase opened into a large room, lit by three floating orbs.

"Halt!"

The Queen stood on the opposite side of the chamber, close to the wall. A rim of yellow marble ringed the outside of the chamber floor while the inner section was white with rose-coloured veins. Odd. The white marble floor shifted when Skyhammer wasn't looking at it directly. Next to the Queen stood two Byndari. One of them was Rantama. Where was the King?

The Queen moved to her left. A small doorway appeared behind her.

Skyhammer advanced into the chamber. The King must have gone through that door.

"Stop!" The Queen waved her hands as she shouted. Skyhammer froze at once. "The center of the chamber on the rose-coloured veins is dangerous. If you step on a vein, it will crack open and suck you inside. Walk on the yellow marble around the edge."

Skyhammer let go of the breath he was holding. He walked around the outside, making sure he ended up next to the Byndari.

"Skyhammer! Rantama is pleased to see you." He leaned in towards Skyhammer. "Your mission was a success?"

Skyhammer's heart was torn. He didn't want to believe what

Spark had said. He couldn't reply to his friend. "I need to speak to the King before this starts," he said to the Queen. "Where is he?"

She gestured to the doorway. His heart dropped. Too late. The ceremony had begun. But Floatilla hadn't crashed.

"You can't go in there. They're conducting the ceremony." The Queen looked at the staircase behind him. "You don't have the Retrograph Sorcerer with you as promised."

Skyhammer watched the two Byndari as he spoke. "I have news that affects the ceremony." He put his hand on the hilt of his sword. "The Retrograph Sorcerer is dead. At the hand of the Byndari!"

The Queen gasped. Rantama and the other Byndari glanced at each other.

"That's impossible, Skyhammer. You know the Byndari are against violence." Rantama's voice had an oddly cajoling tone. "Just stay out here and tell us what happened."

Rantama reached out a sandy white hand as though to soothe Skyhammer.

Skyhammer couldn't take a chance. His sword sliced through both Byndari. While the sand and amoebas were falling to the ground, he stepped through the doorway. "Don't trust any Byndari," he called over his shoulder. He found it hard to speak. His friend was dead and Skyhammer had killed him.

The Queen's mouth gaped open, then she began yelling for the guards.

The passageway was dark. He cursed his lack of light. He ran into a wall but didn't cry out. There was nowhere else to go. A rectangle flashed green. The wall was dense and soft, familiar. He braced himself then passed through the doorway.

When the doorway released him into a completely different location, Skyhammer was not surprised. At least this time the floor was at the same level as the one he had just left. But that was the only similar aspect.

The room in front of him was so enormous he couldn't see the other walls or the ceiling. He was no longer in the Tower, he was certain of that. Beneath his feet was a metal platform. Stairs led down to the main level below. Spaced with regularity along the wall to his left and right, copies of his platform and stairs dotted the walls until they disappeared into the darkness. Perhaps they led to other Towers? He started down the steps, eyes darting around, drinking in the sight before him.

An ordered field of enormous lanterns stretched away into the blackness below. Each lantern hung in the center of a hexagonal hole in the floor, the only sources of light in the room.

Five figures gathered around one of the lanterns. An Aridizan was shaking its finger in a human's face. He could also make out a Katipo, a Nasuchu, and a Flyer. No sign of the Byndari. The human was definitely the King. Skyhammer leapt down the rest of the steps with the intention of racing to the King's side.

The realization that the objects in the hexagons were not hanging lanterns stopped him in his tracks. He stepped close to the nearest hexagonal hole. There was a gap between the metal floor and the lantern. The gap was the length of his outstretched arms, left fingertips to right fingertips. Now he could see the lantern was a sphere, rotating. Skyhammer bent over to see what was holding it up. Nothing! The sphere floated exactly in the center of the hexagon. Its upper hemisphere reached to an inch above Skyhammer's head. Light from the sphere reflected its colours in the metal rim of the hexagon.

Leaning closer, he watched rust-red and grey clouds swirl around the spinning sphere, a sandstorm in a desert. What was the sphere for?

Time was short. He jogged over to the group consisting of three females - Nasuchu, Flyer and Katipo. The rest were males. Royalty of the other races, he supposed. How had they arrived in the human Kingmaker Tower? Where was the Byndari King? They were arguing so loudly that none of them heard his approach.

"Technology is simply a word for stronger magic." The Aridizan king let out an exasperated sigh. "That's why the Wall had no instructions on what we were supposed to do once we were in here. If the lever is on the Magic side then the only option is to pull it to the Technology side. That's what stronger magic means!"

The Flyer and the human were shaking their heads while the Katipo and Nasuchu nodded.

"Do you see any other solution?" The Aridizan turned his back on the group and noticed Skyhammer running towards them. "Who are you? Hey, human. Is this your son or something?"

The crowd of royalty looked over to Skyhammer. He bowed first to his King, then to the rest of them.

"How did you enter the Hall of Worlds?" the King asked. "This is Benjamin Skyhammer," he added for the benefit of the other royals. "He's the Keeper of the Retrograph Vault and a famous Relic hunter."

"Everyone knows Skyhammer." The Aridizan's voice was filled with disdain. "He's the one that will pay the most when the Moksha return and find their sacred Relics in the hands of collectors!"

Skyhammer rolled his eyes. "Actually, they may thank me for gathering the Relics in one place so they don't have to spend their time . . . anyway. That's not why I'm here. Hall of Worlds?"

"We've discovered that each of these spheres is a planet, a whole other world," the King explained. "Every few thousand years, the planet's residents get a chance to change their planet from location-specific magic to magic covering the whole world. The Nasuchu and Katipo queens have been kind enough to share some of their culture's knowledge with us. How did you get here?"

"Same way you came in. Kingmaker Tower. Via the Deadlands, Rainbowcloud, Endless Sands and the Fungal Forest. Not in that order." He pulled back his shoulders and lifted his chin. "My King, I have fulfilled my mission." Skyhammer cleared his throat and waited.

The King raised his eyebrows. "Well?"

"The Retrograph Sorcerer changed my Retrographs and yours in order to warn us of a plot by the Byndari to completely remove magic from Pingala," he said.

Skyhammer heard two gasps of shock and an involuntary chirp.

The Katipo queen snorted. "That's ridiculous." She adjusted the amethyst-encrusted crown on her bright red head, her only concession to her royal status.

"I assure you it's true, milady," Skyhammer said firmly. "In addition, I have discovered that this ceremony is the method by which the Byndari aim to remove the magic. But most importantly, my lord," he looked straight at the King, "if magic is removed from the world, Floatilla and all its residents will fall onto the mountains outside and surely perish. We cannot allow that to happen."

Everyone began talking at once.

The Aridizan king held up his hand for silence. "Why should we believe you? Let's complete the ceremony and return to our countries." His wrinkled black chin shook as he spoke and his black eyes glittered with a keen intelligence. The purple robe became him.

The King looked insulted. "Skyhammer is reliable and honest. If he tells me this is true, then I believe him."

A chirp erupted from the Flyer again. They all saw abject despair on her face. She gained control of her voice. "No magic means the Flyer race will die. We cannot procreate without magic."

Relieved that he had made it in time, Skyhammer began to relax. Time to tell them the rest of the story and let them decide how to deal with the issue. "The Byndari are-"

"Aliens."

Everyone turned to the Nasuchu and Katipo females who were backing away from the rest of the group.

Chapter 28

"Aliens," the Nasuchu queen repeated. Naked like the Katipo queen, grey skin like death, she clutched a small black cup in her palm, the mouth pointed at Skyhammer. The Aridizan king took a step towards her and she trained the black cup on him instead. "Don't move, HriHri."

The Aridizan froze.

Accomplices. Skyhammer's face fell. "That's why there are no Byndari here." He shook his head. "Alien species can't enter a Relic. But it doesn't matter." His voice twisted in disgust. "They have sent two races to do their bidding. So now you're servants to aliens," he sneered in an attempt to distract them. He had to protect the King from that black thing.

The Katipo queen laughed. "We are allies, fool. Once this world is no longer magic-driven, the Byndari will be able to leave Pingala and return to their home world."

"Why couldn't they leave before?" The King asked. "How long have they been here? Who are they?"

The Nasuchu woman cackled. "They tricked us all but in the end they chose Nasuchu and Katipo as their allies. The Byndari's star ship crashed on Pingala thousands of years ago. It crashed because their ship was run by technology, not magic. When they entered our atmosphere, the ship fell into the ocean. They've been here ever since."

"Why didn't they tell anyone?" This from the Aridizan king. "We could've helped them."

"Pah!" the Katipo queen snorted, dropping her arm back at her side. "Do you see all these planets in the Hall of Worlds?" She threw her arms out.

Skyhammer kept his eye on the black cup in her hand. He didn't know what it did but the queen obviously thought it was some sort of weapon. He would treat it as such. He wanted to kill her now, to kill her and the Nasuchu queen. Both women didn't seem to care that changing the world to technology would wipe out at least two races. But he also felt curious about technology. A world without magic? A world where a species' brain power mattered?

"All these planets," the Katipo continued, "are the same as

Pingala and the Byndari's home world. They use either magic or technology. One or the other. Every few thousand years, the planet's intelligent species can change between the two. The Byndari knew they just had to wait. They just didn't think it would be as long as it was. They realized that the species on Pingala didn't know about the system. When they found the Relic from the Pinnacle, the piece of wall, they knew it was their only chance to escape."

She sounded so sympathetic. Skyhammer's lip curled in disgust. She cared nothing for the other species on her planet. "What else did the Byndari promise you?" he asked.

"Katipo and Nasuchu will run this planet with the technology our new alien friends have shown us." The Nasuchu queen had pointed the black cup at the Aridizan King again. He took a step back.

"What is that thing, Nasuchu?" the Flyer queen asked. "What do you mean by 'technology'?"

"A weapon, Flyer. A gift from our new allies. Technology is what the Relics are based on. That's why the Relics don't do anything."

"The Retrograph Vault works," Skyhammer muttered. The King and the other Royals nodded.

The Nasuchu queen tapped her chin with her finger. "Ah yes, the Retrograph Vault."

"And the Kingmaker Towers," Skyhammer added. It bugged him now. Why would these Relics still work when Pingala so clearly operated on magic? "Unless they aren't Relics and they operate on magic."

"The Towers are access to the Hall of Worlds so they must always work if the planet's species are to be able to change between magic and technology," the Flyer queen said.

The King looked at the Flyer. "I agree. If these changes have been going on for thousands of years then maybe the Moksha lived through both technology and magic and created objects that could be used in both."

Even the Nasuchu and Katipo queens nodded.

"We want to keep Pingala a magic planet," the Aridizan King said in a firm voice. "Majority rules."

"We're wasting time," the Nasuchu said to the Katipo. "When will they learn that technology rules now?" The Nasuchu moved her finger. A bolt of blue light shot out of the opening and into the Aridizan king. A reek of burning flesh and clothes arose. His head hit the floor face first, then his body crumpled over it.

No one moved. Even the Nasuchu looked surprised. She and the Katipo queen exchanged smiles.

"This will be even easier than I thought," the Nasuchu said to the Katipo. "Rantama was right."

Skyhammer flung himself to the left behind the nearest sphere, pulling the King after him. He heard two more shots as he moved farther away from the turncoat queens, pushing the bewildered King in front of him. He didn't allow himself to think about the Byndari name he had just heard. He pushed it down inside and concentrated on saving the King.

They crouched behind one of the spheres. The King breathed heavily. Skyhammer turned his face to the floor in order to hear better. He started in surprise. Set into the metal hexagonal floor was a black rectangle. In the middle, silver letters spelled out SATURN. On the left side of the letter 'S' was a crown symbol with a circle around it. Directly opposite, on the right side of the letter 'N', was a lightning symbol. A light under the crown picture shone a dull red. A bright green light emanated from under the lightning symbol. Skyhammer glanced over to another sphere. The same symbol board with green and red lights sat under each sphere.

"Humans, we know you are in here," the Nasuchu sang out. "Our weapon will not rest until you are both dead." She paused. "Go press the lightning symbol," she ordered the Katipo queen. "It's flashing yellow. Our window of opportunity will be closed when the eclipse is over. It's only a few minutes away." Then she screamed to the ceiling, "You are the only two left, humans. Two against two. But my lovely new weapon tips the balance!"

If the Katipo queen pressed the button, Floatilla would fall. Not on him, this room was no part of the Tower in Quasianti. But Higgins was out there. If the whole city crashed on top of the Tower, she and Mute would die. "I have to get back to the Pingala sphere," Skyhammer whispered to the King. "They can't be allowed to touch the lights. Make your way back to the stairs while I distract them."

The King nodded, eyes wide, and shook Skyhammer's hand.

"One more thing, King."

The King turned, mid-crawl.

"Don't let Higgins come in here." He glared at the man.

The King nodded and continued on his way.

Skyhammer moved in a large circle until he was opposite the staircase. He could hear the Nasuchu and Katipo queens clomping around on the metal platform.

"Hey corpse eater!" he shouted. "You can't get me, crazy cannibal!" He jumped up and down until he was certain the Nasuchu queen had seen him. Then he dropped to his belly and slithered back in the direction of the Pingala sphere, always keeping spheres between himself and the queen.

The Nasuchu stalked past him on the other side, muttering to herself.

He moved in towards where the Pingala sphere was. Close enough to see the red feet of the Katipo queen. She knelt in front of the symbol board. The crown was still green but the lightning symbol was flashing yellow.

The tiny Katipo queen leaned forward, both hands in front of her, closing in on the yellow symbol.

Skyhammer crept up behind her. Here's hoping the gap is a really deep one, he thought, then grabbed her ankles and tipped her over the edge. The Katipo queen toppled forward, screaming.

The Nasuchu raced back, firing at Skyhammer. He crouched down and pulled the dead Aridizan king's body in front of him as a shield. When the yellow stopped flashing, he would kill the Nasuchu queen.

"Stop where you are, Nasuchu," a familiar voice called out behind him.

Skyhammer's head jerked up. Higgins. She wouldn't know about the weapon. "It shoots, Higgins, be careful," he yelled. Popping his head out from behind his makeshift shield, he noted the Nasuchu queen had stopped running and was taking careful aim.

"Higginsdownnow!" he screamed.

A bolt of blue left the Nasuchu's hand and shot over his head.

THUD. Higgins' body hit the floor behind him. He was too late.

Chapter 29

Higgins is hurt. Higgins is hurt. Higgins is hurt. That was all Skyhammer could think. He rose, holding the Aridizan body at his back as a shield, and ran to her.

Higgins lay on her back, her left arm severed just below her shoulder. He pulled her around the nearest sphere, blocking them both from the Nasuchu's weapon, and kneeled beside her.

"Skyhammer." Her eyelids fluttered open. "Save magic. Save Floatilla." Her eyes closed. Skyhammer's eyes registered that Higgins' severed arm and shoulder weren't bleeding but his heart could only see her still form and a lonely life without her. He inhaled. She wanted him to save magic. This time he wouldn't fail.

STOMP. Skyhammer raised his head and peered around the sphere. The Nasuchu queen had used her foot to press the technology symbol.

His heart stopped beating. Time stopped passing. He blinked, then stood up and faced the Pingala sphere.

The Nasuchu cackled and danced around the sphere, firing blue bolts into the endless ceiling. Now the lightning symbol was green, the crown red.

Skyhammer drew his sword and stalked towards the Nasuchu, heedless of anything but the need to kill her and a sinking sadness about the millions of tragic deaths he knew were now occurring outside the Tower.

He floated across the metal floor, a cloud of darkness and death. A smouldering ball of anger burnt inside him.

The queen heard him coming and turned. A look of fear crossed her face then she raised her arm, weapon clutched in her hand, and gave him a contemptuous smile. "Your sword against th-"

With a snarl, Skyhammer lunged. He batted her hand aside with the point of his sword then drove it into the queen's chest. With a sigh of surprise, she toppled to the floor. Skyhammer glared at her lifeless form.

After pushing the queen's body off his sword with his heel, he rushed back to where Higgins' body lay prone on the floor. Her eyes stayed closed. Her left arm lay some distance from the rest of her body. He noted the lack of blood but he leaned in close to listen for her breath. A small puff of air filled his ear.

Skyhammer collapsed over her body in relief. The edges of the wound appeared burnt; the weapon must have cauterized it.

He looked around at the dead bodies, former Kings and Queens of Pingala's most intelligent species. Death reigned inside and outside the Hall. The red and green lights under Pingala's sphere caught his eye. Maybe he could change it back. He jumped up and pressed his foot on the glowing red crown. Nothing changed.

He didn't know how long he sat there, waiting. So quiet in the Hall of Worlds now. He stroked Higgins' face and kissed her cheek and called her name. She didn't respond. He looked at Higgins' hand and back at her body again. Skyhammer grabbed the arm and pressed it to her shoulder. Maybe if he held it long enough it would grow back together. He wanted to get her medical help but it was hopeless - Floatilla and all the people living there would be dead. Silence enclosed him in a small world, him and Higgins alone. He listened to her breath and talked to her, recalling aloud the development of their friendship, telling her over and over how much he cared.

Some time passed. Images of Floatilla residents' descent to the jagged mountains around the Tower filled his mind. He shied away from the thought, terrified that he had wished this upon them and it came true. He stared at Higgins, willing her to awaken.

Finally she stirred. Her eyes opened. A small smile creased her face. "Saved you . . . again," she whispered.

He gulped, nodding, not trusting himself to speak. He covered her hand in kisses.

"Take me out."

He sat her up ever so gently but her face still spasmed in pain. He bound her left arm to her shoulder with a piece of material torn from the Aridizan's cloak. Then he tied her arm across her chest. Pain filled her eyes. He smiled encouragingly to be strong for her since he couldn't take away her pain.

Then Skyhammer carried Higgins from the Hall of Worlds and back into Quasianti.

* * *

When Skyhammer emerged from the passageway to the Hall of Worlds carrying an unconscious Higgins, the first sound he heard was sobbing interspersed with whispered conversation. He halted. The chamber in the Kingmaker Tower was almost pitch black. Since the Tower was a Relic, it had not been destroyed by the fall of the floating city. Across the chamber, a very faint square of light was blocked by dark figures. Why was it so dark? No more magic, he realized. Of course. Before, human magic had always lit the chamber. None of the humans who had taken refuge from Floatilla's destruction would know how to light a fire or would have even prepared for that eventuality. "My King?" he called out. "It's Skyhammer." The room fell silent.

A voice came from the other side of the chamber, near the light. "Is it over?" The King's voice.

Skyhammer felt as though the whole world were listening. Then he realized this was his whole world. The remains of the human race. He adjusted his grip on Higgins. "All the other royals have been killed, my lord." He swallowed. "But the world cannot be returned to magic."

The refugees started muttering amongst themselves and Skyhammer heard some start crying.

The King spoke. "My people." He paused. "My people," he said again, voice choked with tears. "We have to go out now into . . ." He took a deep breath. "We are going back to the nearest town. Gather as much food as you can on the way and check for survivors." The words tumbled out. "We will return soon to honour and bury the dead." The King went down the stairs.

A silent procession followed him. Skyhammer recalled the Queen's warning about the center of the room and trod with care around the edge until he came to the doorway. He carried Higgins down the brightening staircase until they stepped out into the warm sunshine. A small hand touched his arm. Mute.

The boy looked up at him. He wrote: "I afraid you dead. Glad you not."

"The three of us will stay together, Mute." Skyhammer took a deep breath, his glance darting everywhere around the Tower.

The sun blazed, despite the heart-rending debris piled up

around the Tower. The wreckage of millions of lives lay around him. Because of him. Closing his eyes, he ordered Mute to find some material so he could put Higgins down until they found a wagon.

Higgins stirred. "I'm alright," she whispered. "I should be able to walk. As soon as I get my strength back." Her eyes fell shut and she was asleep. Skyhammer kissed her forehead.

Mute returned with a filthy piece of blue material. "Best I see. Sorry," he wrote. He laid it out on the flagstones surrounding the Tower's base. Skyhammer settled Higgins on her back and then looked around. The majestic quiet of nature that usually soothed him now emphasized the lack of human noise.

Groups of people were clearing a way across the plateau so they could get to the path that led down to Cheshire. Most of Floatilla had fallen onto the mountains and into crevices around the Tower, unreachable without flight. Maybe they could get the Flyers to help. He hoped they had flown away before Floatilla had fallen.

He forced himself to look at the disaster around him. Objects and bodies mangled or broken. He stared at his feet, unable to face it for a moment. Mute stood beside him, one shoulder digging into Skyhammer's waist, touching him for comfort. Skyhammer knelt and hugged him, long and hard. A child his age shouldn't have to see this. He stood up holding Mute's hand. His mind was frozen. He knew he should be out there looking for something to carry Higgins but he couldn't move, didn't want to start dealing with this new world. It was too soon.

A woman brought them a salvaged wheelbarrow, resting her hand on Skyhammer's arm for a brief moment before walking off. Skyhammer couldn't get the words out to thank her. The metal was dented but the wheels turned. Before Floatilla's fall, no one had ever been kind to him like that. Mute covered the bottom with material. Skyhammer lifted Higgins into the wheelbarrow with Mute's help. They trundled down the path.

Couches, kitchen utensils, flowers, books, all the normal evidence of human life, littered the ground. As did maimed, bleeding bodies. A small girl's body lay horribly twisted, her slate clutched in her fingers, face smashed beyond repair, pink dress stained. Magic couldn't save her. Skyhammer forced himself to focus on Higgins. He told Mute that if he saw any food, he was to pick it up. And that Mute should find a bag in which to carry it. And find a bag for Skyhammer because he could carry food as well.

Mute walked off, reluctance on his face. Skyhammer and Higgins moved in silence except for the squeak of the wheelbarrow. They were the last group to leave the Tower.

Following the path winding down the mountainside, the remnants of humanity trudged back to Four Hills.

Chapter 30

Higgins stood, right hand on the wheel, a bright yellow flower tucked behind her ear. Sails billowed above her, gleaming white in the sunshine. The left sleeve of her tunic had been removed and the resulting hole sewn up.

Skyhammer paused at the top of the steps to admire her, shifting the disc he carried to his right hand. "Flora?" he called out with a grin.

She winked and smiled.

"Helen?" Mute wrote in capital letters, sticking his head and writing board out from under the stairs where he was coiling a rope in the shade. He stomped to get their attention.

They laughed, together, as Higgins shook her head. "You'll never guess."

"No, you'll just never tell." Skyhammer wrapped his arms around her and they kissed for a long time. Mute started clapping. When they came up for air, Skyhammer pointed at the flower. "Where did you get that?"

"From Four Hills. With Floatilla's shadow gone, things are growing!" She smiled and rested her hand on her belly.

Green shoots had been visible in the dirt beside the road as they travelled from the Palace to the Bay of Biscuits a few days ago. Life was returning; it had been six months since the fall of Floatilla. Skyhammer sat down on a cushioned bench behind Higgins and stretched his legs out with a contented sigh. He and Higgins had decided to take a few weeks' break, with Mute, and sail out to the Pinnacle and back.

The remaining humans were still cleaning up around the Tower as much as possible. No one had seen a Byndari since the ceremony.

Skyhammer set the disc beside him and opened his Retrograph Whorl. He had been avoiding his changed Retrographs. Now, looking at one from the Deadlands, he imagined Spark moving the items like pieces in a board game, trying desperately to figure out a way to communicate the danger to him. She was at peace now, he believed. He hoped she knew that her declaration of love had freed his heart and mind for Higgins' love. An incredible gift.

He closed the Whorl for a moment to watch his partner. Within the happiness he saw in Higgins' eyes, a seed of sadness would always remain. Her family, all Floatilla citizens, had perished in the fall. She was adapting well to having a single arm. Mute adored her and helped her whenever he saw a chance.

Whorl open again, he stared for a long time at a Retrograph of Rantama. His jaw began to ache from clenching. This creature had professed to be his friend, then turned around and almost destroyed his species. How could Skyhammer not have noticed anything unusual that last visit? Higgins kept telling him to get over it - no one else knew either. Why should he?

"Hanamun did," he had pointed out.

Higgins had nodded. "She knew the Byndari were trouble but she handled it badly. Her paranoia ruined her integrity."

"Who knows what the Byndari threatened her with though?" The guilt he felt at destroying Rantama had waned since the Fall of Floatilla, as he had learned about the Byndari's careless disregard for all the species on Pingala. The Byndari would have to repair their ship before it could leave the planet. Skyhammer wanted to find it before the aliens left. Perhaps people were still imprisoned in their ship. But what payment could possibly be enough for all those deaths?

On the other hand, he had a hard time blaming only the Byndari. They had provided the Nasuchu and Katipo queens with the weapon and convinced them of the benefit of technology but the queens made the final decision to change Pingala to technology and cause Floatilla to fall.

The King had ordered Skyhammer not to tell anyone about the Katipo and Nasuchu queens' actions in the Hall of Worlds. He did not want the other races to take revenge on the innocent citizens of those countries. Skyhammer wasn't sure they were innocent, but he obeyed the King and kept his mouth shut.

The Nasuchu seemed to have disappeared anyway. They no longer attacked travellers on the traders' road through the Deadlands. Rumour had it that they were dying, now that their magic power was gone, because they'd lost the taste for raw flesh. Skyhammer suspected that it wasn't that simple. The Flyers too had retreated from contact with the other races. Their race would soon die out without magic to facilitate the tree/Flyer reproduction system.

As for the Katipo, a couple of weeks after the ceremony, two humans had emerged from the Fungal Forest, bewildered but healthy. The Katipo had held them in a kind of zoo with members of other races as well as a range of animals. In the same manner as they controlled the spiders, the Katipo were able to control human minds. They had kept this aspect of their magic power a secret from other races, but had kidnapped and used members of the other races for many years. The Katipo usually affected the humans' minds so that they had no desire to escape but that wore off a week after magic was gone. The humans, a young woman and an older man, told stories of the animals in the swamp that had turned on their Katipo masters - the cruel ones, at least.

Skyhammer stared out at the wash behind the ship; silver fish flew through the creamy water. He inhaled a large breath of strong salty air. They had heard nothing from the Aridizans since magic disappeared, which bred suspicion in Skyhammer. Had they know what was going to happen? If so, how?

In Four Hills, a welcome change in attitude towards Skyhammer had taken place. Partly because the King had released an official story of how Skyhammer had vanquished the Retrograph Sorcerer. Humans would take a while to get used to their lack of magic powers. He figured the fact that humans still had Retrographs helped. He had always just wanted to be like everyone else, to be able to do magic. He chuckled. It wasn't really funny. Since the Fall he was respected by humans because of his survival skills. Much of his time had been spent teaching people how to live without magic. He had assumed that many humans from the farming and forestry villages would have survived. Unfortunately, most of those people had also made the trip to the Kingmaker Tower for the ceremony and died there. So yes, Skyhammer was a respected and accepted member of the human race. Only now, the human race consisted of a few hundred people, not a few million. He finally had something he wanted in life, just not in the manner he would have chosen. Skyhammer knew he would happily go back to his non-magic status if it meant Floatilla had never been destroyed.

"Hey, sailor!" Higgins blew him a kiss.

Perhaps things had changed for the better after all.

Skyhammer smiled. After all, he had gotten something else he wanted too. He stood up and held out the black disc. "What do you think this is?"

She peered at the Relic and shook her head. It was made of a non-metallic material that was common to Relics. Unfamiliar symbols were written in silver on the front between two dark blue oblong pads.

"Remember? We found it a couple of years ago and I didn't want to sell it because of the symbols," he reminded her. "We left it outside in the sun and dunked it in some snow to see if anything would happen."

"No clue." She shrugged.

Mute bounded up the stairs to look.

"I left it out on the deck yesterday and accidentally stepped on it this morning. Watch this!" He threw the disc on the deck, then placed both feet on the pads. The disc lifted him into the air.

Higgins clapped a hand over her mouth. Mute grinned.

"A flying disc!" Skyhammer called from the air above them. He put more pressure into his heels and zoomed out over the water, then came back and travelled along at the same speed as the ship. "The Relics are controllable now!" He landed on the deck. "Do you know what this means?" He passed the disc to Mute.

"The Moksha may have died out because of a change to magic," Higgins surmised. "From technology. But how come the Towers and the Retrograph Machine still worked when magic did?"

Skyhammer shrugged. "Maybe as more Relics get used we can figure out what really happened to the Moksha."

Mute stamped his foot on the deck and pointed to an island off the port side.

Skyhammer squinted. On the island's beach, figures were jumping up and down.

Higgins whipped out her mini telescope. "Byndari. Why aren't they repairing their ship with the others?"

Skyhammer and Higgins stared at each other for a long minute.

"We have questions." Her face was sober.

"They might have answers," Skyhammer said. "Do we want to know?" He paused. He could choose to leave it alone. To accept what had happened and move on with his life. He laughed, inside. He needed to know more.

Skyhammer nodded to Higgins, who spun the wheel and sailed their ship toward the island.

THE END

Thanks for reading! If you enjoyed this book, please consider leaving a review on Amazon, Createspace and/or Smashwords.

I love to hear from readers so feel free to connect with me online:

Email: skyhammer1@nicolesheldrake.com
Website: www.nicolesheldrake.com
Twitter: NicoleSheldrake
Facebook: The Adventures of Benjamin Skyhammer

ACKNOWLEDGMENTS

For her fabulous work on the cover art, map and formatting, thank you, Paola van Turennout.
If you want Paola's services for your own book or website, contact her at paola@graphitize.com.

Thanks also to my editor, Aynsley Friesen, for her patience with my atrocious punctuation and grammar. Any errors still in this book are the result of my bad choices, not hers.

My writing group peeps, Louisa, Bridget, Renee and Laura, provided valuable feedback, friendship and motivation - you guys rock!

And of course, big thanks to my family and friends who read, encouraged, poked and prodded this book to completion.

SKYHAMMER BOOK 2

Interested in reading more adventures of Benjamin Skyhammer?
Send me an email at Skyhammer2@nicolesheldrake.com and I'll let you know as soon as the next Skyhammer adventure is available.

www.ingramcontent.com/pod-product-compliance
Lightning Source LLC
Chambersburg PA
CBHW071605030726
47593CB00001BA/321